Roll On

A Trucker's Life on the Road

FRED AFFLERBACH

ACADEMY CHICAGO PUBLISHERS

Published in 2011 by
Academy Chicago Publishers
363 West Erie Street
Chicago, Illinois 60654

© 2011 by Fred Afflerbach

First edition.

Printed and bound in the U.S.A.

For Sweetums

and

the ones who don't fit in.

"There was nowhere to go but everywhere,
so just keep on rolling under the stars."
—JACK KEROUAC

"When you're traveling, you are what you are
right there and then. People don't have your past
to hold against you. No yesterdays on the road."
—WILLIAM LEAST HEAT MOON

PROLOGUE

"GRANDPA, TELL US A GHOST STORY, please, but not too scary."

"Okay, okay. Out on the long highway, late at night after all the big trucks have gone to sleep, a nasty creature rises up out of the ditch. It smells like a sewer, has a pointed nose and pointed chin and is covered with green slime. The animal has cactus needles on its face and wings like a buzzard and likes to fly high above the trucks, always circling. Sometimes when it's feeling evil it picks out a rig and lands on top of it. And with a long, sharp fingernail it scratches an X on the roof. The next day, lightning could strike that truck and the driver gets all burned up inside the cab. Or a tornado might pick up the rig and swing it around like a whip and smash it into the ground, crushing the driver inside. Or the rig could drive off a bridge into a bottomless lake. And sometimes when the creature casts a spell, the trucker's heart just explodes out of his chest and nobody finds him lying in the bunk for days and days. It's awful."

"What's the creature's name?"

"The Ditch Dragon."

"You ever seen it?"

"Nope. I tell everybody out on the road, stay away from the Ditch Dragon."

ONE

THE GREAT TRUCKS THUNDERED across the desert floor. Flatbed rigs with steel pipes stacked and chained to oak floors, refrigerated box vans stuffed with California strawberries, and shiny aluminum tankers pregnant with fresh milk kicked up sand and gravel as they rolled past Joshua trees and thorny ocotillo shrubs. The midday sun had baked the asphalt to mushy, black putty. Heat hovered above the highway in a foggy blanket, distorting the road ahead so it appeared wet. But the puddles remained a mirage, distant, out of reach, always a mile or so ahead.

One by one, the long and heavy rigs eased up behind an old Peterbilt ambling down the right lane. Like a tumbleweed, the solitary rig rolled along at its own pace. A stubborn crosswind bucked the trailer and pushed it toward the shoulder. The driver sat hunkered down behind the steering wheel, hairy left arm dangling out the window, creases etched into his forehead and around his eyes.

The trucks kept passing. Merging into the left lane. Pulling up beside the old timer. A quick glance and a nod and a hand lifted from the steering wheel. Rear turn signals blinking. Mud flaps fluttering. Then, back into the right lane and into the distance. Goodbye, Pops.

"I'll catch you on the pass," the old man yelled into the empty desert. "You'll be dropping gears. Radiator boiling. Transmission overheating. I'll walk right up beside you like you're a scarecrow."

The afternoon wore on and the temperature approached one hundred degrees. Hazy mountain peaks in the distance slowly took shape, a metamorphosis from soft silhouettes to jagged outcroppings. The trucks pushed harder, passing the old man, three days gray stubble on his chin and sweat stains under both armpits.

"Any rig can run flat out on a table top. Wait till we hit the mountain. That grade'll slow you down . . . like brake shoes dragging on eighteen wheels."

Glancing often into the rearview mirror, the trucker watched the sun turn from white-hot to a glowing ember on the horizon. Like the years before, he knew he would soon climb past the same rigs that had earlier slipped by. He knew he would soon be dodging their cheap, blown-out recapped tires, called gators, on the CB radio because they look like alligator carcasses. He knew he'd pick up radio chatter about monitoring pyrometers and tachometers, drivers fretting over rising transmission and coolant temperatures as they began a series of downshifts needed to make the grade. He knew these rigs would soon slow to a crawl. Then it would be his turn. With his engine and transmission working in harmony, and a steady hand on the wheel, he would tightrope along the inside stripe, watching the rigs that had passed him disappear in *his* rearview mirror.

"You fools," the old man barked out the open window, his words drowned out by the roaring exhaust and rushing wind of another passing rig. "You got them transmissions and gear ratios set up so you can run a hundred miles an hour. Don't make no never mind on the grade. This is where we find out which rigs got the guts and which ones couldn't buck a headwind if a locomotive was pushing it."

The man remembered that the four-lane, divided highway would soon narrow to a single lane in each direction and enter a canyon. Oblong and weathered boulders would loom from above like gargoyles. The road would then round a corner, exit the passageway, and hover on the edge of a deep cliff like a long, narrow balcony. The driver's only safety net would be a low, steel guardrail. Dented and scarred, it offered little protection for an out of control rig.

The old trucker pushed the Pete along, anticipating the exhilaration of catching a rig laboring up the mountain pass, distant taillights growing brighter as he gained ground. With gnarled fingers gripping the wheel, he could feel the road through the tires, shock absorbers, springs and system of u-joints that worked their way up inside the cab through the steering wheel, through his hands, and into his nerve center. What he sensed puzzled him. Resistance from the steep grade had melted away. Pulling a forty-five-foot trailer loaded with office furniture, the truck should be laboring, demanding a series of downshifts to prevent the oil and coolant temperatures from overheating. Instead, he downshifted only twice. He double-checked the gauges. Normal. The diesel engine purred. The transmission hummed. One white stripe at a time, the heart of the mountain disappeared under his wheels.

The old man shifted his weight. Seat springs groaned. Where were those ancient boulders? Rounded by eons of wind and rain, stacked and balanced by some divine hand in odd formations that defied gravity, painted by lovers pledging their allegiance to Debbie, Katy or Diane, or high schoolers immortalizing the class of 63, or maybe 68, depending on how the paint dripped and later faded. And what about the rocks desecrated with four letters intended to shock? Although painted over, the crass words burned through, remained defiant.

Instead of these old landmarks, the trucker passed through a valley of fresh-cut rock. Limestone walls, raw, like the earth had been cut open yesterday, lined both sides of the road. Then, a flicker of light in the mirror, the faint glow growing brighter. Now two lights. Headlights. Gaining. The driver pushed the accelerator to the floor. Black smoke billowed above the rig and it surged forward. The tachometer needle twitched and pointed toward the right until it touched the red line. Still, the lights behind him grew brighter. He eased off the accelerator and wrapped bent fingers around the shifter handle. With a gentle tug he pulled the lever down, pausing as the stick reached the neutral position, and eased the transmission into a higher gear. Back on the gas. More black smoke. The rig surged forward. But the headlights were now several truck lengths behind. A voice jumped out of the CB speaker.

"Need a push?"

The rig moved into the passing lane, sidled up to the old truck, and passed, right turn signal blinking. Obligated by the code of the road, the old man flashed his headlights off and on, a signal to the other driver to merge back in the right lane. The faint glow of red trailer lights grew dim on the horizon.

At last, the summit, where the mountain peeled away, revealed a starlit sky. The truck driver spied cone-shaped silhouettes on the right—tepee replicas at a rest area. A sign and a quick exit. Everything his headlights touched looked clean. New concrete tables nestled under the tepees for shade. Barbecue grills made from fresh-cut stone. The driver pulled into the parking area reserved for truckers. Set the air brakes. Whoosh. Puffs of white dust drifted from under the trailer.

"This can't be Peligroso Pass," he said.

Then a low rumble and a sleek, black Kenworth—CB handle, Hubcap, painted on the truck door—pulled in the slot beside him. The door slammed and a tall man with a paunch hanging over a huge silver belt buckle walked saddle-sore toward the restrooms.

The old trucker sat stupefied for a few minutes, checked his road atlas, and then stepped out on the edge of his rig. He clutched the handrail next to the vertical steel muffler strapped behind the sleeper compartment. Stretching and lowering one boot to the ground, his other heel lodged in the step just below the fuel tank. *Sheesh, these new boots take some getting used to.* He kicked at the step once, twice and a bolt rattled loose. The step gave way, sagged just enough to create a snare

"Looks like you could use a hand," a voice said. It was Hubcap, returning from the restroom. The wind buffeted his black felt hat. A turkey feather wedged in a snakeskin band fluttered in the night breeze. "Must be rough. Can't even get down from your rig without getting hung up like a coyote in a trap." The man grinned underneath a shaggy mustache that dripped down the corners of his mouth.

The old trucker glanced over his shoulder. *That sombitch seems to be enjoying this.* He reached up, steadied his boot, unlaced it, and wiggled free his foot. The empty boot hung limp from the step. Leaning slightly—one white sock and one boot side by side—the man extended his hand.

"They call me Ubi Sunt. Been a couple years since I run Peligroso Pass. What happened?"

"Damn if I know. Don't get off the Gulf Coast much. But I heared drivers say before they dynamited and bulldozed that twenty-mile stretch it used to be a hellified climb. Engines overheated going up, brakes overheated going down. Heared some hands drove a hundred miles out of their way just to avoid it. Don't make no difference now," the man said. His hand quickly jumped to the top of his hat and pushed it down so the wind wouldn't carry it away. "Ain't much left of old Peligroso Pass but a little ol' speed bump. Hell, I only had to drop one gear, hit the summit doing fifty-five."

Ubi Sunt wiggled his boot free from the step. Balancing on one leg, he thrust his foot back in his shoe and stood upright. He shook his head.

"They cut the heart right out of the mountain."

"That's progress," the man said. His open hand remained on top of his hat, pushing down. "Well, looks like you won't need my help after all."

He hoisted himself onto the rig. Rolls of fat oozed over his belt and the truck leaned to the driver's side. Twin CB antennas bolted on outside mirror brackets shook like giant tuning forks. Inside the cab, the man pushed in the clutch and forced the shifter into low gear with a thud. Ubi winced. The rig shook and lurched forward. The driver mashed the accelerator. The rpms surged between gears and the rig gained speed. Shift after shift, the transmission emitted a high-pitched whine—reeeeee—and the cab bounced up and down. Screeches from grinding gears made Ubi's neck hairs stand on end. No driving sombitch.

Ubi stood flat-footed, raised his cap and ran his hand through thin straw-colored hair. He fiddled with the broken step. *To hell with it. Fix it later. Clear skies. A sea of stars. Perfect night for driving.* Back in the driver's seat, he reflected on the steep grade. Old adversary, worthy opponent, an assessment or initiation, a trucker's rite of passage that greenhorns like Hub Cap would never know. He mumbled again that they had cut the heart out of the mountain. *Unbelievable.*

Engineers, highway department bureaucrats, and contractors with dynamite and huge scraping and cutting machines may have built a quicker and easier route to the top of Peligroso Pass, but they hadn't been able to soften the sharp curves and six percent downhill grade that continued to challenge drivers' skills and tax their equipment. Mangled steel guardrails and black skid marks provided stark evidence of how easily a driver could lose control.

Ubi quickly slipped through a half-dozen gears—easy on the tranny, let gravity do the work—until he found one that would hold back the rig. Save your brakes, that's how you do it. The mountain continued to pull Ubi's rig downward, but he kept it under control, plenty of brakes left, and the transmission continued to hold back thirty-two tons. Although the gauges reported optimal readings, whenever Ubi faced a long mountain descent, sweat beaded on his forehead and his hands.

That first trip down Peligroso Pass remained vivid, like it happened yesterday, not more than thirty years ago. On that initial run, Ubi got into trouble early in the descent by staying too long in a high gear. Frequent braking only demanded more braking. Smoke from hot brake shoes billowed from under the trailer. Sure, downshifting would slow the rig, but gears and pistons were already spinning and churning as fast as possible. If he tried to downshift, the transmission would come out of gear all right, but he wouldn't be able to shove the stick into the next lower position without chipping or breaking a tooth. The result? Floating in neutral, free-falling down the mountain—called Mexican overdrive by some truckers—strapped inside a sixty-four-thousand-pound missile hurtling along with nothing to stop it but mushy asbestos brake shoes pushing against steel drums. So Ubi hung on until the road flattened out and he stopped on the shoulder. A veteran driver soon pulled over to check on the rig with white smoke billowing from underneath it. After he realized the rookie was okay he offered this admonition: "Go down the grade in the same gear you went up in."

Nowadays a runaway rig can nosedive into a truck escape ramp—a long, straight driveway filled with sand built especially for out of control rigs—but Ubi had no such safety net. And if you crash-land into an escape ramp, expect a hefty tow bill for winching your sunken ship off the sand bar. Now that the mountain was cut wide open so that anyone could fly up the pass in high gear, a driver could easily get into trouble on the descent, runaway ramp or not.

Easing down the steep grade, Ubi took advantage of a quarter-mile straightway to admire the Milky Way, stars close enough to reach out the window and grab a handful. Thank God that hadn't changed. Then the pungent smell of hot brakes, just like that first time, wafted across the highway. His headlight beams reflected off a wall of smoke. Ubi was suddenly driving in a fog. Brake hard, downshift, quick, again and again. Look, there on the shoulder, red fluorescent triangles, and flashing, four-way signals from an eighteen-wheeler. Ubi eased past and stopped on the shoulder. He pulled two levers on the console. Air rushed through a system of valves, hoses and chambers. Brake shoes locked tight against steel drums. The rig rocked forward, then squatted down on the side of the mountain.

Ubi fingered the CB mike.

"How about that hand with hot brakes on the eastbound side? You okay?"

Silence.

Ubi hailed the driver again. A passing westbound driver said the hot brakes smelled like someone had pissed on a campfire, but no reply from the parked rig. Ubi checked his mirror—nobody coming—grabbed a flashlight, and with an eye on the loose step, climbed down from his truck. He reached between the torpedo-shaped fuel tank and the truck frame and grabbed a wooden block. He dropped it, kicked it under a giant tire's downhill side. A football-shaped chunk of limestone caught his eye and he wedged it under a tire on the passenger side. Walking stiffly, one hand braced on his back, Ubi trudged uphill toward the disabled rig. The red glow from a cigarette pointed the way toward the driver. Ubi aimed his flashlight in that direction but the beam bounced back in his eyes, briefly blinding him. It was that gear-grinding sombitch with the big belly and the belt buckle that looked like a hubcap stolen from a '72 Cadillac.

"You all right?" Ubi asked.

"Think so. Brakes overheated."

"No kidding."

Ubi brushed past the man. "The way you tore out of the rest area, what did you expect?"

It was a warm evening, even at five thousand feet, but the man shivered like he had been pulled out of San Francisco Bay in January. Ubi dropped to a knee—cringed when gravel pushed into his kneecap—and peered under the trailer.

"Sheesh. What the hell's wrong with you, driver?" Ubi asked. He straightened up, his hand pressed against his back. "You got no brakes. But you ain't blocked your wheels?"

Ubi shined his light up and down the shoulder, near the guardrail. "What the hell do you think is holding your rig on the side of this mountain? Your Fairy Godmother? Grab some of those rocks over there and sling 'em under some tires. Quick."

After the men had blocked several wheels, the truck groaned and nudged forward. The rocks slid slightly, grabbed hold of the mountain, and held the great rig in place.

"Got a nine-sixteenths wrench? If we tighten up these brakes, you might get down the mountain without killing yourself. Grab some gloves too. These jokers are gonna be hot for a while."

With a fresh cigarette dangling from his lips, the driver fetched a plastic toolbox from his truck cab, but it wasn't latched and screwdrivers and pliers spilled across the shoulder. Ubi's flashlight beam found the man on one knee, scooping a handful of tools and gravel into the cracked plastic shell, now decapitated.

"What a mess. That's all the tools you carry? Oh brother, you couldn't fix a tricycle with that. How are you gonna work on a rig?"

"Company truck," the man said. "They pay me to haul freight, not lie on my back and turn wrenches."

"Well, you might want to learn how to adjust your brakes and some other basic repairs," Ubi said. "I reckon you get paid by the mile, like most company drivers. You don't make any money wait-ing on a tow truck."

Ubi retrieved from his rig a nine-sixteenths wrench and slipped on a greasy, long-sleeve flannel shirt and leather work gloves. Smoke emanating from the trailer had cleared and Ubi slid under the rear axles. With the driver pointing the flashlight where Ubi directed, he turned a bolt and the connecting push rod moved the brake shoes snug against the brake drums. Ubi wiggled on his back from one side of the rig to the other.

"I'm hung up. Can't move."

"Huh?"

"Feels like I'm paralyzed. Probably a Charley Horse. Sheesh, this is the worst one I've ever had," Ubi said.

"What do you want me to do?"

"Reach down and yank me out."

The heavy man set down the flashlight, grabbed Ubi by the same boot that had earlier hung on the fuel tank, and dragged him from under the rig. Using two hands, he grunted and pulled Ubi to his feet. Ubi's flannel shirt bunched up, and long, red scratches stretched down his back. Reaching behind his shoulder blade, he picked out several pieces of gravel that had embedded in his flesh.

"You're going to have to adjust the others," Ubi said. "Time you learned anyway."

An hour later, a heavy young man covered with grease and an old man with a sore back, sore knee, and cramping calves eased their rigs down the mountain and pulled into a rest area for the night. Ubi rummaged around in his sleeper, found a plastic water jug, toothbrush and toothpaste tube. Hadn't brushed in two days, maybe three. Sitting on the edge of a concrete picnic table, he squeezed the toothpaste tube. Empty. He opened his pocketknife, slit the tube, and squeezed white paste across the top and down the sides of the toothbrush. Scrub, slosh, spit. Fifteen minutes later, he was nestled in a cocoon of cotton sheets and furniture blankets as the highway hum lulled him to sleep.

Down the road in the morning to the J&B truck stop: fuel, fill the thermos with black coffee, the jug with water from the men's room sink, pick up a loaf of bread and can of Spam on the way out. Sheesh. Almost forgot. Grab a postcard with the odd-looking Joshua trees, their strange, fuzzy limbs looking like something out of Dr. Seuss. Grandkids love Dr. Seuss. Lick a stamp. Scrawl a message.

> *Dinosaurs blocking the highway slowed me down*
> *Twenty-foot rattler hiding in my nightgown*
> *Crossing this dessert in ten feet of snow*
> *Found a frozen herd of buffalo*
> *Grandpa Truck*
>
> *P.S. See you around Halloween. Tell your mother not to leave the car in the driveway. I need lots of parking space.*

TWO

SEVEN-YEAR-OLD MOLLY BURST THROUGH the front door and into the kitchen waving her skinny arms like a windmill.

"Mama, Mama, Grandpa Truck is coming. That's a big ten-four. Grandpa Truck's coming. We got a postcard."

"Take off your shoes," the mother said, looking up from the kitchen counter, her serrated knife hovering above Italian bread slices. "How many times have I told you?"

The girl's twin brother, Jeremy, slid across the kitchen tile in white socks and skidded to a stop against the pantry door.

"That's a big, big, big, ten-four."

The boy held his arms toward the ceiling and stood on his toes. "Grandpa Truck is coming for real. And I took off my shoes. See." The boy teetered on one foot, the bottom of his white socks now chalky-brown.

Molly kicked off her black school shoes and held the postcard below her face. Silently mouthing the words, her index finger slowly traveled from line to line.

"He's gonna be here next week," her voice cracked. "That's a big ten-four. Grandpa Truck's coming next week. After he finishes his dessert."

The mother, Jeanne, twisted a knob on the kitchen stove, lowering the flame under a pan of boiling water. It was Tuesday, and that meant basketti.

"Let me see that."

She reached down, pinned her shoulder-length brown hair behind her ears. "He misspelled desert, a place of little rainfall and sparse vegetation."

She turned the postcard over. "See. That's a desert. Your grandfather is not well-educated. But you guys are going to college."

"Not me," Jeremy said, grabbing the postcard. "I'm driving a big truck. Like Grandpa. And that's a big ten-four."

Jeremy held the postcard to his bony chest like a teddy bear. "Can Grandpa bring the big truck to school? Stephen's dad drove a police car to school."

Jeanne resumed slicing bread. Pushing hard on the knife's wooden handle, she upended the cutting board and catapulted a slice onto the kitchen floor. The twins squealed and wrestled on the beige tile. Molly came up the winner. Standing upright, she held the bread slice over her gaping mouth.

"Molly, you will not eat that. Give it here. Now."

Jeanne jutted her hand toward the girl, but Jeremy swooped in and snatched the slice from his sister's fingers. He bit off a crescent-shaped piece and started chewing.

"Jeremy. You're behaving like an animal. You will not eat off the floor, and you will not drive a big truck. Ever," Jeanne said, grabbing the bread slice from Jeremy's small hand. "Now, spit that out."

Jeremy swallowed and opened wide, revealing two missing front teeth and an empty mouth.

"That's it. Jeremy, go to your room."

Jeanne pointed toward the kitchen door.

"I didn't work all day long to come home to this. I haven't even had time to change clothes," she said, as if she just realized the fact herself. "Now, to your room. The both of you. And don't come out till I call you for supper."

"But Mama, I didn't do anything," Molly whined.

"I don't care," Jeanne said. She placed her hands on her hips. "Go to your room. And no, Grandpa can't take his truck to your school for show and tell."

"Aw, Mama. Why not?" Jeremy asked, bread crumbs dotting his teeth.

"Because I said. Now go to your room."

"That's not fair."

"Go."

Behind the closed bedroom door, Jeremy stood on his bed, pushed a pin through the top of the postcard with the Joshua tree photograph, and affixed it to the large bulletin board hanging above his pillow. He bounced on the bed softly so Mama wouldn't hear the springs; last time that happened, she broke a wooden ruler over his backside. His blue eyes scanned dozens of picture postcards pinned to the bulletin board: an alligator sprawling on a riverbank, four presidents' faces looking out from the side of a chiseled mountain, and what seemed like the biggest McDonald's arch ever—but only half of it—was all lit up at sunset, like a giant rainbow. "Jeremy, come look where Grandpa Truck sent the post-card from."

Molly pushed a brown pin into the bottom, left corner of a United States wall map hanging above her bed. Jeremy leaped from his mattress onto his sister's, grabbing her arm as he landed.

Molly had talked her dad into hanging the map. She used col-or-coded pushpins in each state that Grandpa Truck sent them a postcard from. Their father chose the colors, dividing the country into regions, and one night at bedtime he explained their signifi-cance. Blue for the Northeast because that was the Union troops' color in the Civil War. Likewise, gray for the South. Brown for the arid Southwest. Yellow for the Midwest, where most of the corn and wheat grows. White for the snow-covered mountain states such as Colorado, Wyoming and Montana. Green for the Pacific Northwest because that rainy country grew magnificent pine and fir and spruce trees. And pink for California, because they were running out of colors and their dad didn't like red.

"I'm going to all those places when I grow up," Jeremy said, carefully bouncing on his sister's bed. "In a big truck."

* * *

Late that night—hours after the twins filled their small bellies with basketti, finished their homework, bathed and brushed and slipped into bed—a short thirty-something-year-old man with kinky black hair turned his key in the front door lock and slouched into a kitchen chair at a small, square table.

"Another postcard from Daddy today," Jeanne said. "He's headed this way." She poured red wine into two long-stemmed glasses that she set before a steaming plate of spaghetti, bread slices hanging over the edge.

"Jeremy wants him to take the truck to school. The twins are acting like Santa Claus is coming to town."

"If I'm seven years old, this is better than Santa Claus," said Jeanne's husband, Martin, dipping bread into thick, red sauce. "They get to ride in the sleigh."

"Oh no they're not. My children are not riding in that smoky old truck with papers and maps blowing around and empty coke cans rolling on the floorboard. Pretzel and potato chip bags on the dashboard. Believe me, I've ridden my share of miles in that truck. And God knows when was the last time he washed the sheets in that bunk."

"I thought Ubi quit smoking."

"He has. About a thousand times."

"I say let them have their fun," Martin said. He twirled the noodles on the end of his fork and slurped. "Let him take the rig to school. The twins will be heroes for a day."

Jeanne handed her husband a white, cloth napkin.

"I don't want them getting the wrong idea. Truck drivers are not role models; they're misfits," she said, leaning against the kitchen counter, swirling the wine inside her glass. "They come and go at odd hours, miss holidays, birthdays, live like hoboes, sleeping on the side of the road. Oh sure, he called me on college graduation day, from Little Rock. If I remember, we went to school together in Connecticut."

"Aren't you being a little hard, honey?"

"Maybe so. And I'm trying to let go of the past. But Mom flew in, spent a week here for graduation, and two weeks when the twins were born, not Daddy."

Jeanne stared into her wine glass. "If they want a hero, they should talk to me about their grandmother, not their grandfather."

Martin unfolded the napkin and draped it across his lap. "Jeanne. Honey. Please. How many times have we been down this road?"

"That's exactly the problem. He's always just going down the road. Never staying put. Like he's scared he might have to get close to someone," Jeanne said. She flopped into the chair next to her husband and crossed her long, thin legs under the table. "He doesn't know the meaning of the word stationary, much less could he spell it."

"Where'd that come from?" Martin asked, wiping spaghetti sauce from his upper lip.

"He misspelled desert on the postcard. How embarrassing, a grandfather who can't spell."

"You want to tell Ubi that the kids can't ride in the rig because he has musty sheets and can't spell? That's going to break not just two hearts, but three. Those kids are all he's got," Martin said, running a piece of bread across his plate and wiping it clean. "Why don't you offer to wash the sheets?"

"It's not just about the sheets, or poor grammar, it's about everything," Jeanne said, squinting at her husband. "Your manners aren't much better than the kids, by the way."

Martin swallowed and folded his napkin on the table. Choosing his words like he was conducting an interview at work, he said, "What would you like to do, honey?"

"I'm going to tell him to shut it down. Sell the rig," Jeanne said, pulling her long torso up straight at the table. "We can find him a place close by. Maybe he can land a job driving a school bus or local delivery van. If he wants a relationship with his grandchildren, he needs to stick around and end this fairy tale."

Martin sipped the red wine. For a moment, a tense silence hung over the small kitchen like a chess game where one player had the opponent's king in her sights.

"Why do you want to clip his wings, honey? The road . . . since your Mom died, that's all he has. And you know he can't handle the East Coast; way too crowded for a nomad like Ubi Sunt."

"He's a worn-out old man in a worn-out old rig who can't face the truth. I'm going to tell him. Straightforward. It's my way, or the highway. Literally."

"Okay, honey, but I rode with him one summer as an undergrad. Remember? Ubi and that rig, Old Ironsides, they reminded me of Paul Bunyan and Babe the Blue Ox," Martin said. He reached under the table and held his wife's hand. "Maybe that sounds silly, but lots of parents in rest areas, restaurants and motel parking lots, they were crazy about that rig, took pictures of Ubi and their kids standing in front of that friggin' beast. Come on, Jeanne, you gotta admit Old Ironsides is unique—looks like a locomotive, or a Sherman tank, as much as an eighteen-wheeler. And the truckers were constantly hollering at him on the CB or coming up to him at the truck stop coffee counter."

Martin looked down at the table, smiled and shook his head. "I'll never forget the family in that Chevy wagon at the rest area outside Ogallala, luggage piled on the roof. All six kids climbed behind the steering wheel and blasted that horn until it ran out of air. Ubi cranked up the engine and built up more air pressure and they started all over again."

Martin stood up, rinsed his plate in the sink, crammed it inside the overflowing dishwasher, and twisted the knob to the start position. "And don't forget all those safe driving and contractor of the year awards, those decals running down both sides of the cab like Army medals. He's still in decent health, sixty-whatever he is, not that old. Why do you want to take that away? Why do you want to put an eagle in a cage?"

Jeanne swirled the Merlot inside the long-stemmed glass. Staring into the tiny whirlpool, she said, in a low voice, "He's no eagle. He's a lost little boy."

THREE

A DOZEN DIESEL TRACTOR-TRAILER RIGS galloped along the Arizona interstate, kicking up dust like buffalo. They pounded cracked sections of concrete highway slabs that were slipping away from each other. They buckled and pitched, jostling the drivers who clutched their steering wheels with iron grips, cigarettes dangling from mouths. Despite the crumbling highway, they roared on at high speed—more than seventy if nobody's reporting any Smokey activity on the CB—and if the radar detector, called a bird dog, is not barking. They weaved from lane to lane, and sometimes onto the shoulder, to avoid the craters and broken sections of road. Hit a big pothole head on, it'll rip the wheel out of your hands. The jarring and vibrating sent tremors through floorboards, into seats, and up drivers' spines. And those seats, some with a small shock absorber at the base, some with an air cushion ride, bucked and tossed the drivers like they were riding a mechanical bull.

The pounding took a toll. Hoses and wires rubbed against frames and each other, shorting out or leaking oil, diesel, or coolant. Heavy-duty steel springs and shock absorbers stretched until they hung limp and ineffective. And tires often exploded, shaking both rigs and drivers. Suffer a blowout and you could lose half a day, either waiting on the roadside for the tire man or limping with a flat into Winslow or Holbrook. Hope they got the right size. If not, could be tomorrow. *So when are they going to pave these roads? How long has Arizona been a state anyway?*

Everything in the bunk—shaving kit, overnight bag, extra pair of shoes—was bouncing around like it was inside a clothes dryer. Back in the trailer, a pallet of dog food or plumbing fixtures could have spilled, rubbing a hole through the inside trailer wall. That'll be a mess at the dock in Dallas.

The herd continued across the Western expanse. Safety in numbers. They told jokes on the CB—preachers, truckers and hookers their favorite subject—and worked the westbound drivers for information on speed traps; Arizona always has several patrolmen hiding below an embankment or on a ramp. *Damn fifty-five mile an hour speed limit, takes an extra half-day to get from coast to coast.* Speaking of fifty-five—"slow-moving rig in the right lane," the leader announced on the CB. The pack roared past Ubi Sunt and Old Ironsides, coaxed them to join, but the driver ignored them.

Let 'em run, all bunched up in a herd. Ubi knew he'd pass them down the road, maybe in Gallup, or Grants when they stopped for about their third time this afternoon. One stops, they all stop. That's not trucking. That's not independence. And it's damn sure not freedom of the road.

Ubi continued at a moderate pace, past a giant hole in the desert floor that was formed when an asteroid crashed into Earth more than twenty thousand years ago. He crossed the Painted Desert—a shimmering landscape of pink, lavender, and gray hues reflecting off layers of sandstone and clay that were exposed by millions of years of erosion. And Ubi skirted the Petrified Forest, ancient pines entombed by volcanic ash and sediment that now lay naked on the desert floor. The tree trunks that had turned to stone in their cocoons below a prehistoric ocean were almost the size of the rigs that swept past.

The bunch slowed to a crawl at the Arizona weigh station. A small complex of brick buildings and an open hangar with a sheet metal roof jutted out of an expansive, gravel parking lot. Westbounders waited in line, showing their manifest to agriculture inspectors. If you're carrying plants or outdoor furniture, better have the gypsy moth proof of inspection or they will quarantine your rig, if they let you in at all. But the eastbound herd had it easy. They downshifted through several gears, their engines and transmissions and mufflers growling as the rpms shot upward with each succeeding shift. They inched up to a state policeman wearing a flat-brimmed hat standing on scorching pavement. He waved them through. The trucks sprinted into New Mexico.

Just across the state line, past the sign reading "Welcome to the Land of Enchantment," the group pulled into the port of entry and, with engines idling, set their brakes. They climbed down from their rigs and ducked low into the wind. Holding bound, vinyl permit books over their faces, the truckers shielded their eyes from blowing sand. Inside the portable building that pitched in the wind, the patrol officer looked up from his girlie magazine and ground a smoldering cigarette butt in the overflowing, glass ashtray. Black and white TV on a nearby desk, the screen flickered off and on. Hollywood Squares. The truckers opened their books, flipped past pages of state permits, and stopped at New Mexico. The officer stashed the magazine behind the counter.

"Where you headed?"

"Houston, Texas."

"You know how to get to Texas?"

No answer.

"Go east till you smell it, and south till you step in it," the officer chuckled. "Any stop offs?"

"No, sir. Going straight across on the interstate."

The officer wrote in a ledger the name of the trucking company, unit number, and miles traveled. "Logbook current?"

"Yes, sir."

"Have a good trip."

The truck drivers climbed back in their rigs and ran through the gears, building speed. As they roared out of the weigh station,

Old Ironsides drifted in. Ubi Sunt twisted the squelch button on the CB and the chatter emanating from the pack stopped. *Who wants to hear that crap?* He dismounted from his rig, careful to avoid the loose stirrup, and ducked into a headwind across the parking lot, head down, forearm up. Ubi climbed shaky wooden steps attached to the portable building and turned the steel doorknob. The wind ripped the handle from his grip and pinned the door against the outside wall. Inside, papers stapled to a bulletin board fluttered and tried to tear free. Ubi grabbed the doorknob with both hands and pulled.

"Close the goddamn door!" someone yelled.

"Sheesh, whaddaya think I'm doing? Playing tiddlywinks?"

Ubi stumbled over a piece of loose linoleum at the threshold. The room looked, smelled, and sounded the same as it always had—blackened ceiling tiles and stale cigarette smoke, window unit air conditioner rattling, blades knocking against the grill. A middle-aged trucker wearing long, gray sideburns and a greasy red Kenworth cap counted out fives and tens and handed them to the trooper. Without a state permit, it's pay as you go. Cash only. And who knows how poor the trooper's memory might be. Forgot to enter a few rig numbers in the ledger. Oh, well. Need to take the wife out to dinner tonight.

A young co-driver stared out a window covered with a film of dust, except for a peep hole someone had wiped in the center. He fiddled with a silver chain dangling from his belt loop. The chain led to a fat brown leather wallet that protruded from the rear pocket of his jeans.

Ubi smiled, nodded at the young man, and pointed at the pitiful floor. "That's why they call 'em chicken coops."

"That your rig, mister?" the youngster asked, gazing through the dirty window.

"Ten-four."

"Sombitch. That thing ought to be in a museum."

"You'll play hell mothballing Old Ironsides. She'll outpull anything you can find today," Ubi said. Then he remembered Peligroso Pass. "Back in California, they had to cut through the heart of the mountain for the other rigs, but Old Ironsides keeps on climbing."

The driver at the counter folded and tucked the receipt in the pocket of his sweaty t-shirt and turned around. "You driving Old Ironsides?"

Ubi nodded.

"Come on, son, you gotta see this rig."

Ubi showed the officer his permit and the three men escaped the chicken coop without the front door getting ripped from its hinges.

"Would you look at this? She's got a snout like a locomotive," the kid said, hands running across the front bumper. "What the hell is it?"

Ubi pulled a tan bandana out of his back pocket and wiped the dust from the football-shaped red emblem attached to the front grill. "Nineteen fifty-six Peterbilt. Only had one wife, only owned one Pete. When she goes, I go."

"Which one, the rig, or the wife?"

Ubi felt his stomach tighten. He twisted the bandana like he was wringing out a wet dish towel. "You boys need to get on down the road. Catch up with your buddies."

"Ten-four on that," the kid said. "Supposed to hit that steakhouse in Amarillo tonight. The hand driving the green Freightliner, called Tiny on the CB, he's going to eat that seventy-two-ounce sirloin and get his picture in the paper again. Done it twice already."

The last of the herd disappeared into the brown, New Mexico mountains. Ubi again pulled out his bandana and buffed a scratch on the front fender. He spat on the passenger side mirror, dabbed away the dust, and wiped the road grime from the hand-lettered name on the passenger side door—*Sassy Sherry.*

FOUR

DADDY FORBADE HER MARRYING a trucker, especially an older, cross-country driver. But this one had bright brown eyes, wind-blown coarse, sandy hair, wide shoulders and narrow hips that led to long legs. *Sorry, Daddy, but he cuts a nice figure up at the Concho Dance Hall. Even if he spends most of his time shooting pool in the back. Even if he's gone for long spells.*

Sherry Kosper, her three sisters and their friends, danced till closing at the Concho almost every weekend. The trucks rumbled into the gravel parking lot at sundown: stake beds for hauling hay bales, barbed wire, and cedar fence posts, four-wheel drive pick-ups used for negotiating muddy ravines and creek bottoms and limestone outcroppings, and some high-sided pickups, their beds littered with empty feed sacks and rusty baling wire. The assortment of trucks often crammed into the lot three and four deep. If you wanted to leave early but were blocked in, push the other guy out of the way. Sombitch shouldn't have parked there anyway.

On a muggy, summer evening, one rig dwarfed them all. The stack pointed toward the sky like a stovepipe. It barely fit under the string of naked yellow light bulbs that stretched above the parking lot, tied to towering pecan trees' upper branches. Even in the dim light, the truck's red paint gleamed from a recent scrub-bing. The steel wheels sported fresh white paint, and the tires were chest high. You had to climb a set of steps and pull yourself up on a guardrail just to peek in the window. And on this humid Saturday night, that's what Sherry did. Nose pressed against the glass, she peered inside and found gauges like in the cockpit of the Watson boys' rebuilt World War II fighter. Standing on the top step above the front wheel, she heard footsteps and a voice.

"Help you, ma'am?"

Ubi had returned to fetch his cigarettes and found hanging on the side of his rig a shapely young woman: watermelon-red lipstick, plaid shirttail tied in a knot at her waist, tight blue jeans tucked into blue cowboy boots.

Sherry turned around, still gripping the handrail. *Mmm, look who's back in town. The good-looking guy who likes pinball and pool and Pearl beer more than dancing. Gotta get him on the floor.* She held out her hand. He helped her down, forgetting the pack of Luckies.

Inside the dance hall, Ubi was a minnow flapping around inside a bait bucket. Sherry was the big hand swishing around in the water behind it, trying to catch the elusive prey. He turned one way, she went the other. The polka, with its nonstop skipping in long circles, the somewhat slower schottische, and the cotton-eyed Joe where dancers lined up in long rows with arms around each other's waist—all a disaster. He went left, she went right. She dipped and twirled, he staggered and tripped. The only dancing Ubi had ever done was the simple Texas two-step. But a local dance club chose that night for its annual party and it controlled what the band played. These dance numbers required lots of practice and quick feet. Ubi was out of luck on both counts.

During a break, when the fiddler and two guitarists stepped out back to tackle several longnecks, the skies opened like Niagara Falls and rain pounded the dance hall's tin roof. A loud crack shook the building and lightning splintered a mesquite tree just outside the front door. The lights flickered, once, twice, and went dark. A few folks panicked, raced to their trucks and cars, slipping in the mud on their way. But the Concho's owner pulled out a box of candles. He showed the waitresses how to melt a little wax on the bottom of empty tin cans and affix the tall, white sticks to it. They set up homemade lamps that way and offered half-price beer. The crowd had thinned and for the first time all night Sherry and Ubi could talk without screaming in each other's ear. And the die-hards like Sherry's sisters and friends hung around until last call.

Back outside, the storm had passed, and Ubi walked Sherry across the muddy parking lot, pointing out the larger puddles along the way. By now, he knew where she lived, and although Ubi was too shy to ask for a phone number, he knew whose porch steps he would be walking up tomorrow around sundown.

Ubi watched the DeSoto that Sherry was driving pull out and cut the corner too tight. The car slid to the bottom of a muddy ditch. Sherry's terrified friends and sisters, packed into the front and back seats, squealed and yelled all the way down. With the girls trapped inside, truck after truck tried pulling out the heavy sedan. Chains wrapped around frames and onto bumpers, groaning, pulling, wheels spinning and smoking. Clutches heating up, smelling like burning tires. Burning tires smelling like the highway department was putting out fresh tar. Drivers bragging, then cussing, finally throwing up their hands.

Leaning against his rig's front bumper, smoking a Lucky Strike, Ubi took it all in. He had dropped his trailer in town, at an empty lot behind Patek's Hardware. After everyone who had tried to rescue the sedan had failed, Ubi waded into the muddy ditch. He felt cold water seep into his leather boots. He leaned over into the driver's side window. "Don't do nothing," he said, "until you hear my air horn. That's when you grab the wheel with both hands and hang on." Sherry's breasts heaved and Ubi caught a quick glance down her blouse. He'd never seen a pink bra before.

Ubi cranked his rig. The diesel engine caught immediately and emitted a deep growl from six pistons clattering in unison. Then a perfect puff of black smoke rose from the vertical stack and drifted into the night sky. Ubi backed up to the edge of the ditch and took hold of the chain that was already wrapped around the DeSoto's chassis. He looped it around his truck's rear frame and climbed in the driver's seat. Ubi tugged on the cord hanging from the truck ceiling and the air horn signaled to Sherry *Let's go*. Ubi's left foot came off the clutch and his rig lurched forward. The chain made a snapping, popping sound and stretched tight. The DeSoto came out of the ditch like someone retrieving a yo-yo with the twitch of a finger.

The next night, Ubi Sunt and Sherry Kosper went on their first date, in a '42 GMC, to the drive-in at Twin Forks, a much larger city twenty miles north. Everyone was talking about a racy new movie, "Dawn of Desire." Ubi parked in the back row, so as not to block anyone's view. Inside the rig, a vinyl curtain separated the sleeper compartment from the cab. Long haul truckers were covering ground faster than ever before and they were demanding comfort. No more of this head down on the wheel, forearm for a pillow, or body curled up in the fetal position in the front seat at night. Truck builders had already cranked up post-war production, but they also started manufacturing more and more rigs with sleepers. And mechanics, even shade tree operators, were welding makeshift bunks onto the older models. Grab a little shuteye in the back bunk, then a cup of java, and you're good for another four hundred miles.

"You're not going to try and get me in that sleeper, are you? Because I won't."

"Nope," Ubi said.

"I bet you've had other girls in that bunk. Right?"

"It's for sleeping. On the road, when I don't have time or money for a motel."

"What's it like?"

"On the road?"

"No. In the bunk. That's what we're talking about."

"I thought you said you weren't interested in getting in there."

Up on the screen, a couple swam in the moonlight and the older man asked an innocent, young woman to loosen her swim-suit top so her breasts touched him when they kissed.

"Well, I'm not. But maybe I'm curious, just a little bit. You got a mattress?"

"Of course, I got a mattress."

"Got a pillow?" Sherry asked.

"Yeah. Two, actually."

"Blankets?"

"Yes. Several. Now, can we watch the movie?"

Suddenly, the cab felt stuffy. Ubi rolled down his window, wiped his brow.

"The end of this movie is stupid," Sherry said. She opened her purse, pulled out a tube of red lipstick and a small mirror.

"You've seen it?"

"Mmmhmm," Sherry said, applying a fresh coat. "I'd say Paisano County is just like the movie. The way everybody runs around on each other, then gossips."

"Why didn't you tell me you'd seen it?"

"You didn't ask."

Ubi didn't know what to think of this sassy female. She was several years younger, but self-confident, especially on the dance floor. She liked leading, and doggone it, just when he was catching on, she'd stop and sit down. And now, she said one thing, but Ubi reckoned that's not what she meant at all. Maybe that's what he found attractive.

"You sure you don't want to see the inside of the bunk?"

"That's what I said."

"I'll show you anyway."

"How many pillows?"

"Two. Like I said."

"Okay. I like pillows."

Sometime in the middle of the night, the theater owner banged on the cab door and shooed the big truck home. And for the next two weeks, with Ubi hanging around town waiting for a load, the couple went out every evening in that rig. It was Ubi's only vehicle and Sherry liked riding high in the shotgun seat, peeking over fences into back yards. Sherry and Ubi enjoyed picnics all over the county, restaurants and shopping in San Angelo, and on Saturday a day trip and a baseball game in San Antonio.

His last night in town, before leaving for Waco to load office furniture, Ubi met Sherry's parents. Sherry still lived at home, working as a waitress at Sam's Steak House. She had been saving for her own place going on three years, but whenever her bank account looked about right, a girls' trip to Galveston or Padre Island cleaned it out and she had to start over.

Sherry had manipulated her dates with Ubi so that her parents weren't home when that red GMC rolled up out front. And they stayed out past the old folks' bedtime. But Sherry's dad knew what his fun-loving daughter was up to. Several times, long after midnight, he heard that rig rumbling down the block, then the front door creaking and Sherry's footsteps on the wooden floor. One night, he peeked between the blinds in time to catch Ubi's face in the front porch light. He must've been thirty now, but looked like one of those children, orphans, or troublemakers, who grew up on the boys ranch run by Jesuit priests several miles outside town. Once every few months, the priests brought the little brats into town and bought them clothes, shoes and ice cream at the drug store. Durn little runts ran around town like wild Indians.

* * *

On an unusually warm and clear January day in 1918, a passenger train with more than a dozen orphans aboard pulled into the San Antonio depot. The children were from the bustling northeastern cities and had been shipped out because they faced bleak lives back home. East Coast orphanages at that time were typically short on funds and space. So, a well-meaning group of New Yorkers arranged this system in which some orphans were put on trains bound for the South and West. Through newspaper ads and flyers hung up at churches, word got out about the kids needing a loving family. But not all adults waiting for the orphan trains were motivated by benevolence. Looking for cheap farm labor, they often picked over the children like they were animals. Poking in mouths and peering in ears, the adoptive parents chose all the strong and healthy children first. When the train rolled into San Antonio, various adults selected the remaining orphans, except a sandy-haired two-year-old.

The conductor said the kid was inconsolable. He started bawling every time the train pulled into a station—from Baltimore, across the South, and into Texas. But when the train chugged out of the depot, he would quit crying—until the next stop. No wonder he'd been passed over in numerous states. Now at the end of the line, nobody knew what to do with him, until a Jesuit priest stepped up. And that priest harbored a sentimental thread back to his childhood in Ireland. Drawing on his Latin classes in the seminary, he named the kid Ubi Sunt, part of a Latin phrase that roughly translates: Where are the snows of yesteryear?

While growing up at Blue Sky Boys Ranch, Ubi could never sit still. In the classroom, church, or cafeteria, it didn't matter. His foot, or knee, or pencil was always tapping, bobbing, shaking, moving. Teachers scolded him, threatened him, counseled him, pleaded with him. The boys at the home laughed and teased him about his nervousness. They gave him names: Jitters, Jumpy, Edgy. But what the students and teachers and priests didn't know, what the counselors' and therapists' tests and evaluations couldn't determine: Ubi was at peace only when he was moving. It wasn't running to something. It wasn't running from something. For Ubi, moving meant peace of mind, and peace of mind meant moving.

Blue Sky was large enough to accommodate young Ubi's ramblings until he reached age ten. By then he had explored every corner of the fourteen-hundred-acre tract that was mostly covered with a mesquite and juniper tree thicket. As he grew older, his legs grew like green shoots in springtime. On organized hikes he covered ground faster and longer than anyone at the ranch. But the facility had little interest and no money for athletics. Cross-country track wouldn't have cost much, but it was unheard of in a 1930s low-budget remote boys ranch in the Texas Hill Country.

The first dozen times Ubi ran away, he was caught meandering country roads only a few miles from the ranch. Ubi sometimes hiked the back country, eating tomatoes, corn, and cucumbers pilfered from farm fields and vegetable gardens. He once paddled a canoe down the Comanche River, catching channel catfish and cooking them over campfires before a game warden nabbed him. One spring he spent weeks working on a second-hand bicycle, and during Easter services he quietly slipped away down a trail that led to a gravel road that led to a county road that led to a state highway. He was only seventy miles from Laredo when a sheriff found him on the side of the road trying to patch a flat with a piece of an old shoe he had found. Later, in his mid and late teens, he ventured farther out. He often hitchhiked, sometimes making it to New Mexico or Oklahoma or Louisiana before police caught him and sent him home.

One ramble that had a profound influence on Ubi ended in an Oklahoma truck stop, six hundred miles away from home. Ubi had hiked through a dozen miles of woods to a state highway and waved down a trucker. He lied about his age, said he was going to Tulsa to enroll in college. The lonesome trucker did all the talking, bent the kid's ears all day and almost all night. The driver's left hand gripped both the big wheel and a Camel cigarette. His right worked two stick shifts, in and out, up and down, like a magician. And he narrated with a lisp. The chain-smoking Dutch immigrant had lost his dentures in Kansas City, a wife in Colorado City, and eight hundred bucks at a craps table in Carson City. Although his lisp made it hard for Ubi to sometimes understand, the trucker could make places come alive that to Ubi were only answers to geography test questions.

With telephone poles and white lines clicking away mile after mile, Ubi kept a road atlas in his lap, flipping from page to page following the Dutchman's stories. A wild river that carved canyons through hundreds of miles of rock, a volcano that was simmering like a giant teapot, geysers that spewed steaming water into the air on the hour, every hour, Montana blizzards, Florida floods, California earthquakes, and Gulf Coast hurricanes—teachers could point to these places and events in books, but the truck driver had seen them through the magic lens of his windshield.

One story was no doubt folklore, but the young wayfarer would never forget it.

"This nasty old critter, all green and slimy, called the Ditch Dragon, comes up out of the creeks and bayous late at night while you're thleeping. It's quiet as death and it'll sabotage your rig, cut your tires or loosen your brakes so the next day you crath into the ditch. You don't have to believe me, but it's true. I've heard too many stories, seen too many wrecked rigs in ditches."

Ubi left the boys ranch at age eighteen and moved to Paisano, a nearby community of several thousand. Paisano managed to plod along without much planning and ambition from its leaders because it was the county seat. Government jobs and affiliated businesses pumped enough money into the local economy to keep the population at about five thousand. Ubi landed a job humping furniture for Owen Williams, about the only black man in Paisano, Texas in the late 1930s. As a youth, Owen left Paisano for Galveston and found work in the shipyards. He hung out at a gym, learned to box, and once lasted six rounds with future heavyweight champion Jack Johnson. But a crashing right hand left Owen face down on the canvas and partially deaf in his left ear. After many years living and working on the Gulf Coast, Owen returned home to take care of his ailing mother. Passing through Houston on the trip back to Paisano, he bought a twenty-four-foot box truck painted drab army-green. Everyone in town called it the Green Goose. Always eager to cover new ground, Ubi would jump in the Goose with Owen anytime, go anywhere, and haul anything. Owen pushed Ubi the way he had been pushed as a boxer.

"Don't worry about the mule, rookie, just load the wagon. Boy, boy, boy. If I didn't see it, I wouldn't believe it. You got the frigadator stuck trying to get it through the front door. The back door's wider. Whyn't you look fust. Rookeee."

But Ubi stuck with it, and together the team found a niche in the county, providing a service others either wouldn't or couldn't match. They were a fixture every morning and evening at Rosanky's Coffee Shop. Owen was a good nigger, Molly Rosanky had said, and she allowed him to use a table in the back near the pay phone for an office.

Drinking coffee one morning, Owen's blood clotted in his brain and he died the next day. Ubi used his savings to make a down payment on the Goose, to Owen's widow. For one year, he paid monthly installments and gave her ten percent commission for all the jobs he got from Owen's referrals.

After the Japanese attacked Pearl Harbor in 1941, Ubi tried to enlist. But Uncle Sam learned Ubi owned a commercial vehicle and put the Goose to work hauling assorted military goods to and from Army posts across Texas. For three years, Ubi saw more of San Antonio and El Paso than sleepy Paisano.

After the war, Ubi returned to the business Owen taught him, but those longer, wartime trips ruined him for regional driving. Hundred mile turnarounds, forget it. The long road beckoned.

Coming back from a delivery in Odessa one day, the Goose picked up a ten-penny nail in one of the rear tandem's. Owen had always carried a spare, and had taught Ubi how to change a tire. With the truck jacked-up on the shoulder, a driver for a nationwide moving and storage company stopped to help. The driver said his company's home office in Denver was looking for cross-country drivers who were good with furniture. The war had changed everything. People were on the go, moving coast to coast for good jobs. Call a mover. Throw the kids in the car. Time's wasting.

Yearning for the freedom of the open road, and saving for one of those truck tractors the interstate drivers roared down the road in, Ubi lived like a peasant for another two years. He finally unloaded the Green Goose for almost nothing and caught a ride in a tractor-trailer rig to Denver. Up in the mile high city, he bought a used GMC from a local beer distributor and signed a contract with Deaton Van Lines. Several years down the road, he bought the Peterbilt that would someday be known as Old Ironsides. Ubi returned to Paisano infrequently. But one spring the loads were scarce, so he hung around town for a few weeks, spending most of his time at the Concho Dance Hall.

* * *

Unlike young Ubi, grass growing under Cotton Kosper's feet wasn't an alarm sounding or call to action. Born in Paisano County, he would live there the rest of his life, rarely venturing more than two or three days away from home. A family vacation was an overnight trip to the Alamo or the state capitol in Austin. Cotton's plot in the city cemetery was secured near three generations of Kospers; the first came to Texas from Czechoslovakia shortly after the Civil War. Cotton never got over having no boys to help with chores. Embittered, he felt God had played a cruel joke, burdening him with four daughters and no sons. In Cotton's eyes, there were women jobs and men jobs. Period. Working outside the home— men. Inside the home—women. Except for house and car repairs and yard work, household chores were the women's responsibility.

"Where's my paper? Where's my dinner? Where's my socks? You girls, get the laundry off the clothesline before dark. Dishes and homework have to be finished before turning on the radio. Help your mother once in a while, for the love of Christ."

Cotton carried a bologna sandwich, chips, and Coke in his steel lunch box every day to his job at the city water treatment facility. The four girls behaved while under his thumb, but once out of high school, they never missed a dance or party. Cotton had to accept it, his wife said, the girls were now women.

A father without a son, and a son with no parents, it looked like Ubi and Cotton might find some comfort in each other's company. But they couldn't stand each other from the get go. On his first and last official visit, Ubi had just leaned back on the couch and was fidgeting with a glass of iced tea when Cotton fired the first salvo.

"Didn't you work for that nigger?"

Sherry jumped to her feet, stamped her foot, hands on hips. "Daddy!"

"Is this why I was invited over?"

"I'm just trying to remember, you had that truck, the color of pea-green soup."

"That man was like a father to me. I learned a lot from him."

"Learn what? Moving stuff? That's a highly skilled trade."

"Daddy, that's rude."

Ubi eased the sweaty glass onto the round, plastic coaster with the image of the Alamo on it. The ice cubes rattled around and clanked against the glass. He walked toward the front door and turned around.

"Good night."

The door fell solid behind him. Sherry bolted, grabbing for Ubi's hand on the front porch. Walking in full stride, he said over his shoulder: "When are you going to stand up to him?"

Sherry jerked Ubi's arm back and yanked him to a stop. "I'll stand up to him whenever I want."

"No you won't."

"I'll show you."

"Okay. Then marry me."

"I've only been dating you a couple weeks. You're crazy."

"We can get married in Vegas on the way to Sacramento."

"I can't marry you. You roam the country in that truck," Sherry said. She looked up at Ubi, tall and slender. "You roll into town, then you just roll on. What kind of girl's going to marry someone like that?"

The next morning, his rig parked near a friend's house, Ubi heard a knock on his sleeper. He rubbed his eyes and, peeled back the curtain. Sherry was standing there, tight blue jeans, blue cowboy boots, and hair in a ponytail. She had about six bags of all different sizes and shapes piled at her feet, and a wooden rocking chair handed down from her grandmother. Clutching her favorite pillow, she was putting on watermelon-red lipstick.

FIVE

SHORTLY AFTER UBI crossed into New Mexico, he pointed Old Ironsides north, toward the Colorado line. The highway narrowed until the shoulder disappeared and there was no place to pull over in case of breakdown. The road was now a patchwork of asphalt repairs, uneven and haphazardly connected. Pencils, caps, coffee mugs, and eight-track tapes all bounced around inside the cab. The pounding worked its way up through Ubi's vinyl seat and into his spine. But above the rig, wispy white clouds drifting across a backdrop of rich blue sky looked like a finger painting. With the road deteriorating by the mile, Ubi slowed the rig and a silhouette on the horizon began to take shape.

At first it looked like some sort of a clipper ship, sailing across a desert sea, frozen, and now a permanent part of the landscape. Old Ironsides purred along at an even pace, and what the Navajos called the "Rock with Wings" grew taller through the periscope of Ubi's windshield. What a work of art, 1,700 feet straight up, disappearing into low, thin clouds. The rig moved closer, dwarfed by the great rock. To get a full view, Ubi bent over the steering wheel and looked up until his neck popped. The truck circled southeast around the guts of a twelve-million-year-old volcano that the white man now calls Shiprock. Ubi turned off the CB, removed his cap and rolled down the window. A pickup zipped past in the opposite direction. Old Ironsides hugged the shoulder to give the driver some wiggle room. Wind whipped the sleeper curtain back and forth and threw Ubi's thin, silver hair straight up. Swirls of dust danced across the desert floor. Ubi took long, slow, deep breaths. The nerve endings in his face and on the top of his head tingled, like he'd sucked down one too many cups of coffee. No wonder the Navajo considered sacred this odd formation jutting toward the heavens like a great bird. Over the course of the next half hour, looking through the prism of his rearview mirror, Ubi watched the volcanic formation slowly diminish into the landscape.

Despite the rugged mountain driving, when his schedule permitted, Ubi preferred back roads for pleasures such as Shiprock. Rather than run with the pack on the interstate, lined up in formation, he pursued the same spiritual connections the Navajo did with their folk tale about how the rock was once a great bird that saved their ancestors from their enemies, transporting them across the continent and dropping them in the southwest desert. *Sheesh. This is what the call of the open road is about. This is the closest thing to being free.*

That night, Ubi put up Old Ironsides for the evening in a small Colorado mining town in the Sangre de Cristo Mountains. He checked into a modest room in a motel that would be overflowing with skiers in another month. Next door, at the Grizzly Bear Saloon, Ubi settled in on a wooden stool and looked up at a fuzzy, wall-sized, color screen where twenty-two men pounced on each other for three hours. Sitting at round tables covered with pitchers of beer, men and women in orange t-shirts howled and danced when their team scored a touchdown against the villains with silver stars on their helmets.

A young lady about the age of Ubi's daughter leaned across the bar, and straining to be heard above the din, explained to Ubi this was a private club.

"You can't drink here unless you're a member. You got a membership?"

Ubi was unwilling to shout only to be told he wouldn't be served. He shook his head from side to side.

"That's okay, baby," the bartender said. "Give me your driver's license, and I'll fix you up. One dollar."

Ubi positioned himself on the stool so he could reach his wallet, which had the girth of a paperback. He extracted his license and one dollar from amongst the diesel fuel and truck part receipts and phone numbers, and handed it to her.

"Happy birthday, Mr. Sunt. Sixty-six. Did the math in my head. You get a drink on the house."

Ubi ordered a draft beer. Shortly, the bartender set before him a frozen glass mug, foam oozing over the top and down the side, saturating the cardboard coaster.

About two sips later, a man wearing a brown felt hat with a large floppy brim almost covering his eyes entered through the back door followed by an Alaskan malamute. The man nodded and asked the waitress for a whiskey and Coke and a Kahlua and cream in an ashtray. The waitress set the drinks on the wooden bar. The man took the glass ashtray, bent over and set it on the floor. "There you go, Jack." He looked at Ubi like the two men had known each other for decades. "Named him after that writer, wrote those dog stories, you know, up in the Klondike."

Ubi nodded, sipped on his draft and twisted the swivel seat toward the man sipping his whiskey—scar across the bridge of his nose, cracked, dried lips that looked like they were about to bleed, long white mustache hairs that trickled down both sides of his mouth.

"I ain't seen another person in two weeks," the man said.

"Must be nice."

"Used to be able to get away, in the back country, placer mining, not see no one for a couple months. Cain't no more. Damned tourists, coming up year 'round now. Why cain't they leave a fellow alone?"

"I used to drive across the country, four, five days, hardly any traffic at all. Just keep rolling. Except for fuel and food, just keep rolling. Now they got tollbooths wrapped around the country like a spider web. Gotta stop and pay over and over. You run through the gears, get moving, then you got to start downshifting and braking again."

Ubi raised his beer mug, but put it back down without taking a drink. "And Oklahoma, by God, has a toll road halfway across the state. From Tulsa to Okie City and partways to Lawton. We pay road use and fuel taxes but that ain't enough, we gotta pay tolls too. And I got this damn beeper my dispatcher wants me to keep on my hip twenty-four hours a day—and that ain't going to happen—so he can bother me and tell me how he needs to change my schedule because he forgot about a load that needs covering."

Ubi raised the mug again and gulped. His Adam's apple bobbed up and down like a fishing cork.

"I hear they're going to put in a ski resort back near Bitter Creek," the miner said. "Imagine the bulldozers rolling through, carving up trees and hauling them away, taking ever last bit of the wildness that made the place what it is."

Jack belched. Ubi looked down, watched the dog circle two times and lie down on the floor.

"Good dog," Ubi said.

"Yeah. Damn shame he can't hold his liquor no more. He got me out of some tight ones when I'd come down and blow off a little too much steam." The man turned the glass up and drained it. He held it by the brim, raised it above his head, and shook it like he was ringing a bell.

"Nurse!" he yelled, and then looked back at Ubi. "I guess we're all getting old."

Ubi sipped the beer, wiped his mouth with the back of his hand.

"Speak for yourself."

The next morning, Ubi and Old Ironsides climbed Wind Creek Pass. Sunlight flickered through the Ponderosa pine needles and cast long shadows on the highway. The shadows danced in front of Ubi's rig and the diesel engine's growl echoed down the mountain in Old Ironsides' wake. He found a favorite pulling gear, rpms hovering around twenty-two hundred. The switchbacks and horseshoes had him twisting and turning up the mountain, hugging the inside shoulder on the right curves, and watching the center yellow stripe when the road veered left.

Almost to the summit, Ubi saw a beer truck sitting still in the climbing lane. A squat man with a heavy beard and a heavy parka bent over and placed three triangular, orange-red reflectors on the highway. Ubi let the rpms drop just a bit, and, without using the clutch, he goosed the accelerator and slipped the shifter into neutral. Continuing the fluid motion, he pushed the rpms back up and eased the stick shift into the next lower gear. The truck offered a low roar. Ubi split the triangles and pulled in behind the beer truck. The driver raised his hands in thanks. Ubi hung his head out the window, cupped his left hand around his mouth.

"What the hell's wrong? She quit on ya?"

"Don't know what happened," the beer truck driver yelled over Old Ironside's idling diesel engine. "Went for a downshift, hit the splitter, and it's like I got no power. Like she's in neutral. By the way, you nailed that downshift. Purty sound. Wished I could jam gears like that."

Ubi set the brakes, climbed down and dropped his chock block behind a set of drive tires. He walked up to the International Harvester rig, "Rocky Mountain Distributing" painted in red on both doors. The driver stood not much higher than the front tires. He unlatched the steel silver clamps on both sides of the hood and peeled it back. Standing on the truck's front bumper, his head disappeared inside the engine compartment.

"It's leaking air. Hear that?"

Ubi leaned forward. "Coming from in the cab."

He opened the driver's door. A soft drink can fell out, hit the asphalt, and rolled down the pass, picking up steam. A gust of wind blew several candy bar and fast-food wrappers out of the cab, swirling in the air about Ubi's face. He swiped at the cellophane.

"Sheesh, driver, you might want to think about cleaning out this truck."

"It's a piece of shit, anyway."

"Ain't no way to talk about a rig," Ubi said, holding his ear against the shifter where it disappeared into the floorboard. "Air's leaking from this spaghetti hose."

"What hose?"

"This little air hose, looks like spaghetti, that runs from your splitter into the transmission."

Ubi peeled back the thick, vinyl cover at the base of the stick shift that keeps hot air and road noise from rushing into the cab. "That's what allows you to drop from high to low range. It got hot and burned clean through. The shifter can't drop into low without air because it's air activated."

Ubi cranked up the engine and the air compressor started spewing air out of the burned hole. "That's what I'm talking about."

Ubi pressed his thumb against the hole and the transmission made a loud click like a key turning in a lock. Ubi returned to Old Ironsides, grabbed a roll of black electrical tape, and wrapped it tight around the spaghetti hose. The gush of air reduced to a slow hiss.

"Okay, let's roll. Grab your triangles right quick and I'll follow you into town," Ubi said. "You'll be all right, as long as you get off that clutch without rolling too far back."

Ubi followed the beverage truck up the mountain pass, back down, and watched it turn into an industrial park on the outskirts of a small town. Old Ironsides continued across the eastern slope of the Great Divide—running downhill and parallel to a swift stream that carried snowmelt toward the Arkansas River and eventually the Gulf of Mexico. Ubi then pointed the rig north on the interstate. Just outside of Pueblo, a familiar series of homemade billboards across an endless barbed wire fence caught Ubi's eye. Some of the wooden posts had rotted and the plywood sheets were leaning toward the ground. Although years of wind and rain and snow had faded the hand-painted letters, the defiant voice behind that paintbrush from years ago rang out.

"I fought in three wars for this country. Now the government wants to take my land. Who's next?"

Another quarter mile and another angry message: "This isn't progress, this is a government takeover."

Top a rise and another one, falling over in a brown pasture: "You'll take this land when my body lies cold beneath it. Not before."

And then a little farther: "Uncle Sam—Keep Off! Others Welcome."

Ubi remembered when those signs first appeared several years back. He tried to get answers on the CB and at a nearby truck stop. Who was this livid landowner? And what happened that pushed him to this point? Nobody knew. Now the signs were almost faded down. Old Ironsides rolled on. Ubi looked out the window at the last one, bent and gray, yet legible. "All Government Agents Will Be Welcomed By My Two Friends—Smith and Wesson." Ubi turned toward the road ahead. Perhaps some questions were better left unanswered.

Rocking down the highway on the squeaky driver's seat, Ubi's left arm dangled out the window and he watched the sun drop behind a silhouette of craggy bronze mountains. Just south of Denver, he pulled into a truck stop with a gravel lot and a rect-angular, flashing yellow neon sign: Curly's Truck Town. A low cloud of diesel exhaust hung over the parking lot. It was only mid-October, but fickle fall was already stirring up trouble. It would be a cold night at this elevation and numerous drivers were idling their engines to warm their sleepers and cabs.

Old Ironsides crept between dozens of rows of trucks until Ubi found an empty slot in the rear aisle. It would be a tough job, backing from the right, the blind side, in the dark, proba-bly why nobody had taken the space. It took three pull-ups, but Ubi wedged the rig between a Kenworth Aerodyne—a new model with a two-story bunk—and a long-nose Mack attached to a refrigerated trailer loaded with frozen beef. Ubi pulled the yellow and red levers on the console and the brakes took hold. The CB had remained quiet most of the day because Ubi kept the squelch knob turned low, filtering out most of the trash talk. The other party had to be right beside you or the radio wouldn't pick up the signal. Then a soft voice, clear and strong, came through the external speaker, mounted on the console with a steel bracket.

"Anybody looking for some company?"

Ubi looked to his right and saw the outline of a woman sitting in the Kenworth driver's seat. Slender cheeks and a long, thin nose. Wavy hair spilling down over her shoulders. Bracelets dangling from a skinny forearm. Narrow fingers clutching the CB microphone.

"Anybody looking for a date? How about that rig, just pulled in, looks like a Sherman tank?"

The woman in the Aerodyne turned her head toward Ubi.

"You want a good time? Take it down to channel twelve."

Ubi turned the key in the dash. The diesel engine shuttered once and quit. Then a different voice jumped out of the CB speaker, suddenly pushing up the needle on the radio gauge that measures signal strength.

"Why don't you damn lot lizards leave us alone? You been pestering us all evening. You beavers got no responsibility, just want to mooch off some lonely old boys been on the road too long. Then when we give in, pay more'n you're worth, you send us home packing a little something more than we bargained for. Got to worry about giving it to our wives or girlfriends. And you just blow all the money on booze, drugs and shit, drifting town to town. Don't give a shit about nobody."

"Why don't you just shut the hell up, driver?"

The woman now held the microphone just inches from her mouth, her hand shaking. "You don't know shit about me. Well, let me tell you something. I got two mouths to feed at home and I don't get no help from their old man. How you think I'm going to pay for groceries, clothes, and rent? Doctor bills, too? Working in the restaurant with the sorry tips you tight-ass drivers leave? Yeah, right."

"Aww, quit your whining, you old whore."

"Why don't you get off her ass, driver," a third voice joined. "It ain't no skin off your nose."

"She's a two-bit whore."

"I ain't no whore. I'm a working mother trying to make ends meet for my kids and I don't need you passing no judgment."

Ubi then watched a man climb out of the Aerodyne bunk, yank the microphone from the woman's hand, reach across the cab, and push the door open. The cab light flickered and burned bright. The woman looked about twenty-one. Ubi turned off the CB and slipped out of the lace-up work boots with waffle soles he had just bought two weeks ago. Twisting to his right, he unzipped the vinyl sleeper curtain and scooted up on the console between the front seats, called a doghouse, and crawled into the sleeper. Ubi rolled onto his back, grabbed a pillow, and felt his neck pop. He reached into a small cubbyhole behind him and pulled out a white, oval alarm clock and a paperback poetry anthology. He twisted the butterfly wings on the back of the alarm clock until it grew stiff. With the steady tick, tick, tick playing in his ear, Ubi put his head back on the pillow, neck throbbing, and opened the book.

"There's a race of men that don't fit in, a race that can't stay still.

They break the hearts of kith and kin and they roam the world at will."

A couple hours later, Ubi opened his eyes. Tap, tap, tap. Someone was at the door, knuckles rapping on solid steel. Ubi sat up, rubbed his eyes, put the book away and looked at the alarm—*you're kidding, three o'clock.* He peered out the curtain. The top of a head was visible through the driver's side window. *What the. . .?* Ubi reached down from the sleeper and popped open the door. Cold air blasted into the cab.

"It's freezing out here. Can I come in and warm up?"

Ubi recognized the voice, the woman on the CB last night. *Boy, she's as tall and skinny as a fence post.* The dome light illuminated her face. It had to be her.

"It's snowing out here."

"Okay. But hurry up. And close that pneumonia hole."

The slight woman grabbed the handrail and pulled herself up the snow-covered steps. Old Ironsides barely flinched. She slid into the driver's seat, and once inside, pulled hard on the door handle with both hands. *Wham.* Ubi lay back down in the bunk. The woman's wavy hair was now wet and matted. A ring of snowflakes formed a white crown on her head. "This Colorado weather changes in a hurry. It was sunshine and sixty degrees this afternoon."

She shook her head and ran her hand through her wet hair. "Thanks. My ride stood me up. And they kicked me out of the coffee shop."

Lying on his side, Ubi looked past the woman's profile at snow falling sideways, illuminated in the parking lot by the yellow sign sitting atop the restaurant. He set a roll of paper towels on the doghouse.

"They kick you out because you're working the lot?"

"You going to lecture me too?" the woman asked. She peeled free a sheet, ran it through her hair.

"It won't do no good. A person's gonna be what they want to be. Preacher, teacher, lawyer, truck driver."

"Hooker."

"I didn't say that."

"You were about to."

"Now you're a mind reader?"

"Yeah, that's it. I'm a mind reader."

The woman reached up and grabbed the CB mike. "Hey boys, get laid and your mind read at the same time. Can't beat that deal."

Ubi placed his forearm over his eyes. "I heard you on the CB last night. Is that true?"

"What?"

"You raising kids on a prostitute's pay?" Ubi reached toward the alarm clock. Tick, tick, tick.

"Maybe we should trade places, Mister. Shouldn't the one who's being analyzed be lying down?"

"Just asking. Don't get sore."

"Don't get sore? Nobody gets sore. We get pissed off. Where the hell you from, Mayberry?"

"I been around the block a few times, girly girl."

The woman peeled off another paper towel, wiped her face. "I got kids. Send money twice a month to their grandparents. Back in Ohio. I'm going back just as soon as I save some money."

"Mom and Dad know you're working truck stop parking lots?"

"Oh, sure, I report to them every night."

"You need to get rid of that chip on your shoulder. Here, make yourself at home."

Ubi handed the woman his pillow and an extra furniture pad he kept in the bunk. The woman sneezed and pulled another paper towel from the roll.

"You're a regular knight in shining armor, you know that? What's your handle, Sir Lancelot?" she asked.

Ubi ignored the comment and rolled over. Maybe he was too hard on her. Maybe he had grown too hard, period. It was sure going to be nice to see Jeanne and her husband and the twins. But first he had to make this drop in Denver and then wrangle a load back East. And tonnage out of Colorado was always hard to come by. Lots of folks moving in, but not many leaving.

When the six o'clock alarm rang, Ubi pushed back the curtain. The driver's seat was empty. The moving pad was gone. He looked on the floorboard. New boots gone, too. In place was a pair of tattered, wet tennis shoes. *That girl has big feet.* Ubi felt in the dark for the light switch in the bunk. Sitting upright, he squirmed out of the stack of thick furniture pads and slid into the driver's seat. His breath quickly fogged the windshield. He slipped on his cap, bright green work jacket, blew on his hands, and rubbed them together. Up on the dash, he found a sheet torn from the paper towel roll with a note scribbled on it: "Thanks for the shoes, Lancelot, just my size."

SIX

TRUDGING ACROSS THE PARKING LOT, Ubi realized how ridiculous he must look, wearing the woman's tennis shoes. But they fit and would have to do until he could dig out his old boots from wherever he stuffed them. Looking down, Ubi found fresh footprints in the snow—boots with waffle soles like his. He followed the trail to the main entrance and found the woman inside a phone booth near the front door, moving pad draped over her shoulders like a poncho. Ubi looked through the glass; she didn't see him. He stood behind a magazine rack, keeping one eye on the phone booth. A couple minutes later the woman raced outside. Ubi followed her to the door, looked outside and watched her jump in a cab.

Over in the restaurant, truckers poured down the coffee, cup after cup, complaining about high diesel prices. Ubi signed a waiting list for a private shower and took a seat in the corner.

"Paid eighty cents a gallon in Monkey Town—eighty cents."

"Ain't nothing, I heard it was almost a dollar in Winnemucca."

"I tell you what the problem is. It's them damn *A-rabs* that's doing it. Got that cartel going. Fixing the prices so they can stick it to us."

"Heck fire, we got plenty of awl right here, but them damn tree huggers got everybody scared to drill. Fraid they might spill a couple drops and get sued."

"We need to get up off that oil in the Gulf of Mexico—start pumping now. We got enough there to last us twenty years."

"There's talk back east 'bout going on strike. A shut down," said a tall man with a full black beard. Ubi figured he was the ringleader. "The big trucking outfits use lots of owner-operators like us. They don't pay for fuel, we do. And the companies that have their own fleet buy fuel in bulk, cheaper'n what we can get at truck stops. Whatatheycare?"

"We need to convoy to Washington. Do something like those farmers did."

"The deejay on that all-night truckers' radio show's trying to get drivers organized for a nationwide shutdown," the instigator said. "I'm all for it. Start right here. Right now. I'll block this driveway quicker'n old Fatty in the kitchen can fry two eggs sunny side up."

Then a voice over the loudspeaker announced the shower was ready for the Deaton Van Lines driver. Ubi left a dollar and change on the counter, stood up, stretched.

"You guys bitchin' about high diesel prices, every one of you ran your engine last night and probably got 'em idling right now, wasting fuel," Ubi said, looking down at the row of drivers at the coffee counter.

"It snowed last night, driver. Do I look like an Eskimo?"

The other drivers snickered, eyes focused on Ubi gathering up his canvas bag.

"I slept without no heat," Ubi said. "Didn't bother me none."

"I ain't freezing my ass off just to save some dinosaur bones," the ringleader said. "Besides, I seen what climbed out of your truck this morning. No wonder you didn't get cold."

More laughter, but louder. Ubi shot the group a glare, stalked off.

"You see the shoes he's wearing?" one driver asked. "And who is that old fart?"

"He's driving that tub in the back row, Old Ironsides. You ain't heard of him?"

"Nope. I stay east of the Mississippi and south of the Mason-Dixon much as I can."

"Old Ironsides is a helluva rig, can pull any pass in the Rockies without even belching. I heard he got that thing set up with gears and a tranny like a logging outfit."

"What's top end?"

"'Bout thirty."

The truckers' laughter followed Ubi into the next room to the fuel desk where he handed the clerk a dollar. The woman pushed across the counter a tiny bar of soap and a thin white towel and wooden tire bumper, key dangling from the fat end, attached by a white string. Shower stall number four. He weaved through a cluster of drivers smoking cigarettes and watching a black and white TV mounted on a wall near the ceiling. Small white letters scrolling across the screen carried notices of loads and their rates. Drivers scratched notes on the back of fuel receipts and envelopes. Dry freight: Colorado Springs to San Antonio—eighty-eight cents a mile. Potatoes: Alamosa to Wichita—ninety cents a mile. Flatbed needed for heavy equipment: Cheyenne to Billings—one dollar a mile.

Ubi glanced at the screen, thankful he was on a preferred dispatch list with Deaton Van Lines. Canvas bag hanging from his shoulder, he headed down the long corridor past pinball and cigarette machines and a row of stools sitting before pay phones. A young black man pushed a cart overflowing with dirty, wet towels in the opposite direction. Ubi stopped in front of a narrow door with peeling veneer. He inserted the key, pushed hard.

Inside, the tile floor was wet and slippery. The grout had turned black. A sixteen-ounce Coors can sat collapsed in the corner. Ubi sat on the commode lid and pulled off the old tennis shoes. He folded the thin towel, dropped it on the floor, and stood barefoot on it. He turned on the shower faucet marked with a bold H and stripped. Waiting for hot water, he pulled on a pair of plastic beach sandals. He held out his hands. Cold water. *Oh well, can't wait forever.*

"Yeeoow!" Ubi's shout echoed down the corridor. Drivers standing in front of the TV laughed and looked over their shoulders.

"Some poor sombitch just froze his balls."

Heaving like he'd run up several flights of stairs, Ubi rubbed a bar of soap across his head and shoulders, under his arms, and between his legs. The water level in the shower was soon ankle deep and began to spill out onto the shower room floor. A small piece of sheetrock flaked overhead and splashed into the water, turning it milky white. Ubi quickly finished showering in the ice water. He leaned out of the shower, and with one hand, dug through his canvas bag and pulled out a faded blue beach towel. After drying off, he slipped out of the sandals and into clean clothes. He managed to shave in the cracked and foggy mirror, only cutting himself once, near his left ear. On his way out of the shower stall, he picked up the soaked truck stop towel from the floor and hung it from a towel rack. Water streamed down, seeped under the door and pooled in the hallway.

Ubi played it safe for breakfast: coffee, toast, and Raisin Bran. This truck stop was not the place to take a chance on an omelet. Ubi and Old Ironsides then sloshed their way up the interstate into Denver. He pulled in front of a sprawling warehouse several blocks long. A new, eight-foot fence topped with barbed wire encircled the spacious, empty parking lot. Ubi set the air brakes—*whoosh*. He stared at the plywood sign attached to the rolling, chain-link gate. *FOR SALE.*

Walking in a daze, Ubi approached the two-story office building, spruce trees growing in raised planters out front. The glass exterior reflected cars and trucks passing on the freeway. For more than three decades, he had leased his tractor-trailer rig to Deaton Van Lines. This was their home office where he signed his original contract. Sure, it had grown and expanded, spilling down the street for five blocks, but this was a refuge, a second home for road drivers, a place where they could meet face-to-face with dispatchers and the girls at the money desk that controlled your advances, and the trip settlement team that cut the checks. At least it was the last time he stopped here several months ago. He checked in last week, notified dispatch he'd be in to deliver today. Nobody said a word about moving the warehouse. And he had left a message with his old buddy's secretary. She said nothing.

Ubi kept walking. Back in his old boots again, his toes quickly rubbed raw. He looked up; a patch of blue broke through thin clouds. Then he saw something that hadn't changed: the old pay phone on the corner. He dug in his pocket, found a quarter. A storage clerk took the call.

"Where are you at, sir?"

"I'm at the warehouse," Ubi shouted, one hand pressing the receiver against the side of his face, the other cupped over his ear. "Why is it all locked up with a *FOR SALE* sign out front?"

"We moved."

"No kidding. Can you give some directions to the new place."

"I don't know where you're at."

"I told you. I'm at the old warehouse."

"Well, I'm not sure where the old warehouse is, *sir*. I just started a few weeks ago, so excuse me."

"Oh, brother. Let me talk to Mick Thorton."

A chilly gust whipped down the boulevard and jerked Ubi's cap from his head. He left the receiver dangling from its silver chord and chased down the cap, which had lodged in the chain-link fence. Back at the phone, he heard a familiar voice.

"Hey, Ubi, I got your message just this morning. I've been on vacation. Man, I'm glad you called. I need to talk to you about the new ownership. Heard you were delivering at the warehouse today. You running late? That's not like you."

"Why did you guys move, Mick? Sheesh. Didn't even tell me. I'm at the old warehouse, locked out, freezing my ass."

"Been some changes in the company. Don't you read your mail?"

"Well, no. Not since everything happened with . . . well, you know. Thanks again for flying out for the funeral."

"Wouldn't miss it. That woman was a saint to put up with you all those years."

"Ten-four, Mick. Big ten-four."

"I tried to find you a load, checked the board. Denver's dead. Nothing going out for at least a week. Sophia says you're staying with us."

"Come on, Mick. You know I don't make a good houseguest. We been through this before."

"Don't care. I got orders from the wife. Kids are on their own and we got all this room."

"Sheesh."

"See you in a few. I'll make sure the warehouseman knows you're on the way," Mick said.

"Okay—but I still need directions."

Click.

Ubi held his hands over his head and looked at the sky. The patch of blue had disappeared. Gray clouds scudded across the horizon and smothered the mountains to the west. He dug in his pockets again. Found some loose change.

By lunchtime, only a small part of the furniture shipment Old Ironsides lugged up from Southern California had been unloaded. The warehouseman and crew broke at noon and left Ubi alone on the dock, refolding and neatly stacking furniture pads that helpers had sloppily piled against a wall. No pride. Ubi yanked on a pad that was folded inside out. The whole stack fell. He bent over to start restacking and heard dress shoes clicking on the concrete warehouse floor.

"Hey, driver, looks like you could use some help," a familiar voice said.

Looking up, Ubi saw his old friend, trim and tall as always, and dressed in his typical brown business suit. But the black strands of hair that he used to comb over that bald spot were filtered with gray specks. And the bald spot had grown considerably.

"Hell, they got these pads folded and stacked bass ackwards. Don't you train these guys anymore, Mick?"

"Been a lot of changes around here, Ubi. Come on, there's a deli across the street, got a good bowl of chili. We got some catching up to do."

Sitting at a table by a plate glass window, the two men slurped down red-hot bowls of chili. Passing cars and trucks sprayed slush onto the sidewalk.

"Our cargo claims are going through the roof. The new owner's breathing down my neck," Mick said, blowing on a spoonful of chili. "You're the best stick man we got. I want you to be a trainer, Ubi, settle down in big D."

"What's wrong with the one you got?"

"He's from sales. You know what that means."

"Probably never loaded a furniture van in his life," Ubi said. He piled a cracker high, bit it in half, and waved his hand before his mouth like it was on fire. "Man, somebody got carried away with the chili powder."

"I can get you a good salary."

"I'll settle for a glass of water."

" I'm serious. Mostly you'll be teaching in our training room. Maybe do some hands-on loading one day a week, and a few day trips," Mick said. "But mostly it will be nine to five, Monday through Friday."

"Come on Mick. I'm not a babysitter. Besides, I work best alone."

"Ubi, this isn't easy to say. . ."

Mick looked out the window, avoiding eye contact. ". . . But dispatchers claim you've lost a step. It takes you longer to get loaded and delivered than it used to."

"I'm not going any slower," Ubi said, dipping another cracker in the chili. He bit off a corner—hotter than hell, but not bad. "Everybody else is just going faster these days."

"You could be a great mentor. I've heard all those Ubi Sunt stories. Stories about you showing drivers how to sandwich loads together to get more tonnage on a trailer, how to thaw out frozen brake shoes, how to load cars, motorcycles, boats. We have a crummy little break room now, coffee's lousy, but look on the wall and you'll see that picture of you hoisting a piano onto a fourth-floor balcony in downtown Denver."

Mick pushed the bowl aside, propped both elbows on the table, and folded his hands under his chin. "You're a part of company history."

"I just don't have the patience," Ubi said, loading chili onto a fresh cracker. "Those kids helping me on the dock this morning, I couldn't deal with that ever day. And what are you going to do when I walk in your office one morning demanding a load because I got the itch again?"

"You got to learn to live with that white line fever, Ubi, sooner or later."

Ubi polished off the cracker, said nothing.

"You might be sorry," Mick continued. "You never know what's around the bend. They're talking about thinning out the herd, no rigs older'n ten, twelve years."

"What the heck is that about?"

Mick leaned back, drummed his fingers on the table, then looked straight into his old comrade's eyes. "Old Ben Johnson drove through a guardrail, off the side of Cabbage Mountain yesterday. That '62 Kenworth rolled to the bottom, him in it."

"Damn," Ubi said, looking out the window. "Damn. Why didn't you tell me this morning?"

"That's not something you say first thing to someone you haven't seen in months. Anyway, that's what's prompting this new policy. Ben's KW was almost twenty years old," Mick said. "By the way, that makes you the senior driver, the patriarch here at Deaton. You're the oldest and been running the longest now."

Ubi pushed his bowl toward the center of the table. "I'm doing the only thing I know, Mick. I can't put up with these kids. Half of the drivers today, they just want to play truck driver. They don't want to work."

Ubi leaned forward and reached for the green ticket lying near the bowl of crackers. But Mick snatched it from the red, checkered tablecloth and held it up.

"Like I said, word over in dispatch is you've lost a step, *compadre.*"

Ubi shook a toothpick from the jar in the middle of the table and stuck it between his teeth. It sounded like Mick tacked that comment on the end of his sentence, *compadre*, just to make it look like he wasn't taking a cheap shot. Ubi looked at Mick out of the corner of his eye.

"Waitress cuts a pretty good figger."

Mick turned his head toward a pony-tailed blonde, tight skirt, sashaying past with a coffee pot. Ubi's left hand swooped in and grabbed the check from Mick's fingertips. He stuffed it in his shirt pocket.

"I may be old, and I may be slow, but there's still plenty of diesel left in the tank."

Walking across the street back to the warehouse, Mick asked Ubi to drop by his office after he was through unloading.

"And bring that pager with you. The one we mailed to your house last year. Dispatchers say you never call back when they send you a message."

Back at the warehouse, Ubi finished unloading at about dark-thirty and paid the two lumpers in cash. They wanted more money, but Ubi held them to the prearranged price of sixty cents per hundred pounds. Ubi counted out the twenty dollar bills one at a time, licking his fingers between each Andrew Jackson. "No stairs, no snow, no piano. And you want more money? You must think this high altitude's gone to my head. A deal is a deal."

Ubi then found Mick's office and settled in an armchair, facing his wooden desk.

"You got that pager, Ubi?" Mick asked.

Ubi dug the plastic object out of his pocket and slapped it into his old friend's palm. "Be my guest. Your little thingamajig don't work."

Mick flicked the on-off switch, then turned the unit upside down and fiddled with a small plastic trap door. He looked up at Ubi, rolled his eyes.

"There's no batteries."

"Sheesh. Batteries? Never thought of that."

"Didn't you ever get your daughter a Christmas present and on the box it said *batteries not included*? You know, a toy car for Barbie or something that she probably broke before New Year's Eve?"

"I wasn't home very often on Christmas. You know that, Mick," Ubi said. He looked at the floor. "I was probably out covering some hot load or shipment that got left on the dispatch board because somebody broke down or said they were sick."

Mick opened the lap drawer to his desk, pulled out two small batteries, and tucked them inside the pager's guts. He flipped the on switch. The screen flickered and black letters on a gray background scrolled past. Mick rattled off several old messages.

"San Diego shipment cancelled. Call dispatch ASAP. That was last April. Got a shipment in Tampa. Good rate. Call dispatch. Also last April. Need a favor; driver broke down, looking for backup to cover a load in Akron. That was in May."

Ubi watched Mick work the tiny up and down buttons with his forefingers like a madman, clicking and tapping.

"You have twenty-three unread messages. Happy birthday, Grandpa. When are you coming to see us? Love, Molly and Jeremy."

"How did my grandkids send that message? They got one of them things too?"

"No, no," Mick frowned. "I'm sure their mother called dispatch and asked them to forward the message." Mick slid the pager across the desktop and leaned back in his wooden armchair. Ubi looked down at the gadget like it was a snake.

"Go on, pick it up. It won't bite."

"No thanks," Ubi said. He squirmed in his chair, a creaky, wooden artifact probably from the early days of the company. "I know how to use a pay phone. At least the toll-free number to dispatch hasn't changed. I check in when I need to. I mean, it's too bad I didn't get the birthday message, but it ain't like it was the twins talking to me on the phone live."

Mick took a long breath and tapped his fingertips on the desktop. The corners of his mouth sagged.

"Go on, say it. You're fixing to fire me. Fire me 'cause I don't want to be a trainer, 'cause I don't want that little contraption strapped to my hip so you can look over my shoulder twenty-four hours a day. Fire me 'cause I won't give up my old rig. You know that load from Tampa? I already filled out in Jacksonville. And Tampa's three hundred miles out of my way."

"Ubi, the day they fire you is the day I quit," Mick said, chopping the air with his right hand, in rhythm with his words. "But you've got to understand. . . . Do you know what they call you and your truck over in dispatch?"

"I really don't care what people say about me," Ubi said. He was getting annoyed. New warehouse, new owner, new gadgets. Why couldn't they just let him be? And now even Mick, it felt like, was turning against him.

"They call you Mike Mulligan and the Steam Shovel."

"Huh?"

"Mike Mulligan. The children's story about the old-timer who wouldn't give up his ancient steam shovel named Mary Anne, even when the new ones were faster and better."

Ubi still hadn't touched the pager.

"I know that story," he said, fidgeting in the chair. "I remember reading it to Jeanne as a little girl, sitting in my lap. In the end, Mike Mulligan races the new machine and wins, but he digs himself into a hole he can't get out of. So they put up a building around his steam shovel and it stays in the basement, heats the whole building."

After an awkward silence, Mick leaned over his desk.

"Ubi, that pager is just the beginning. A few trucking companies are experimenting with satellite tracking systems that can monitor their rigs around the clock. Hook up a little gizmo on the roof about as fast as you can install a CB. That's all it takes."

"Nobody's putting a dog collar on me and Old Ironsides. I'm independent and staying that way."

"The times are changing, Ubi. Let me ask you this. What happened to the open range when they invented barbed wire? And what happened to the Pony Express after the telegraph came along?"

Mick stared across the desk. *Why was Ubi so inflexible? How can you get through to someone like that?* He leaned back in his chair. *Better not push it.* Mick glanced down at the pager, back up at Ubi. Maybe it was a mistake telling him the dispatchers call him Mike Mulligan. And maybe it was a mistake declining that settlement offer from the new owner. After almost thirty years of sixty-hour weeks, his wife deserved more of his time.

Then the phone rang. Ubi flinched and his hands sprung up off the armrests. Mick picked up the receiver. "Hello, dear. We're leaving right now. Chicken and dumplings sounds great."

While Mick made small talk with his wife, Ubi stepped into the hallway. The pager remained on the edge of the desk.

For three days, Ubi stayed with Mick and Sophia, sleeping in an upstairs guest room furnished with Colonial oak dressers, matching nightstands, and a double bed with tall posts on both the head and foot boards. Down the hallway was the piano room. One night Ubi woke from a dream; he was alone, loading all the furniture from Mick and Sophia's two-story house into his trailer. Concentrating on the bedroom that he had been staying in, he eased the stout triple dresser down the narrow staircase using a two-wheel appliance dolly. Then he tackled the upstairs piano by himself. Using a piece of equipment that resembles a gurney, called a piano board, he slid the instrument down the staircase and through the tight corner at the front door. But the ramp into the trailer went straight up. Like Sisyphus pushing a boulder uphill, every time Ubi got the piano to the top of the ramp, near the trailer door, the piano slid back down.

For the next few days, Ubi rode into work with Mick. The dispatch board where the operations department tracked outbound tonnage was as empty as the eastern Colorado high plains, so Ubi kept busy working on his rig. The first day he swept out his trailer several times, and in doing so found a couple of furniture pads that had mildewed. The snow showers had moved east; the afternoon was warm and blue, so Ubi hung the pads like bed sheets on a makeshift clothesline behind his trailer in the back lot. Ubi opened the rear and side trailer doors, and cool, dry mountain air swept through the empty van like air freshener. He went through each stack of pads, and if he saw one that was out of line, he shook it out and refolded it. When he was done, the stitching faced the same direction on every pad and each stack stood perfectly straight, from the floor to the top. The straps that held the pads in place were pulled tight like fence wire.

Another day, Ubi took advantage of the same bright weather and gave Old Ironsides a thorough cleaning. With a brittle whisk-broom he kept under the seat, Ubi swept out the truck tractor. Gravel and dirt and potato chip bags and chewing gum wrappers, a greasy rag, he swooshed them all into a brown paper sack. He sprayed down outside mirrors, glass, and headlights with Windex and rubbed them with a copy of the Rocky Mountain News until all the bug guts and glass streaks disappeared. Then Ubi used a short steel pipe to jack up the cab so it tilted forward. Remembering horror stories about mechanics and drivers who had their skulls crushed by a falling truck cab, Ubi wedged a wooden block near the hinge so even if the hydraulic hose blew out the cab wouldn't fall. Then he checked for oil and coolant leaks. Everything was tight.

Back at Mick's one night, Sophia set the table with the every-day China and pulled out of the oven a casserole dish topped with a layer of bubbling cheese. She poured three goblets half full of red table wine.

With two grown kids now living out of state and her husband working long hours, Sophia found her days long and unfulfilling. She could go back to work, sure, but it had been about twenty years since she held a full-time job. Instead, she fretted over her husband's wardrobe and meals. She kept an immaculate home and sent a well-fed, manicured husband into the rat race, five, some-times six, days a week. But now with a houseguest—Ubi Sunt, the recent widower, longtime driver, and family friend—she found an opportunity to throw a nice dinner party, even if it was only for three.

"I wanted to have a lovely dinner, since it's been such a lovely day and I have the company of these two lovely men," Sophia said, long black eyelashes fluttering.

"This is lovely," Ubi said, unfolding the red, cloth napkin in his lap.

Mick poked his nose inside the wine glass, sniffed and then sipped. Ubi reached for his glass, grabbed the stem, and raised it to his mouth. He tried to steady the brim against his lower lip, but purple drops trickled out the corners of his mouth. With one hand, he raised the napkin to his lips, and with the other he quickly set down the glass. It teetered and fell onto the tabletop.

"Sheesh, I'm so sorry," Ubi said, his face matching the color of the wine. "Let me get it."

Ubi dabbed at the wine with the napkin, and it turned purplish red. Embarrassed for his friend, Mick grabbed the serving spoon and dug into the casserole dish like nothing happened. Sophia's face looked like someone had backed into her Alfa Romeo at the beauty salon. Her head and shoulders sagged, and when she glanced at Mick for help and their eyes met, she realized her dinner might not go as smoothly as expected.

Ubi made it through the salad without any further mishaps. With that feat accomplished, he took a deep breath and looked down at his next challenge: a full plate of lasagna. Fortunately, Sophia turned her attention away from Ubi and toward her husband.

"Honey, the reverend's housekeeper called this afternoon. She wants to ship one of their pianos to a nephew in Baltimore. He's supposed to be another Chopin, supple wrists and fingers that cartwheel across the keyboard," Sophia said. She exhaled slowly and held her hands above the table. "Oh, why was I born with these clumsy digits?"

Ubi negotiated his way through the lasagna, left hand shaking. Almost finished, the fork slipped from his sweaty fingers, bounced under the table, and landed beneath Sophia's chair.

"I'll get it."

"No, please don't," Sophia said, clutching her wine glass. "It's okay."

Too late. Ubi had already bent down. He got his head completely under the table, bumped it, and shook the dishes. Sophia shivered. Mick kicked the spoon across the floor into Ubi's hand.

"Sorry I'm so clumsy," Ubi said, returning the spoon to the place mat. He stood up and slid his chair against the table. "Thanks for dinner. Can I help with the dishes?"

"Oh, my word," Sophia blurted, then covered her mouth with her hand. "I mean, uh, thanks, but it's okay."

Ubi turned toward the staircase and took two careful steps, making sure he didn't bump the table.

"Ubi, can I ask you about your, um . . ."

Sophia paused, searching for the right word.

Ubi stopped, and with his back to Sophia, addressed her. "You can say it. My problem."

"Well, your condition, I prefer to call it your condition. Have you seen a doctor?"

Ubi slowly turned toward Sophia. "Oh sure, got all kind of subscriptions."

"You mean *prescriptions*," Sophia corrected. "So, do they help?"

"They're worthless. They give me headaches and gas and keep me up all night. When it gets really bad, I just get in the truck and drive. Nothing else works. I'm okay as long as I stay busy, keep rolling, you know. But when I'm sitting still, it's like my arms and hands won't listen to me."

Ubi stepped toward the staircase and clutched the banister with his left hand. The wine and lasagna warmed his stomach. "Thanks for asking. Thanks for the lovely dinner. Thanks for letting me bunk here. Good night."

Upstairs in his room, Ubi opened the poetry book his wife had given him for an anniversary present, something to keep him company on long nights out on the road. The hardback cover had suffered a couple of coffee stains, and the pages had yellowed somewhat. Still, that book had been a good friend through the years. And Ubi had bought three more poetry volumes, kept them in the bunk for nighttime reading. Influenced by favorites Walt Whitman and Emily Dickinson, he had coped with Sherry's illness by writing. He never made it past a few pages. Yet writing was like trucking, solitary and therapeutic.

Most efforts landed wadded up in the bottom of the trashcan. Tonight was no different. His attempt to capture how the southwestern sky in El Paso was sometimes blotted out by the copper smelter operation there was another failure. Here you go, in the garbage where you belong.

The next morning, with Ubi and Mick down at the warehouse, Sophia decided it was time to wash the sheets in the guest room. Pulling off a pillowcase, she bumped over the wastebasket and a crumpled piece of yellow paper rolled out. Sophia flattened out the wad, sat down on the edge of the bed, and turned on the lamp. *What's this? A poem?*

> Looking up at Big Blue
> I run my hands
> across the horizon.
> At thirty-thousand feet
> contrails carve up Big Blue
> like a birthday cake.
> Sometimes, a gray curtain
> obscures Big Blue,
> smokestacks, emissions.
> Big Blue is patient, waits
> for us all to go away.

Oh, my word. How sad. Sophia rolled the paper into a ball, held it in her fist, and walked downstairs. Standing before the kitchen garbage can, she thought about Ubi and how his life devoted to traveling was so incomprehensible. She flattened out the yellow paper, opened it, and read it again. Maybe he wasn't as one-dimensional as he seemed.

Still waiting on a load to the East Coast, Ubi hung around the break room and chatted with the warehouseman and a couple of forklift drivers. They were having trouble locating storage lots. Moving a hundred-thousand-square-foot warehouse loaded with furniture had rubbed raw almost everyone's nerves.

Sitting in a chair with brown stuffing oozing from a ripped vinyl seat, Leroy the warehouseman held a Zippo lighter to an unfiltered cigarette hanging from his mouth. He had finally found the storage lot for those folks in Delaware, a mahogany dining set that had belonged to their grandparents. A storage clerk had been hounding Leroy: "They been calling for three weeks—pissed off. They want their shit and I'm tired of taking an ass-chewing for your drunk ass."

* * *

Working at Deaton Moving and Storage was the only job Leroy Mays had ever had. After four years in the Navy during World War II, he returned home, age twenty-two, and found work as a warehouse helper. One snowy November afternoon, the operations manager caught the head warehouseman snuggled under a thick moving pad, napping in a Duncan Fife sofa in a loft reserved for overstuffed furniture. The next morning, the owner promoted Leroy to warehouse manager. For the next thirty years, you could find Leroy anywhere in the warehouse by following the jingling sound of the big, hoop-shaped steel key ring dangling from his hip.

Leroy's bulbous nose and his oversized, potato chip ears made for cruel jokes from a serial cartoonist who drew caricatures on the restroom stalls and warehouse walls. So far, the culprit hadn't desecrated the new warehouse. The new owner issued a memo and hung it on the drivers' room bulletin board promising he would fire anyone who wrote or drew on company property.

During the move to the new warehouse, Leroy was recovering from a long bout with Jim Beam. Standing in the hallway one afternoon, a dispatcher told Ubi the story:

"When his wife died in that car wreck last February, Leroy crawled into a bottle and wouldn't come out. After he backed the forklift through the wall into the ladies room, Mick drove him home and moved in with him. They came to work and went home together, ever day. And Mick's wife, she came over and cooked supper ever night. After Leroy got tired of living with his boss, he quit drinking and Mick moved back home. As far as anybody knows, Leroy ain't touched a drop since," the dispatcher said, running a black pocket comb through his shoulder-length hair. "Leroy said he's glad he sobered up, but he hasn't had a good meal since last spring."

* * *

Leroy scooted back his chair and curled up the warehouse locator sheet in his fist.

"That makes three storage lots going back east," he said. "Let me go tell the boss man."

Ubi was sitting at the same table. He followed Leroy down the corridor toward Mick's office. The two men walked past a pictorial history of the moving company. Framed black-and-white photographs of Depression-era trucks with spoke wheels and uniformed drivers waving from running boards gave way to a chrome-dressed, Kenworth eighteen-wheeler with "Hi-tech Specialist" hand lettered on the trailer. Ubi caught the image of Old Ironsides hanging on the wall. Ubi and Sherry, arms around each other's shoulders, were dwarfed by the bumper, grill and massive front. Ubi stood, frozen, his eyes burning like he'd driven late into the night and got up early the next morning to pound more pavement.

"You coming, hoss?"

Ubi looked up. Leroy stood at the far end of the long, narrow hallway, holding the door open for him. How long had he been staring at that picture? Leroy closed the door and approached Ubi.

"You fixin' to go through hell, Ubi. I ain't lying. I know. I been there. Sure, I fucked up the way I handled it, staying drunk and all. And Mick helped me pull out of it. But just 'cause I'm sober don't mean it don't hurt no more. And you know what? I hope it don't ever stop hurting."

Leroy jutted his Durante-sized nose into Ubi's face. Red and purple veins stood out. His tobacco breath burned Ubi's eyes even more. "A man that don't feel no pain, well he ain't no kinda' man at all. No count. That's what I'm tellin' ya, Ubi Sunt."

Leroy and Ubi then walked through a large open room crammed with dispatchers seated elbow to elbow. With telephone earpieces lodged in the crook of their necks, and fingers furiously chasing letters and numbers on keyboards, they peered into black computer monitors they called "the tubes." These dispatchers delivered marching orders to several hundred drivers daily. Ubi paused and watched one slam his phone into the cradle.

"Driver musta' turned down a load," Leroy said. "Probly didn't want to deadhead from Yazoo to Kalamazoo."

Inside Mick's office, Leroy shoved the locator sheet inside a plastic tray already stuffed with white and yellow papers. Mick handed him a folder with another missing storage lot. Leroy flipped through it and quickly left. After the door closed, Ubi placed his palms flat on Mick's desk and leaned forward. "How many of those lost storage lots you got that need to go back east?"

"Half-dozen. Maybe more. Seems like Leroy got overwhelmed with the move. We got shit scattered everywhere. And that's just one of my headaches. Real estate issues. The Interstate Commerce Commission's breathing down my neck about logbooks.

Dispatchers are getting squeezed because the new owner doesn't know why a driver can't deliver in Sacramento and San Diego the same day. They're both in California, so he thinks it shouldn't be a problem."

"It's no secret they're five hundred miles apart, Mick."

"Tell that to the owner."

Mick then opened the lap drawer, pulled out a plastic bottle, and shook it like a baby rattle, little pills pounding inside. He twisted the cap and poured two antacids into the palm of his hand. "Go through about six of these a day."

He threw back his head, grabbed the water glass that sat next to the phone, and swallowed hard.

Ubi leaned over the desk. "I want all those little storage lots going back east."

"Come on, Ubi. You know I can't get directly involved in dispatch. Playing favorites," Mick said, slipping the pill bottle back into the desk drawer. "We got drivers waiting for loads longer than you've waited. Two, three weeks."

Ubi stood up straight. Stuffed his hands in his pockets. Took a long, deep breath. Exhaled slowly.

"I'm pulling rank. I was hauling for you guys before most of these dispatchers heard of Rand McNally. And by the way, half of 'em still haven't, but that's another story."

Ubi looked down at Mick, the desk covered with files and papers, the red message light on his phone flashing nonstop.

"I'm helping you clean up this mess, Mick. Gimme all your little lots that are going to the Northeast. I need to see Jeanne and her family. And I'll clean up the docks in your warehouses from here to Omaha. Twenty shipments, I'll take 'em all. And I'll take that grand piano at the preacher's house too. The one your wife was talking about at dinner the other night."

It was Ubi's time to cash in on all the good will he'd accrued over the decades, for all the hot loads he covered with little sleep, for all the extra miles he ran when his logbook was out of hours but he drove anyway, dodging the truck scales and weigh stations, for all the backtracking and deadheading. He'd been making deposits for decades, and now it was time for a withdrawal.

"Besides, nobody hustle's for a load like me. They're all spoiled; want a full wagon from coast to coast. I know what your dispatchers call those drivers—barges, 'cause all they want is the high-paying, easy loads going pond to pond."

Ubi paused, pulled his hands from his pockets, and dropped his arms to his side. First, the left hand started twitching, fingers tapping on his pants leg. Then the right hand started shaking. Ubi looked down at both arms, his fingers tap dancing out of control against his legs.

Mick stood up, leaned over his desk. "Can you stop that?"

Ubi's face turned crimson and the veins in his neck stood out like red lines on a road map. This time he shoved his hands into his back pockets, but they continued quaking.

"Yeah. Get me back on the road!"

SEVEN

Reverend James L. Dagney had been at his favorite spot in his split-level log cabin mountain home for more than an hour when the moving van pulled up out front. With his left hand hanging limp at his side, the right hand maneuvered up and down the ivory keys of a Steinway baby grand piano. Four fingers, long, thin, and nimble, darted and danced across the keyboard.

Ubi banged on the door until his knuckles turned red. Yet the reverend, left side of his body paralyzed by a stroke, continued playing, unaware the man and his two helpers waited on the front porch. Then, a round woman with a feather duster in her hand opened the door. The rush of cool air stirred the room and the reverend slowly rotated on his piano stool.

"He's saying goodbye," the housekeeper explained. "Been playing since the sun come up. You fellas ever know somebody who played Carnegie Hall?"

Before Ubi or his two helpers could answer, the woman continued: "Didn't think so. Well, now you do. Play another for them, Reverend. You fellas sit down on the couch over there. I'll bring some hot tea."

The man played for another fifteen minutes while the threesome sat dutifully on the couch sipping tea. Ubi had two more stops that day, one in Glenwood Springs and the other in Longmont, so he wanted to get going. Still, as the partially paralyzed reverend played, Ubi relaxed. At the end of the sonata, all three men stood and clapped. The reverend slowly climbed to his feet. He bent over the piano, kissed the black and white keys over and over, and slowly closed the keyboard cover.

The moving men then removed the harp-shaped lid and wrapped it in thick, soft furniture pads. Ubi crawled under the piano like he was adjusting trailer brakes. Grunting and squirming flat on his back, he looked up at the piano's underbelly. He unscrewed the foot pedal assembly and handed it to a helper. The reverend stood in a corner and watched the operation. The helpers stood at opposite corners of the piano, lifting slightly as Ubi unbolted two legs and set them aside. The three men then tipped the piano on its edge. Ubi unbolted the third leg. The trio wrapped the piano with furniture pads and strapped it on the piano board. Ubi then slipped a four-wheel dolly under the instrument.

The reverend slowly approached the piano, arms outstretched, and rested his head on top of it. He said something to the men, but they couldn't make sense of the jumbled words. The stroke had left one side of his mouth drooping and misshapen. The woman stepped in and interpreted.

"This is the first piana he ever had. Bought it with money he saved over ten years working as a timber cutter. He cain't play it like he use ta could. Now he wants his nephew ta have it." Ubi and the helpers awkwardly hung their heads, unsure what to say. The woman continued. "You may not know Reverend Dagney, but he's recorded seven albums, everything from Mozart to Beethoven to Duke Ellington."

By now the reverend had wiped his eyes and raised his head from the piano. When he heard the housekeeper say Duke Ellington, his eyes lit up. "Geeev . . . thaim . . . an albwum."

The three men squinted.

"He wants ta give you fellas an album. Hold on, I'll be right back," she said, holding up her index finger.

"Don't worry about me," Ubi said. "I don't own a stereo."

"What you mean?" the housekeeper asked. "You live out of that truck?"

Ubi nodded. "Mmmhmm."

The woman turned toward the basement stairs, took three steps, paused, and with her back toward Ubi, she pointed toward the ceiling and repeated, "I'll be right back."

After the woman disappeared down the stairwell, the crew rolled the piano across the threshold, down the concrete sidewalk and up the loading ramp into the rig. Ubi strapped the piano to the trailer wall and returned to the house to get a signature. The reverend scrawled his initials on the bottom corner of the inventory sheet and insurance certificate.

"Maybe I shouldn't say this," Ubi said, looking across the room and then back into the man's face. "But I'm sure sorry for what happened to you."

With raised eyebrows, the reverend handed over the paperwork.

"Your piano. It's like that truck to me. I don't know what I would do if something happened and I couldn't drive no more. Just don't know," Ubi continued, looking down at the red tile floor, unable to fix his gaze on the reverend's sagging face. "Reverend, I guarantee you one thing. Nothing's going to happen to that piano. Guaranteed. I know you can't play like you used to, but I'll get that Steinway to your nephew safe and sound. You have my word."

Ubi held out an open right hand. The reverend wrapped his sinewy fingers around Ubi's stubby knuckles and squeezed tight.

"Whuut kind uh truuck?"

"Fifty-six Peterbilt. Got over two million miles on her. She can pull a herd of elephants over Pike's Peak." Ubi forced a smile.

The reverend's droopy face remained unchanged. But Ubi sensed a touch of laughter in his eyes. The men held hands until heavy footsteps on wooden basement stairs broke the trance.

"You got an eight-track stereo in that submarine-looking truck of yours?" the housekeeper asked, holding out a small plastic box about the size of a paperback. "Now you can hear how good the reverend was when he played with bof hands."

Ubi and Old Ironsides spent the next few days together mountain climbing. Steep, winding roads carved from mountainsides makes herding an eighteen-wheeler up and down narrow passes difficult even in good weather, but Mother Nature was once again digging in her bag of tricks. A couple inches of snow fell in the higher elevations and one morning just after the sun poked its head into the rearview mirror, Ubi left the Continental Divide eastern slope and entered a two-mile tunnel bored through the throat of a thirteen-thousand-foot mountain. Inside the tunnel, Ubi flipped the toggle switch on the dash and his headlights cut through the darkness. Then a small red convertible, top down, zoomed past. Two heads bobbed up and down in the front seat. The radio blasted, echoed off the white tunnel wall, and eclipsed the diesel engine's drone. Crazy kids. Top down in this chilly weather. A faint glow soon appeared ahead and gradually grew brighter—the end of the passageway. Ubi noticed the road was wet and he tapped the air brakes. Back in the tunnel, snow had been falling from vehicles' hoods, trunks, and roofs and melting when it hit the road. Water then meandered down the tunnel floor until it hit the cold highway outside and promptly froze.

Only a few hundred yards after leaving the tube, Ubi saw the red convertible spin around in the middle of the road. It bounced off the concrete wall on the left shoulder and skidded toward the right side guardrail. Old Ironsides skidded on the thin layer of ice and went into a jackknife. Truckers call it a jackknife because, like a pocketknife snapping shut, the eighteen-wheeler is trying to fold in half at the point where the truck is attached to the trailer by the fifth wheel.

It's a sick feeling, trailer gaining on you in the rearview mirror; like falling from a tree in slow motion, grasping at branches as the ground grows closer. With luck, the rig will straighten when the driver takes his foot off the accelerator. You could also pull a hand lever that activates trailer brakes, but it's a tricky thing. Too much brake makes things worse and you could end up playing crack the whip with a sixty-foot rig. A jackknife is typically the result of driving too fast on wet or icy roads, or braking too hard. The beginner who escapes his first close call with a jackknife will drive away with valuable experience. After his heart stops pounding and his sweaty palms dry, he'll never look at truck driving in the same way.

Ubi's trailer wheels continued to roll free and push the tractor sideways. He gently pulled the trailer brake attached to the steering column and felt a little tug, like a catfish taking bait, and the skidding truck slightly straightened. Up ahead, the convertible bumped against the guardrail and continued slowly downhill, backwards. When Ubi and Old Ironsides approached in a half-skid, the passengers covered their eyes.

"Easy now, girl."

Ubi gently pulled the hand brake lever. The trailer obeyed and realigned behind the tractor. Ubi drifted past the convertible and onto the shoulder where the road rose slightly uphill. He hit the brakes hard and skidded the last ten feet before stopping. But his rig sat slightly cockeyed, looking as if it had just come around a corner, and hadn't completely straightened out. "Damn black ice."

Ubi set the air brakes. A scratchy voice on the CB speaker announced the highway department had just closed the tunnel behind them. The red convertible continued sliding backward downhill, toward Old Ironsides. The driver fought the steering wheel, trying to turn the little car around. Fresh scars ran down both sides of the vehicle like racing stripes. The driver got the car pointed forward, but it spun around again and smacked into the side of the trailer. It screeched against the rig, steel on steel, until the tiny car lodged against the giant truck's door.

Ubi peered down from his open window into the convertible. Breathing hard in the thin air, the couple was either high on something, insane, or having the time of their young lives. The driver's long reddish hair was mussed and covered her face. She turned up the collar on her long-sleeved blue denim work shirt. The tails of her red scarf—loosely tied around her neck—flapped in the wind and slapped her in the cheeks. She yanked at the knot, loosened the scarf and pulled it over her ears and the top of her head. The passenger reached under the seat, pulled out a windbreaker, and crammed long skinny arms into the sleeves. His head was shaped like a football. Ubi reckoned they couldn't be older than twenty-five. He remembered the Florida plates he saw in the tunnel—figures.

"You kids okay?" Ubi yelled.

"Yeah. Thanks for playing backstop," the man said, panting. "If you hadn't been here, we might still be sliding."

"What the hell are you doing way up here? This ain't the Everglades you know."

"We're grad students. Researchers," the young lady said, her head pitched back, looking at this strange man in a strange truck. "I'm Amber. Journalism candidate for a master's degree." Amber gripped the windshield for balance, climbed on the front seat and shook Ubi's hand. She then introduced her co-pilot.

"And my friend, Larry, is a candidate for a master's in photojournalism," she said, pushing stubborn hair strands from her face.

"I'm Ubi Sunt, and if you want to get down this mountain without breaking your necks, I suggest you wait a while for the sun to melt this black ice."

"Black what?"

"Ice. That's this slippery stuff you been sliding on like a hockey puck."

The two looked at each other and frowned. Ubi continued. "It's actually clear ice that freezes on the road. Mostly at night. But you can't see it because it's clear. You see the blacktop highway below, think it's dry road. Then, next thing you know, you're spinning like a top down the middle of the highway."

"How long till it melts?"

"Hard to say. Could be soon. Could be hours."

"We need to get going," Larry said. "We're on a journey to find the real America."

Amber shot Larry a look colder than the black ice. "Just look at the dents and scratches on my new car. And all you can say is, let's get going."

The convertible was only a few weeks old, a graduation present from Amber's parents that she named Little Red Riding Hood, and it already looked like it had been in a demolition derby.

"You inconsiderate knave."

Oblivious to Amber's insult, Larry climbed on the back of his seat, sat down, and spun his body toward Old Ironsides. "Amber, when I push against the truck with both legs, you let off the clutch and hit the gas," he said.

Amber thanked the trucker again and turned to Larry.

"What about Little Red Riding Hood?"

"Don't worry, we'll take it to a body shop when we get home. I know someone," Larry said. "Now, on three, you pop the clutch."

In a whir of spinning tires and leather Dingo boots pounding on a semi-trailer, the car broke free from the rig like a lifeboat from an ocean liner. Ubi watched Larry talking and waving from his perch on the back seat as the car disappeared down the mountain.

"Damn fools," Ubi shook his head. "Better go check on them. Might roll that little Match Box car into a canyon."

Ubi released his brakes, put the truck in gear, and engaged the clutch. The drive wheels broke free and spun around, emitting little puffs of steam. Old Ironsides didn't budge. Ubi climbed down and rummaged through his side box, a compartment accessible only from the ground that he used for storing snow chains, a fire extinguisher, red triangles, several cans of Spam, and other stuff that would seem like junk to anybody else. To keep from slipping on the ice, Ubi had to keep one hand wrapped around a handrail. With the other, he dug deeper into the side box until he found a small carton containing laundry soap and a quart of bleach. He worked his way around the eight drive tires, pouring several ounces of bleach under each one. A few minutes later, Old Ironsides broke through the ice and Ubi eased the rig down the pass, braking only when the road leveled off and he knew he could get firm footing. He continued this pattern until the road met a stream bed and ran parallel to it. Down in the valley, he took in the view—a swift mountain stream and a fly fisherman hopscotching across it on river rocks, remnants of ancient boulders that tumbled down from the mountain above. The nimble fisherman, wearing forest green waterproof pants and a windbreaker, turned toward Ubi and waved both hands above his head, crossing them over and again. Then, a bright flash reflecting off something in the river. Something the color of lipstick, or the inside of a watermelon. Little Red Riding Hood.

No place to pull over. Ubi stopped in the right lane. Flung open the truck door. He then performed a spin move he perfected shortly after he bought the truck, when he was young and cocky. One hand on the rail, one foot on the top step, he vaulted away from the truck and landed like a cat on both feet. He'd pay for that tomorrow.

The lanky fly fisherman was suddenly in Ubi's face, eyes pinned open, stammering something about a red convertible that almost hit him as it crashed into the rapids and washed downstream. Ubi looked up. The two kids were standing on the front seat yelling. The car was wedged against a boulder, rocking back and forth. Swimming or wading into the stream was impossible. The whitewater would pound against the rocks any fool who tried. It looked like the little car was safely pinned against the rock; still, the look on those kids' faces told another story. For all he knew that car could at any moment break free and continue downstream. They had to do something.

Ubi was no fisherman, other than bringing in a few channel catfish back at the home when he was a kid. And he knew little about the mysterious gyrations that fly fisherman used to launch their tiny lures into mountain streams. He pointed at the tall fishing rod that rose a couple feet above the man's head.

"You any good with that thing?"

The fly fisherman flipped up the lid on the basket hanging from his hip. Three rainbow trout squirmed inside.

"I have my days."

"I hope this is one of them," Ubi said. "Cause we're going after a big one."

Ubi swung open the rear trailer door and fetched several cargo straps he used for securing furniture inside the van. He tied them together until he had more than one hundred feet of line. He tied the last section so the steel turnbuckle was hanging free. This would be the anchor. Then he told the fisherman he would have to cast his lure into the convertible's front seat. The men tiptoed the rocky stream bank to a great boulder with a flat spot on top. The fisherman stood on Ubi's bent knee and slithered up the rock. Lying face down and still hugging the boulder, a wave crashed against the rock and soaked the fisherman. Ubi watched the man rest his head on the rock. Water trickled down his canvas hat and onto his shoulders. Ubi caught a little spray too. He felt a shiver run down his backbone. The man pulled his hat tight, climbed on all fours. Ubi handed him the fly rod.

"How many pounds test is that fishing line?" Ubi asked, watching the man gain his balance and stand up.

"Eight pounds. Not enough to pull no car out of the rapids."

"It'll do."

The fisherman twisted, turned, and waved the rod in the air. Fishing line floated above his head like a spider web. Ubi couldn't understand how all that line would not get tangled. With a flick of the wrist, the fisherman's tiny homemade lure soared in the air above the car and landed on the hood.

"Misjudged the wind," the fisherman yelled above the spray.

"Sheesh. Are you kidding me? That's perfect. Now yell at them to pull the line. I know they think we're crazy, but tell them keep pulling."

The fisherman cupped his hands, yelled, and the wind carried his orders to the couple. They yelled back, but whatever they said was drowned out by wind and the roar of the rapids. But the kids pulled on the line until the fisherman's reel was empty. Ubi then tied his cargo strap to the end. The two men waved and yelled for the couple to keep pulling. A few minutes later, the young man in the convertible reeled in the end of Ubi's yellow cargo strap. Ubi relayed orders to the fly fisherman, still atop his perch on the boulder, to tie the strap to the steering column. The fisherman yelled. The youngsters obeyed and waved back through a prism of soft sunlight and white foam.

The angler looked down at Ubi, shouted to him that the kids had the strap tied off. He yelled again. But Ubi couldn't hear. Looking up at the fisherman standing on the boulder with rapids crashing around, Ubi fell into a trance. Standing on his pedestal, the fisherman looked like he was carved in stone.

"Hey trucker," the man yelled again. Another wave crashed at Ubi's feet and he snapped out of it. "How many pounds test is that yellow strap?"

"We're fixing to find out. Maybe two thousand. Good thing it's a tiny car."

The fisherman nodded. "Let's reel her in."

The angler slipped down the boulder and onto the bank. Ubi then backed his rig to the edge of the soft slope, near the water's edge where it looked like the car had left the road. He climbed back down from the driver's seat and slid under the trailer. He tied the strap to a steel beam that held up the wooden floor, made the sign of the cross, "Father, Son, Holy Ghost," and headed back toward the driver's seat. Then he heard a scream like someone was riding a roller coaster for the first time—the car had broken free from the boulder and was bobbing in the stream, held in place only by the strap. Ubi hitched up his pants, pointed at the fisherman.

"You're my eyes and ears. I can't see them from my rig. You got to stand somewhere you can see me and the car at the same time."

Ubi dropped the transmission in low gear. With a soft touch, he eased out the clutch. The bend in the road just ahead should give him the angle to pull the car out of the current and near the shore. The kids could scramble out then. A four-wheel-drive pickup roared by, swerved around Old Ironsides, and the driver leaned on the horn. Ubi continued inching forward into the right lane. He felt a strong tug. Looked out the window, but no fisherman. Damn. Ubi reached for the air horn, but the lanky man appeared in the mirror, standing on the water's edge, waving his arm for Ubi to continue. A Ford Bronco drove up, slowed down. The driver stared, but continued. The fisherman continued bobbing in and out of view, waving at Ubi, and then disappearing to check on the terrified couple. Ubi felt a bump on the end of the line, like the car was stuck. Then he heard a loud, *whoa, whoa, whoa*. The fisherman's red face suddenly appeared in the passenger's window. Hanging on the side of the rig, fighting for air, his body heaved up and down.

"We got 'em. The car caught a boulder on the bank, and they climbed out. We got 'em. Thank God, we got 'em."

"Damn fools," Ubi said. "I told them to take it easy." A station wagon swished past, narrowly missing the front bumper. Ubi backed the rig out of the road, set his brakes, climbed out, and grabbed two furniture pads from the trailer. He approached the wet couple.

"So, we meet again."

The two youngsters grabbed the dry pads and wrapped them around their shoulders. Seconds later, a heavy wave splashed against the little car and the strap came untied at the steering column. The car drifted downstream, out of sight.

The young woman sat on the riverbank and put her head in her hands. Her long hair fell limp and matted on her shoulders. She sniffed, choked back tears, and rubbed her eyes. Finally, she held up her head.

"I can't believe it, Little Red Riding Hood, gone," she said. "My graduation present from my parents. Gone. Floating down the river. How am I going to tell them?"

"Well, at least you're alive," Ubi said.

"Yes, you're right. We are alive. And thank you so much, for the second time today," she said. "We're alive, but that car was . . ."

The woman dropped her head into the crook of her arm.

The angler looked upstream, his mind on trout. Then he turned and faced the wet couple.

"You kids need a ride or anything?"

Before anyone could answer, car wheels crunching river gravel interrupted the conversation. Everyone turned and looked.

"Never mind," the fisherman said. "Here's the sheriff."

The sheriff interviewed the youngsters. The fisherman tiptoed up the riverbank, around a bend. Ubi followed, caught him on a point bar where the current slowed to a lazy pace and the water softly gurgled.

"What makes you come out here?" Ubi said.

"I just like to be left alone."

"I like being left alone too," Ubi said. "That's why I drive that rig. But it's not that simple. What else?"

The angler's mouth dropped open, and his head tilted a few degrees to the left. Clearly annoyed, he said, "If you're looking for something like the meaning of the universe, trucker, why don't you climb up that mountain?" The man pointed his rod at a snowy peak. "See if you can find some prophet, maharishi, or guru, or whatever up there."

Ubi looked at the ground, kicked at some pebbles, rolled them under his boot soles. The angler tied an artificial insect on the end of his line, spit on the knot, and pulled hard on the end with his thumb and forefinger. When he looked up, he was taken aback by the expression on Ubi's face. How could a sixty-something-year-old man with the ingenuity to save those two kids be so tortured? The man leaned against a stump, propped his fishing rod against his leg.

"Because I find something here I can't get anywhere else. Booze, sex, religion, I tried it all. Nothing gives me this tranquility like trying to outsmart these beautiful animals. I don't know why. I've got a wonderful wife, kids. Ain't rich, but ain't poor. But this works for me," the angler said.

A minute passed. The stream bubbled nonstop. The men's ears adjusted to the sound, a backdrop to their conversation.

"The road does the same thing for me," Ubi said. "Sometimes it got to where I wasn't worth nothing at home. My wife would finally say, 'go on get outta' here before you drive us both crazy.' She understood me like nobody else. But now she's gone, and if I'm hanging around too long in one place, I get this rash. Like poison ivy."

The angler stared into the river, stone-faced, and without looking up, said, "Fishing works pretty good for me."

A silent minute or two passed. Then the men noticed a figure on the riverbank headed their way. "Aw, heck. Look here. The sheriff," the angler said, pointing upstream to a burly man wearing a brown jacket and fuzzy brown hat with the earflaps folded up. "You do the talking. I've got fish to catch."

The angler tiptoed upstream. A sudden rush of water splashed against a boulder. When the spray and mist settled, the fisherman was out of sight. The trucker and the sheriff walked back toward the road, chatted about the incident, and Ubi gave a statement. The would-be journalists were leaning against the sheriff's car, furniture pads still draped across their shoulders. The sheriff said he was on his way to Loveland to pick up a prisoner wanted for auto theft. Salvaging the automobile that washed downstream would have to wait.

The sheriff asked Ubi to take the youngsters to a nearby town so they could call folks back home. Twenty miles later, Old Ironsides rumbled into a small community that was once a thriving mining hub, but now consisted of a post office, a few bars, and a restaurant. After everyone made their phone calls from a pay phone hanging on the side of a utility pole in a muddy parking lot, the youngsters insisted on riding with Ubi and Old Ironsides.

"Why don't I drop you off at the nearest bus station and you can head home? Sorry, Amber, but you can write off this trip to youth and inexperience."

"We don't give up that easy," Larry shot back. "We're out here to find the spirit of America, the heartland."

Larry was now wearing a Dartmouth cap, and he pulled on the bill, determined to continue the trip.

"Please," Amber added. "We can't go home failures. Even though we lost the car, we can save our story."

Ubi looked down at Amber's pleading brown eyes and thought about his daughter, Jeanne, and how she used to bat those long eyelashes and get whatever she wanted—movie tickets, new clothes, sleepover at a friend's. "Okay, get in," he said. "But I ain't no babysitter."

EIGHT

FOR THE NEXT THREE DAYS, Amber and Larry helped Ubi stack cartons, furniture, and household appliances in the trailer, using vinyl straps and plywood decking to separate the loads. Calling dispatch daily, Ubi found enough tonnage to fill his trailer.

They moved a small-town lawyer returning home to Boston. He didn't want to pull a rental trailer across the country and agreed to pay moving costs to ship his law books and furniture from his one-bedroom apartment. Ubi and the youngsters carried everything down from the third floor. Next gig, an antique dealer on a hunting trip had bought a jukebox and several pinball machines from an old saloon in the Colorado mining town of Meeker. He needed it shipped to his store in Reading, Pennsylvania. And, that same day, they loaded a nine-hundred-pound gun safe in Rawlins, Wyoming that a New Jersey banker and gun collector bought on vacation and wanted shipped back east. Ubi paid his new helpers cash. Bunking in the trailer at night, Amber and Larry sat cross-legged underneath a flashlight hanging from a trailer wall and recorded the daily events in their journals. The thick furniture pads kept them warm, even when the Rocky Mountain nights dropped to freezing temperatures.

Ubi's patience with small loads that most drivers refused paid dividends. Interstate shipments are priced according to miles and weight. And when you're buying anything in bulk, the more you purchase, the less it costs, whether it's sold by the gallon, bushel, or, as in the moving business—per hundred weight. With a No. 2 lead pencil and a Big Chief tablet, Ubi did the math. A trailer full of minis, as dispatchers called them, paid twice the revenue of one household that filled a rig. And unlike some drivers who like to just throw it on, throw it off, Ubi enjoyed sniffing out the small loads, often going out of his way to grab an extra shipment other drivers turned down. Ubi relished the challenge of rearranging his trailer, shuffling shipments around so he could make room for that 1957 Indian motorcycle a Milwaukee man inherited and ordered shipped from his uncle's place back in Laramie, Wyoming. That one shipment paid for a tank of fuel.

After adopting this strategy ten years ago, Ubi ordered a custom forty-five-foot trailer, the longest one available, with extra doors on both sides. This low-slung beast, called a double drop frame, had more cubic feet inside than conventional moving vans. And in the furniture hauling business, cubes are what counts. By studying the road atlas in his bunk at night, Ubi knew how to load the shipments for easy access when he made his deliveries. When Ubi was trying to fill his trailer, he kept in close touch with the Denver office, hustling, scratching, calling for more tonnage from public telephones in truck stops and cafes. And he pulled it off without a pager.

"Dispatch . . . I got five-hundred cubic feet open. You got anything in Western Colorado going to New England? No, I'm not full . . . because I got this big wagon and I load tight. Okay, I'll take that shipment to Erie, drop it on the way across. Whattya got in Erie when I drop that? A load to Providence. . . no problem."

But there was a drawback to dragging that big boxcar across the continent. The middle of the trailer could hang up, or high-center, on railroad tracks and humps in the road. That happened only once, at a low water crossing in the Texas Hill Country near

Kerrville. It took Ubi two hours with his hydraulic jack and blocking timbers to wiggle the beast free.

Ubi and his new crew loaded his last shipment, a half-dozen desks and credenzas from an oil company office in Cheyenne; his next stop—a military base in Rapid City, South Dakota. Ubi slipped through four gears in low range, hit the air-assisted knob on the shifter, five more shifts, and the rig soon hummed down the highway. Up and down, winding through the back country on a two-lane road, sometimes Old Ironsides would catch a pothole that shook the cab, and open drinks would fall over or spew their contents through the pop-top.

With Amber riding shotgun and Larry sprawled out in the bunk, the couple picked up the thread about searching for America. Like the earlier conversation outside the tunnel, Larry led the charge.

"We want to know what everyday people think about government oppression and imperialism, corporate greed, malfeasance, and the destruction of the environment," he said with a booming voice. "We're the next generation of Woody Guthrie, Jack Kerouac, T.S. Eliot, Hunter S. Thompson. We're the new counterculture. We're writers and prophets, philosophers, poets, anthropologists and environmentalists. We're going to tell the story that will define our generation. Do you know what that exhaust from your truck is doing to the polar ice caps? Well, do ya? Do you know with every mile you drive you're helping carve a whole in the ozone, not to mention damage to . . . "

"Okay, okay, okay. Larry, don't get carried away," Amber interrupted. "Will Rogers said he never met a man he didn't like. Larry never met a conversation he didn't like. Even in the middle of nowhere."

Ubi pushed Old Ironsides along at a steady clip. Fast enough on the downhill side to easily scale the next grade, the diesel engine hummed along like a marathon runner. No sense to get in a hurry. These Black Hills, or Paha Sapa according to the Lakota Indians, were something to behold. They could make you feel a little spooked if you let them. Ubi learned from literature he read on an earlier trip that the hills were named for their dark appearance from a distance. Some of the granite and gneiss outcroppings had remained steadfast through eons of erosion. But expanding ice in deep crevices had cracked and weakened the rock, and wind and rain and gravity pushed boulders down below, where they broke into pieces. What remained upright sometimes looked like sentries, guarding the sacred Lakota land. Eerie—yes, a little. But more than that, serene.

Ubi's left arm dangled out the window. Right hand steady on the wheel. The nervousness that dogged him in Denver had melted away like snow falling from those cars back in the Colorado tunnel. His brown eyes were clear and sharp.

"You have any music?" Amber blurted above the wind whistling through the windows. It was a warm afternoon, and Old Ironsides had no air conditioning.

Ubi had forgotten about the reverend's jazz tape. He had meant to give it a try, and just yesterday unwrapped the cellophane, inserted it in the eight-track's open mouth, but never pushed it completely in. With a flick of the wrist, the reverend's piano that was riding in the trailer came to life inside the cab. The solo intro to "Take the A Train" echoed off the doors, the bunk, the windshield. Ubi pushed the rig around a bend. Amber smiled, sat up straight, placed both hands on the dash like it was a keyboard, and ran her fingers back and forth. She shifted her weight in the seat as the top-heavy rig swayed around the curves. Larry sat up in the bunk and rolled Ubi's road atlas into a cylinder. When the trumpet player broke in, he held the horn to his lips, gyrated back and forth like the jazz musicians they saw last week in New Orleans. And, unknown to the other two, Ubi's clutch foot rhythmically tapped up and down on the floorboard.

"Jazz, unbelievable," Larry roared from his perch in the bunk. "Riding through the Black Hills in an eighteen-wheeler listening to jazz. Friggin' unbelievable."

Through the evening, the reverend's piano ushered the trio down the long and winding road. After the tape had gone around once, clicking from track to track after every two or three songs, Ubi turned down the volume. By the second time around, the scarlet sun had dropped behind the distant hills to the west. Larry had fallen asleep lying on his back in the bunk, mouth wide open. In the shotgun seat, Amber's narrow chin kept dropping on her chest. She'd wake with a startle, eyes popping open, and sit upright for a few seconds before her head began another descent. Ubi reached across the cab, touched her shoulder, and nodded toward the bunk. Although Amber and Larry put forth that their relationship was platonic, Ubi sensed otherwise. He'd seen how they looked at each other, an unspoken language all lovers learn at some time. Amber crawled into the bunk and snuggled up to Larry. Ubi reached behind him and pulled on a string near the truck ceiling. A vinyl curtain rolled down and the bunk was suddenly dark inside.

Alone with his thoughts, Ubi drove into the night. Rounding a long curve, the front right tire dropped off the shoulder, and the truck shook and pitched to one side. Amber bounced awake and heard the driver's seat squeaking under Ubi's weight. Ubi pulled the wheel hard to the left, and the truck righted. But the jolt pitched a heavy brown paper bag from a small shelf above Amber's head and it softly landed on the mattress near her chin. In the dark, she crunched the brittle paper between her fingers and pulled out a hardback book and pencil-thin flashlight, probably for night reading. She flipped the flashlight switch and propped herself up with her elbow. She opened the book and found the yellowed title page: *The Complete Works of Walt Whitman.* At the bottom, she read a faded inscription, something about a happy anniversary. But a signature at the bottom was clear—Sherry Sunt. Although the date was scratchy, it looked like about the same time Amber was born—24 years ago. Amber carefully thumbed through the pages. A twinge of guilt—like she was snooping in someone's diary or she was a peeping Tom—flirted with her conscience. But she couldn't control her trespassing fingers and wandering eyes. Numerous favorite passages had been underlined, and someone had scrawled notes in the margins. A breakfast receipt from a truck stop marked where the reader had left off.

> *When I sitting heard the astronomer where he lectured with much applause in the lecture-room,*
> *How soon unaccountable I became tired and sick,*
> *Till riding and gliding out I wander'd off by myself,*
> *In the mystical, moist night-air, and from time to time,*
> *Look'd up in perfect silence at the stars.*

The flashlight soon dimmed and Amber closed her eyes, holding the book to her bosom. Suddenly, she didn't care if the old trucker discovered her transgression. It seemed okay, maybe because she had discovered something tender out on the hard road.

Ubi continued pushing Old Ironsides through the Black Hills. A headwind buffeted and rocked the rig on almost every turn. No matter, the highway was empty, no oncoming traffic, and the sky was loaded with stars. The diesel engine's steady hum and the rig gently swaying felt to Amber like she was an infant back in Florida, rocking in her mother's arms.

Just before midnight, Ubi found a wide swath of gravel on the right shoulder and pulled over. He set the brakes. Valves on the dash popped. Air hissed. But the young couple did not stir. Ubi climbed down from the rig. Standing on the roadside, he took a deep breath, tilted his head back, and exhaled. Vapor formed a funnel above him and drifted away. Ubi found the Milky Way, a cluster of stars so thick it looked like a low cloud. Would a celestial trucker someday zip from planet to planet dropping off and picking up stuff the way he drove across North America? Or would transportation in the sense he knew it become obsolete? Maybe they would send goods across galaxies the way voices are transmitted on the CB. Load whatever kind of freight that would be needed into a transmitter, and by pushing a button like the key on the microphone, the goods would materialize in another world.

Ubi looked down briefly, rubbed the crick in his neck, and raised his head once again toward the heavens. He liked the idea of a space trucker better. An independent contractor with his own rig, flying twice the speed of light, making deliveries across the universe. Ah, what foolishness. Can't let go of this tired old rig—rebuilt the engine three times, transmission once. How can you wrap a mind around the mysteries of the universe? And sometimes mysteries are better left alone. Just keep it simple. Town to town. Day to day. That would have to be enough. Let tomorrow take care of itself. Right now, gotta get some sleep. Gotta drop this shipment first thing and make it to Minneapolis tomorrow night.

Ubi sauntered around the back of the rig, crawled inside the trailer, rummaged through a milk crate and found a large yellow flashlight. Working in dim light because the batteries were old, he made a pallet from several moving pads. He reached in his jacket pocket, pulled out a small alarm clock, and twisted the wing nut on the back. The steady ticking soon lulled him to sleep. Ubi was a light sleeper and had an innate sense of what time it was even when he was crossing time zones on a regular basis, so the alarm was backup. A few hours later, the morning light slanted through a small crack in the trailer door where Ubi had strapped it shut. Lying on the moving pads, he stretched and groaned and threw off the covers. Shortly, he had the pads perfectly stacked and strapped against the wall. The alarm in his pocket rang—6 a.m. Standing outside the trailer, he heard a steady rocking sound coming from the front of the rig, like someone was standing on the truck frame bouncing up and down. Outside, he walked toward the rig's front and stopped beside the passenger door. The cab again bounced slightly up and down, squeaking just a little on the mounting brackets. Ubi's eyes found the faded letters on the rig—Sassy Sherry. He smiled a wistful smile. Rolled a stone back and forth under his foot.

* * *

"It's chilly in here."

"Let me pull the covers up. How's that?"

"Nice and warm when I put my head on your chest. Like this."

"That's real nice. Tickles."

"Want me to stop?"

"No. How did you sleep?"

"Like that log at the park entrance. That soft rain on the roof was soothing. Like a waterfall. You?"

"Slept like a baby. I'm going to poke my head out, see if it's stopped."

"Okay . . .what do you see?"

"Nothing. Still dark."

"Good. Come back under the covers."

"When do you have to catch that bus again?"

"Later. Don't worry. We got time. If I miss the nine o'clock, they'll be another one."

"I wish you didn't have to go. It's different when you're on the road with me. It doesn't matter if things go wrong, a load cancels, or I'm late because I blew a tire."

"We have a two-year-old now."

"I know."

"Grandma and Grandpa said they would keep her for only a week. Then they're going to the coast."

"I'm just talking."

"I know."

"Maybe I'll give up the road. I'm a good mechanic. I could stay home, work on cars, trucks."

"Honey, you would drive everyone crazy. Remember when you took off all December last year? You changed the oil in my car three times."

"Well. I 'm just talking. Here comes the rain again. Hear it?"

"I love it under the covers, with you, when it's raining."

* * *

Ubi circled the tractor-trailer, kicking tires, looking and listening for leaks. Compressed air for the brakes, engine oil and coolant, and diesel fuel all ran through a spider web of hoses that at any time could rub raw from the constant jarring. Facing the front bumper, he reached up and opened a small door just under the windshield. He yanked a metal hook and slowly extracted a five-foot cable with a flat piece of steel that looked like a tiny ruler on the end. Holding the snake-like cable with both hands to keep it from dragging the ground, he saw black motor oil just below the line marked *add*. He shoved the dip stick back in, grabbed a funnel and a plastic gallon jug from the side box, and poured rich, thick dark yellow oil down the funnel's throat. *Second time this week*, he thought. Ubi stooped over and looked under the rig, but saw no oil spots on the ground. He stepped back from the rig and looked at Old Ironsides like a doctor examining a patient. Then he heard footsteps crunching on rocks and gravel below a steep ridge. *Aw heck, here comes old loudmouth Larry with a camera, probably taking pictures of the sunrise. Didn't see him climb out of the bunk.*

"I'm going back to bed," Larry said, brushing past Ubi. "Wake me up when we get to town."

While Larry climbed through the driver's door, Amber spilled out the passenger side with a couple sheets of paper towels clenched between her teeth. She grasped the handrail and her toes danced on the side of the truck, feeling for steps. Ubi could tell by the look on her face she needed to use the ladies' room.

"I'll watch for traffic," he said, "just go behind the truck. Nobody will know."

A few minutes later, Amber returned, a little-girl grin on her face that again reminded Ubi of his daughter. Ubi quickly pulled his water jug and a tiny bar of soap out of his side box and poured water over Amber's hands. Then, like a magician, Ubi was suddenly holding out a hand towel that he had washed with a load of laundry while staying with Mick and Sophia back in Denver. Clean. Dry. Soft. Amber held it against her cheek.

"You got a little bit of everything in that storage compartment, Ubi. What do you call it?"

"I just call it my side box."

"Magic box is more like it."

Amber then fussed with her hair, piled it in a bun, let it fall. Running her hands through the long matted locks, she looked at the water jug and the soap.

"Can I wash my hair right quick? Here on the side of the road?"

Ubi nodded. "Why not? Done it myself that way many times."

Amber bent over with the bar of soap in her hand and Ubi turned the plastic jug on its side, careful not to let any water trickle down her neck.

"That's cold that's cold that's cold!" Amber squealed, stamping her feet. In less than a minute, her head disappeared inside bubbles and white soap suds. "This water makes such a rich lather, Ubi. Where'd you get it?"

"Pure Rocky Mountain river water. No chemicals. No additives. No filtration. Got it yesterday when I was fishing. Pulled out a real whopper."

"No kidding. Okay, rinse me off."

Ubi poured more water over the young woman's head. The soapsuds formed a white foamy puddle at her feet. Inside the rig, Larry snapped away with his camera, shooting through the open passenger side window. Then he pulled out a small note pad: "Roadside Baptism."

An hour later, Ubi backed up to a dock on the Air Force base. The trio unloaded the office furniture with no trouble. Dropping at a warehouse was usually a treat; no stairs, no long hikes through office lobbies, and Amber had those furniture pads folded and stacked like a pro. The youngsters made phone calls back home. Ubi checked in with dispatch. Old Ironsides was eastbound again by noon. Back on the interstate, a long day's drive across a wind-swept prairie stood between the travelers and Minnesota. Amber again rode in the shotgun seat, eyes fixed on the faceless horizon. Larry reclined in the bunk in his favorite position, head propped on a pillow so he could see out the windshield. Flat, open and boring, the drive soon became monotonous to Larry and Amber. But for Ubi, the open road was breast milk, a tonic, herbal tea, shot of tequila, or a Rosary recited on bent knees.

"Don't you get bored?" Larry raised his head and fluffed the pillow. Wind gushed through the driver's side window into the bunk. The atlas flapped open, pages rustled like tree leaves. "I mean, sheesh, Ubi. There's nothing out here."

"That depends on what you're looking for," Ubi said. His left arm dangled out the window. Old Ironsides cut a straight path, chewing up white stripes. "You're looking for the real America, right? Well, this is your backyard. It's my backyard, Amber's back-yard, it's all of ours. Don't overlook it because it looks desolate."

"But I like people. And America is all about people. Where are the people?"

"Larry, when you say nothing's out here, meaning people, well, that's the appeal," Ubi said over wind whistling through the truck cab. "Look to the south horizon, out Amber's window. See that single tall tree, leaves turning bright yellow. Probably a cottonwood. What's the story behind it? How did a seed fall and germinate in that one spot? Why no other trees? How old is it? Has it been struck by lightning? What about fires and blizzards and droughts?"

Ubi adjusted his weight in the truck seat. He turned his head toward Larry who was now lying on his stomach, half out of the bunk. "Solitude is not a dirty word. It's the chance to be alone with your thoughts."

"So, you're misanthropic."

"Come on, Larry," Amber said, annoyed. "Let the man talk."

"I'm not sure what that means, Larry. But a man shouldn't be afraid of his own company."

"Okay, then. You're like that tree," Larry answered. "Standing tall and alone against the winds of change."

"Maybe so. Except one thing."

"What's that?"

"That old cottonwood is growing in a ravine, so it must have put down deep roots."

Ubi returned his gaze to the highway ahead. Thump, thump, the truck bounced over a large crack in the asphalt. Thump, thump, then the trailer. Ubi squinted. Not one vehicle in sight. Nice. He leaned forward and wrapped his arms over the top of the big steering wheel. "Sheesh, y'all, all I know is the feel of the road under my wheels. It's like a soundtrack to a great movie. Old Ironsides hums along and I got a front row seat to the U. S. of A."

Quick to change the subject, Larry asked, "Do you smoke?"

Ubi shook his head no. That was a never-ending struggle, but for almost a year he hadn't touched a cigarette.

"Chew anything—tobacco, toothpicks, gum?"

"Gum, yes, but that other stuff, no sir."

"Do you take pills to stay awake? I heard some truckers pop 'em like candy."

"No road dope. If I can't get there on caffeine, I don't go."

"Ha," Larry said. He sat up straight in the bunk, leaning forward with his head rubbing the ceiling. "Everybody's got a vice, an addiction. What about sex? I hear truckers pay those prostitutes at truck stops for a little action."

Amber's mouth dropped open and her brown eyes flared. She wrapped her fingers around her ponytail so the wind wouldn't slap her in the face with it and turned toward the bunk.

"That's enough, Larry. Leave him alone."

"It's okay," Ubi said, leaning forward. With a crumpled paper towel, he wiped dust from the dash. "There's only one truck for me, and you're riding in it. And there's only one woman for me, but you missed her by about six months. She lost her fight with The Cancer earlier this year."

"I'm sorry, Mr. Sunt. Sometimes Larry can be so intrusive."

"It's okay. I gotta learn to live with it."

"Uh, Mr. Sunt, excuse me," Larry said, oblivious to the conversation up front. "But you just compared your wife to a truck. Is that typical of your breed?"

"Good God," Amber yelled into the bunk, still clutching her ponytail. "The man pulls us out of a river, saves us from drowning, gives us a job, a ride, a story about life on the road, and you want to grill him like a hamburger?" Amber turned toward Ubi, his left arm dangling out the window again. She cleared her throat. "Ahem, I apologize for my friend's boorish behavior."

Larry raised up on all fours, crawled half out of the bunk. "I too, sincerely apologize, Mr. Sunt, for my inquisitive nature. But we're going to write a narrative about America, about the ephemeral nature of life, about the—"

"Not again, Larry, come on," Amber interrupted. "For once, shut the hell up, let the guy do the talking. Everywhere we've been on this trip, you run your mouth at." She leaned over the dash, peeking at the tachometer. "How many rpms is this engine going right now?"

"Eighteen hundred."

"You're running your mouth at eighteen hundred rpm-sRPMS," Amber scolded. "You're supposed to listen when you interview someone. Remember what they taught us?"

Larry retreated into the bunk and pouted, a game he played with Amber when he got carried away and she cut him back.

After a couple of quiet miles, a flatbed rig carrying a piece of red farm machinery passed in the opposite direction. Ubi held up his left hand; the trucker raised two fingers from the steering wheel and nodded. Then it hit Ubi like slamming into a pothole at seventy miles an hour.

"Larry," Ubi said, reaching up and adjusting the CB volume and squelch knob. "You want to understand the road, you like people, you should talk to some of these ratchet jaws on the CB."

"Interview someone on the CB?"

"Ten-four. That's what I'm sayin'."

"Oh, God," Amber said, putting her hand to her forehead and looking down. "That's all we need, loquacious Larry on the two-way truckers' radio."

Ubi held the mike toward the bunk. Larry took it and the corkscrew cord stretched tight. Ubi showed him how to push down on the black button to transmit.

"Breaker, breaker," Larry chirped. "Got any good buddies out there?"

Ubi's face reddened. He yanked the cord and the microphone flew across the cab like it had been launched from a slingshot. It smacked against the front glass.

"Sheesh! You trying to pick a fight? You don't call anybody a good buddy on the CB."

"Why not? That's how it's done on TV, in the movies."

Ubi returned the mike to the small latch hanging on the side of the CB. "I guess we need a little instruction on CB manners and lingo. First off, a good buddy is a fag. It's one of the worst insults you can toss out there. You don't call anybody a good buddy unless you're ready to pull over and duke it out."

Amber raised her eyebrows. "I beg your pardon, sir. A fag? You mean a homosexual, or a gay person, don't you?"

"Yeah, that's what I meant. Sorry."

Ubi remembered the day Sherry admonished her dad for calling his old friend and mentor, Owen, a nigger. He didn't want to be like that, but that *was* how truckers talked on the CB. Ubi shook off the feeling of shame and continued.

"Anyway, if you want to talk to someone, you gotta recognize him by what he's driving. Like this," Ubi said, picking up the mike. "How 'bout that westbound large car pulling that reefer? Seen anything back toward Mitchell?"

"Got one taking pictures. Your side, about the 284."

"Ten-Roger that," Ubi said, "You're looking clean and green back to Rapid City." Ubi hung up the mike and Larry leaned forward.

"Why did you ask that guy about a reefer? Is he smoking pot?"

"Aw, hell naw, Larry," Ubi said, making a flat grin. "A reefer is that refrigerator unit on the front of his wagon, or what you would call his trailer. From the name on the side of his rig, El Primo Foods, he's probably hauling frozen dinners to grocery stores. And taking pictures means a radar gun."

For the next thirty miles, Ubi explained the slang, colloquialisms, and code of conduct that had evolved on the truckers' channel nineteen.

"You don't need to say break one-nine just because you're on channel nineteen. Sheesh, only folks on nineteen can hear you anyway. Just get after it. You might ask where the cheap fuel is—and remember, always fuel, never gas—or if the chicken coops are open at Yankton, or if the Snow Chi Minh Trail across Wyoming is still closed at Rawlings. And don't tie up the channel with a bunch of tripe. We don't care how you ran around the scales on

I-44 through Missouri because you were five thousand pounds overweight and four days behind on your logs. Remember this, Larry," Ubi said, waving at a passing empty flatbed. "The only difference between a fairy tale and a trucker's story is that the fairy tale starts, 'Once upon a time,' and a trucker begins with, 'You ain't gonna believe this shit.'"

"Also, you gotta keep up with mile markers. On the interstates, they start on the western state line at zero and count up from there. Now, interstates running north—south start at the bottom, like Laredo, Texas, and count up from number one to the state line, at Oklahoma, that should be about the four-ninety. And that means it's four hundred ninety miles back to Laredo."

"Now, interstates running east to west are all even-numbered. They begin with low numbers down south. For example, I-10 runs from Los Angeles to Jacksonville, Florida. And they work their way up higher and higher. I-40 through Tennessee, Arkansas, Oklahoma. I-70 across Illinois, northern Missouri, Kansas and into Colorado. And I-90 runs from Seattle through that section of Idaho that looks like someone's finger pointing, then across Montana and North Dakota, into Minnesota and Wisconsin. The north—south interstates are odd-numbered and count up from I-5 on the West Coast to I-95 on the East. In the middle of the country, you got roads like I-25 through New Mexico, Colorado and Montana and I-75 through Kentucky, the Buckeye, and into Michigan."

"What's the Buckeye?"

"Aw heck, that's Ohio. We got names for everywhere, everybody and everything. Crescent City? That's New Orleans. Amarillo is the Armadillo, and Albuquerque is Albaturkey. Baton Rouge is the Red Stick, Chattanooga, the Choo Choo, and Chicago, Shy Town. San Francisco is the Gay Bay, sorry 'bout that Amber, I'm just telling you what the drivers are saying. Montgomery, Alabama is Monkey Town. Nashville is The Guitar. St. Louis is the Gateway, Big D can be either Denver or Dallas. Sheesh, there's so many other names I can't remember 'em all. Like Los Angeles is Shaky Town and Missouri is Misery 'cause whenever you pull in the chicken coops, if they feel like it they're gonna' get in your wallet. Fire extinguisher out of date, or a light bulb burned out on the top of your wagon, or your rig's a couple inches too long, or a few pounds too heavy, they're going to fine you—cash. If your wallet's a little light, they give you a free ride into town to get money wired. And that ain't no fairy tale."

"Now what was I was talking about? Oh yeah, CB lingo. Only rookies, or a dad on vacation in his Ford wagon with a new CB trying to impress the family, would say Smokey Bear. It's a speed cop, or just plain bear. And the grass in the middle of the road is called the comedian, not the median."

Ubi fingered the CB mike. "Like this here. How 'bout it, west-bound ?"

"Yeah. Go ahead."

"Got a speed cop in the comedian at the two twenty-four."

"'Preciate that. You're looking good back to Sioux Falls. Ain't seen nothing but a gator in the hammer lane at the ninety-two."

Ubi hung up the mike and said to Larry, "Okay, quick translation: gators are the big, black blown-out recaps you see scattered across the road all the time. The hammer lane is the left, or inside track where you put the hammer down. You know what put the hammer down means, right? Same as pedal to the metal. Hammer lane is supposed to be the passing lane. 'Course ever now and then somebody in the left lane gets to lollygagging along at double nickels, that's fifty-five miles an hour, and everybody's gotta pass in the right lane and that's normally a big no-no."

Telephone poles passed in never-ending succession, and Ubi found himself talking more than at any time since Sherry passed away.

"Here's another one for you. Hauling sailboat fuel—that's running empty, no load, also called deadheading." Ubi rolled up both shirtsleeves and draped his left arm out the window again. "A construction zone where concrete barricades make a long, narrow lane is a dog run. Brake check is when everybody suddenly stops. On the CB, it goes like this: Northbound, you got a brake check just before that dog run at the one-fifteen. You copy that? Got a copy means did you hear that? A hand is a driver. A glad hand is a clamp that connects air hoses between the tractor and trailer. And you know a tractor is just another name for a truck. So, right now you're riding in a tractor-trailer rig. You copy that? "

"Big ten-four, good buddy," Larry said. Amber quickly slapped at him with her spiral notebook. "Just kidding." Larry held up his hands. "Couldn't resist."

Ubi continued. "Now if you're talking and somebody picks up their mike and interrupts, talking over you 'cause they got a more powerful radio—you just got stepped on. When another rig passes you, it's your obligation to flick on and off your headlights when he's clear to switch lanes. Either that, or tell him on the CB 'you missed me.' Then he's got to either say 'preciate it,' or something like that, or flash his trailer lights at you a couple of times. That's just courtesy. Code of the road."

"What else was I saying? Lingo? Okay, marijuana is smoking dope and the other stuff that keeps you up all night is called road dope. Road dope can be pocket rockets, yellow jackets, West Coast turnarounds, black mollies, bennies, and ain't none of 'em worth a dang because they leave you worse off down the road than if you took a nap. Don't know any driver out here who lasted more'n a couple years who took a lot of road dope. Smoking dope? That's what some of the kids like to do in the back row of the truck stop before they go in and eat a bunch of junk food and go to bed."

A fast-moving Peterbilt pulling a refrigerated trailer in the hammer lane then shot past Old Ironsides. Ubi flashed his headlights, and the driver merged back into the right lane, twinkling his trailer taillights off and on.. Mud flaps with chrome silhouettes of a shapely women glinted in the sun. Amber looked up from her spiral notebook, pointed at the rig with her pencil.

"What about that?"

"I know, I know, Amber, a lot of truckers got them gals splashed on bumpers, caps and all, but that's just gutter slurping. Yosemite Sam holding up two pistols saying 'back off' or the cartoon guy with those big feet that says 'keep on trucking' they're okay with me. But splashing them chrome girls all over a rig like a pinup, well, it's—"

"It's sexist," Amber said, her top lip curling up.

"Speaking of naked ladies, lot lizards is the term for hookers who work the truck stops. That's a sad story, girls going door to door in the back row, jumping from bunk to bunk. Some use the CB to recruit business. Just breaks you up thinking some daddy's little girl doing that. And you won't like this either, Amber, but a lot of truckers on the CB refer to women in general as beavers. Hope that don't offend you none."

"Beaver. How crass." Amber said. She stopped writing, bit on her pencil.

"I'm not saying all of us talk like that, okay? I'm just telling you the truth. Look here, let's change subjects," Ubi said. "On the CB, truckers have a class system according to the rigs they drive. A Peterbilt is called a Pete, or Petercar. Fella' named Peterman bought a truck-building outfit back in the '40s and manufactured logging rigs for the Pacific Northwest. If you want to get laughed at on the CB, just get one of those bumper stickers that say 'Old truckers never die, they just get a new Peterbilt.' Some hands say Pete drivers act a little stuck up. With the slogan 'class,' they got calendars that instead of those chrome gals, these ladies are decked out in long, formal nightgowns. Looks like they're going to be a bridesmaid or something. Next up, Kenworth. Those drivers think that's the best rig out there, call 'em Kaywhoppers or a KW and they are a damn good truck. Drop a Cat or Cummings engine in one and you're set for a million miles. Freightliner bought out White trucks a while back and nobody really understands what's the difference, White-Freightliner or whatever. But now, most of the Whites have fallen apart, or stay close to home on local runs. Freightliners are sometimes called Freightshakers, or Rattleliners. Some of those drivers don't especially like that. International takes about the same place in the pecking order as Freightliner. They worked their way up out of the Midwest, hauling grain. Some folks call them corn binders. Macks grew up during World War II. Helped defeat Hitler and the Nazis, but they run mostly along the East Coast bouncing over some of the roughest roads in the country. Some drivers say that's the main truck back East because anybody who spent the kind of money it takes to drive a Pete or KW doesn't want to see it beaten to pieces on the Atlantic Coast. Mack has the bulldog on the hood, and everybody uses the term, 'Like a Mack truck,' for a comparison to something solid, but ask some truckers and they say that dog just don't hunt."

"Some obscure trucks like Diamond Reo are fading away 'cause they can't keep up with the big mass-production models. But we got a new kid on the block called the Western Star. Ain't never drove one, but word is you got a Western Star, you got a piece of craftsmanship. Probably at the bottom of the heap lies the GMC, or Jimmy. And Ford's got a few models they made over the years, but you won't see too many serious truckers running those rigs. They're for greenhorns or short haul."

Ubi looked around the cab at Amber and Larry. He figured that he'd probably put them to sleep. But Larry was sprawled half-way out of the bunk, staring at this enigmatic trucker, and Amber was still taking notes. Poetry, jazz, road etiquette. Who would have guessed?

"What about different body styles?" Amber asked. "See that rig pulling a flatbed, it's got a different front grill from Old Ironsides."

"All right," Ubi said, adjusting his weight in the seat. "Besides name brands, there's another way to classify trucks. First, you got the long-nose, a big snout sticking out six feet from the windshield. With a chrome bumper and big grill, it's the classic look. Then you got the cabover, like Old Ironsides." Ubi patted the dash.

"It's got the flat front, like a sheet of plywood. It's called a cabover because the cab sits over the engine. Driver's seat is right on top of those monster pistons churning up and down," Ubi continued, pointing to the floorboard. "Like where I'm sitting right now. And a cabover rides rougher'n a long-nose because you got a shorter wheelbase."

"So, why drive a cabover?" Amber asked. She was having trouble reading her notes, bouncing in the truck, but she kept scribbling.

"A cabover turns tighter than a long-nose. And folks like me who haul furniture—we're called stick haulers or bed-buggers by the way—we like them 'cause we're going into neighborhoods, apartment complexes, tight downtown streets to move people. We got to get in and get out, or waste time loading everything on a little U-haul and deliver it like on a ferryboat. Also, we can carry a longer trailer by shortening the length of the tractor. One way to look at the difference between the long-nose and the cabover is in the song 'Give me forty acres to turn this rig around.' It's about a trucker who cain't back up too good. Long-nose truck drivers think they're a notch above the cabover drivers. One old saying, 'If it ain't got a hood, it ain't a truck,' explains it all. Us cabover drivers, we act like we don't care. I can make more money hauling furniture anyway."

"Ubi, say that again, about furniture haulers. What are you called?"

"Stick haulers, or bed-buggers, which ain't no lie. I moved some folks, you wonder how they live in that filth. Cockroaches jumping around the house like jackrabbits. I've probably hauled more critters coast to coast than Barnum & Bailey. Anyway, other terms, let's see, you got car haulers called portable parking lots and a livestock trailer is just a bull wagon. And a plain old freight trailer, just call it a wagon, or a dry box. Speaking of wagons, you've probably seen those drivers pulling two trailers, about thirty feet long each; we call 'em wiggle wagons because they're always weaving down the road, don't track straight at all.. Ain't gonna be no test on this, Larry, but it's something you outta' know so you don't get all embarrassed on the CB. Oh, and like I said earlier, a highway patrol car is a Smokey; those guys dress like Smokey the Bear. City cops are called local yokels. And if some law enforcement is driving an unmarked vehicle, it's a plain wrapper, depending on which color, like you would say, 'westbound, you got a plain white wrapper rolling at the four-twelve, bubble gum machine on.'"

"What's a bubble gum machine?"

"I didn't tell you that one? Sorry. That's the lights on top, all those blue and red and white lights look like a bubble gum machine."

Running into a strong headwind, Ubi kept an eye on his gauges. He had to run the engine at higher rpms than normal to keep Old Ironsides rolling about sixty. He knew he could fudge the fifty-five mile an hour speed limit a little.

Ubi handed the CB mike back to Larry. A couple miles down the road, Ubi pointed toward an oncoming tanker truck.

"How about that westbound, got a copy?" Larry asked.

"Ten-four," the driver replied. "Who's that over there in that old Petercar?"

Larry looked at Ubi and asked, "What do I say now?"

"Aw, heck. We forgot to give you a handle, Larry."

"What's *your* handle, Mr. Sunt?" Larry asked, leaning forward on his elbows. "I know you don't use the CB all that much, but you do have one. Don't you?"

"My wife called me the Southpaw because I like to hang my left arm out the window. The best handles are ones someone special gives to you, something that describes some kind of quirk," Ubi said. He looked at Amber. "What about Larry? Any ideas?"

"Motor Mouth."

"That's been done. Lots of Motor Mouths out there, unfortunately, Ratchet Jaws too."

"How about the Bloviator?"

"Bloviator? That sounds like something that bolts on to the exhaust manifold. Or a nickname for a volcano. What's that you called him the other day, low something?"

"Loquacious. It means talkative," Amber said, looking up from her spiral. "Hey, why not Loquacious Larry?"

"Naw, too hard to say," Ubi said, shaking his head. "And nobody would understand what it means. Tell ya what. Let's go with the next best thing. How 'bout Double L? CB handles gotta be short. Initials work good. You can be Double L."

The tanker truck had passed out of earshot, but Larry keyed the mike, looking for a friend on the endless expanse. "You got the old Double L over here. I'm talking to everyday folks, traveling the country. With my fellow researcher, I'm writing an empirical story about America."

Three rigs hauling beer out of Milwaukee appeared out of nowhere, sailed past in the opposite direction. No answer. Ubi told Larry to try talking more like a trucker, but Larry ignored him, waited a couple of miles and tried his pitch again when a westbound International blew past. This one took the bait.

"Well, I can tell you ain't no trucker just by the way you talk," the driver said. "But here's the skinny. Truckers is a bunch of misfits, loners. Can't stand no eight to five work, gotta keep moving. That's us. Hobos with a steady job, that's all we are. Ain't no glorious occupation, neither. Hard on the backside. Hard on the gut too. They say eat where you see a buncha' rigs parked out front 'cause the truckers know where the best food is. Wrong. We eat where we can park our rigs. Bad roads. Bad food. Tall tales and tall trucks. That's all it is."

Amber frantically scratched down the trucker's words on her note pad.

"Ten-four," Larry said. "What about money? I heard you guys make enough to sit up for weeks at a time, drinking beer and fishing and taking it easy."

"Some do," the driver replied. "But this ain't no shift work. You don't get off the same time ever day. And you got to be mechanic, bookkeeper, and if you want to work with these dispatchers playing favorites, you got to be a politician too. Heck, the ones who get the good loads ain't always the best drivers. They're the ones who come to the home office and grab the tab at the bar or drop an envelope of cash in their dispatcher's desk drawer."

"You take road dope?"

"Negatory on the pocket rockets," the driver said. "Like old Dave Dudley said, it's Rolaids, Doan's Pills and Preparation H that moves America's freight."

Ubi grinned and explained that Dave Dudley, along with Red Sovine, were top hands in the trucking music genre. And that the driver sounded like a trucker Ubi knew who went by the handle Big Dummy. He ran with his wife, Little Silly. Last time Ubi saw them, they were hauling furniture for a Florida moving company. Ubi told Larry to ask the driver for his handle, and it was Big Dummy indeed. But the trailer he was dragging had T & H stenciled on the side. T & H was notorious for low pay and slow pay. Ubi reached for the mike and hailed the driver.

"Hey Big Dummy, what are you doing driving for old Tired and Hungry? Wasn't bed bugging bad enough? What are you trying to do, Dummy? File bankruptcy?"

"Is that you over there, Southpaw?"

"Ten-roger. Me and Old Ironsides, still plugging along."

"I'll be a monkey's uncle. I didn't get a good look at the rig or woulda' recognized Old Ironsides. My back done give out humping sticks, so now I'm just bumping docks. My wife says I've gone from a humper to a bumper. Ain't that some shit? Anyway, I just open the trailer door and let the forklifts do the work. Mama's watching the books real close, so we're doing okay. Tell old Double L, us truckers are fixing to go on strike with diesel prices going up. That's all they're talking about down South."

The driver's voice faded, but before it was out of earshot, Big Dummy told Ubi he would catch him on the flip flop. Ubi explained that CB conversations between truckers headed in opposite directions were usually brief because the signals travel only five or fewer miles, and flip flop meant return trip, or just somewhere down the road.

By now, the young journalists had grown used to the bumpy ride. Old Ironsides was built on top of leaf springs and shock absorbers, unlike the new rigs assisted with air bags. These rubber bags are about the size of a large basketball, filled with air of course, and designed to take a pounding. Not long ago, Ubi rode in a friend's new rig. It had air bags. The ride was smooth, but it was still a truck. Ubi didn't understand why some drivers thought a truck should ride like a Cadillac. But that pounding took a toll on Amber's kidneys, and she asked Ubi to—*uh, well*—stop at the rest area.

"You mean, time to check the tires, Amber. Sure, that ain't no problem."

Double L spent the next one hundred miles interviewing drivers on the CB while Amber took copious notes. Worried her scribbling would be illegible, she filled her spiral—the more the better. Just outside the town of Mitchell, Old Ironsides rolled past a billboard glorifying the mighty Corn Palace. Ubi took the exit and a strange building came into view. Minarets and teardrop-shaped spheres rested on top of the two-story building, which sat on the corner of a downtown street. But what made Larry stick his neck out of the bunk like a giraffe and Amber sit up straight—the building was covered with a mural made of corn kernels and dried grasses.

"It looks like it should be in Moscow," Larry said. "That architecture, unbelievable."

"What the hell is it?"

"I guess you missed that billboard. It's the Corn Palace," Ubi said. "Built about fifty years ago. Used to have basketball games here. Now they got everything from rock and roll concerts to the annual Corn Festival. And some local artist decorates the outside with a new theme every year, made of corn, or course. That's what you're looking at."

Amber and Larry climbed down from Old Ironsides and walked slowly around the building. About a half hour later, they returned to the rig. Ubi had just finished updating his logbook. Amber looked up; even when Ubi wasn't driving, his left arm hung out the window.

"Why do you always dangle your arm out the window?"

Ubi didn't hear. He was lost in the road atlas. Minneapolis was more than three hundred miles away. Amber cupped her right hand around the side of her mouth.

"Mr. Sunt, we decided this is where we get off. We think we can get some good interviews here. We're going to hang out for a day and then head back south."

Ubi looked down and smiled. "Ain't it something? Prairie folks got a helluva' imagination. Built something like this way out here."

Ubi climbed down from the rig and arched his back. His spine popped. Amber heard it and winced, held her hands over her face.

"You need to get that checked out, Mr. Sunt."

Ubi ignored the comment. Women worried too much.

"How are you and old Double L getting back to Florida?"

"Bus station's right around the corner," Amber said, pointing. "We got just enough money for a cheap motel, bus fare and a couple meals. This will be our third mode of transportation— gone from Little Red Riding Hood, may she rest in peace, to Old Ironsides to a Grey Dog."

Amber stood on the balls of her feet, wrapped her arms around Ubi's neck and pulled him close for what seemed to the trucker an hour, or a day, or a lifetime. A young woman hadn't hugged Ubi like that since his daughter had said "I do" at the Catholic church back home on her wedding day. How long ago was that? Ten years?

Next, lanky Double L walked up and gave Ubi a bear hug. Boy, this new generation was something else. Men hugging men. Ubi patted Larry on the back and when they released, he grabbed the young man's hand, squeezed hard. Felt like putty, smooth and soft, but still a genuine grip. That's what counts.

"You take good care of her, you hear, or I'll . . . I'll . . . "

Ubi felt his eyes begin to water and his voice crack. *Damnit, stop that.* ". . .I'll tie you to the front of this rig like a hood ornament."

Double L smiled and nodded, handed Ubi a matchbook from one of the trucks stops they visited. A phone number was scrawled inside. "We'll catch you on the flip-flop," Double L said, remembering the CB lingo.

Ubi climbed in his rig and slipped the transmission into low gear. Old Ironsides growled sweet and low. The truck pulled away, Amber and Larry watching.

"Good-bye you rover and rambler, wayfarer and drifter, wanderer," Amber yelled and waved. The truck grew smaller and smaller, until it disappeared around a corner. "You, you, you old . . . " Amber's voice cracked, and she turned and buried her head in Larry's chest.

An hour later, Ubi and Old Ironsides rolled across the state line into Minnesota. That night, at a truck stop outside Minneapolis, Ubi squeezed into a private phone booth inside the driver's lounge and closed the folding glass door behind him. The operator told him he could dial direct and save money, but Ubi said he wasn't interested.

"Just put me through and charge it to my . . . Aw heck, I forgot again. Had the home phone shut off months ago, operator. What's that? Call collect? Oh, no. You don't call your daughter and son-in-law and grandkids collect."

Ubi walked toward the cash register. His eyes misty, he bumped into a waitress who almost dropped her coffee pot, and brushed shoulders with a young, slender trucker who turned and gave Ubi a *go to hell* look. No home phone number because there's no home anymore. Hadn't thought about it like that. No phone meant no home. Ubi rolled those two words around inside his head—no home—over and over until a ruddy-faced man wearing an apron and a big grin asked Ubi if he needed some coffee. "Sure looks like you could use some," he said.

Ubi held out a twenty, asked for pay phone change instead. Back at the phone booth, he had to wait for a half hour for another driver to finish his conversation. At last, he squeezed in the booth and stacked a pile of quarters on top of the pay phone.

"Hello, this is Jeremy."

"And this is Molly."

"We're not home right now," Ubi heard two young voices in unison. "And neither is Mom and Dad so leave us a message."

"Hey everybody, this is Grandpa Truck calling from Minnesota. Seems like it's taking forever to get out there. I keep getting more loads to pick up and drop off along the way. But I'm getting closer. Reckon it'll be just a few more days."

Ubi slowly cradled the receiver. When it was safely in place, he said, "And I love you guys."

Ubi squeezed out of the booth, and a heavy driver wearing overalls asked him if he was already through with his phone call. "Yeah, she's all yours," Ubi said, "nobody home."

NINE

THE INVESTOR GROUP—American Star—that now owned Deaton Van Lines had sold the downtown Minneapolis warehouse built in the fifties and set up shop in an unfinished industrial park on the city's north end. Old Ironsides rumbled through a double-wide steel gate that was bent and sagging from a recent collision with the packing material van, and Ubi swung the rig wide toward the back of the lot to make a U-turn. The lot was covered with a thin coat of road base that in patches had worn through to the black dirt below. The front tire caught a pothole, and although the truck was moseying along in low gear, the cab pitched to one side, and Ubi's head jerked back. The truck then slipped past a small shed and sidled up to a cluster of portable buildings connected by covered ramps. Mostly new faces inside. Only a few of the old dispatchers, salesmen, or drivers left. The general manager remembered Ubi from the time he moved a star hockey player to town from Calgary.

"If it ain't Ubi Sunt; half Davy Crockett, half Sam Houston and half Bigfoot Wallace."

The manager snuffed out his cigarette in a metal ashtray and brushed ashes from his thick, black moustache. He stepped around a steel desk and pushed through a high countertop that swung open on hinges and served as a roadblock to keep out the pesky over-the-road drivers who smelled bad and tied up their phones.

After a long hand-pumping session, the manager addressed a young man wearing heavy boots and hooded sweatshirt who was sitting in one of several small, wooden chairs in a corner.

"You know who you're working with today? Look here," the man said, pointing to a black-and-white framed photograph hanging on the wall. "See that safe hanging in the air above that rig? That's Ubi Sunt standing on the ground there. He moved that hockey player into an eighteenth floor downtown penthouse that his wife bought when he retired. Job took three days."

The young mover stood, glanced at the photograph, shuffled his feet. It was cold for late October, even in Minnesota, and he didn't look forward to working outside.

"How do you like the new digs, Ubi?" the manager asked, holding out his hands. His suit coat sleeves slid almost to his elbows. "Complete with a portable john out back. How'd you like to take a crap out there in mid-January?" He pointed out a small window toward the shack that Ubi had just dodged. "Hell, I got an ice-fishing shanty on Lake Minnetonka bigger'n that."

The man reached inside his coat pocket, produced a one hundred millimeter cigarette, and popped it in his mouth. He flipped back the top on a silver lighter. A low flame met the cigarette, and white smoke curled toward the ceiling. "New owners sold the downtown warehouse for a cool million, and moved us into this."

"I know. I just left Denver," Ubi said. "Where's your storage? The warehouse?"

"Got a rented space couple miles away. Nothing like the old one."

"Sheesh," Ubi said, scratching his head. "Sheesh."

"You hear much about the strike?" The manager asked, puffing the cigarette. "Most of the long-haul drivers coming through here say it's bound to happen. Fuel's pushing a buck a gallon. Something's got to give."

"I don't listen to the CB like I used to," Ubi said. "Too much trash talking. Everybody wants to outdo the other. But I heard some grumbling out west about getting organized. Maybe a protest—one of those rolling roadblocks. But I don't pay it no never mind. I pretty much keep to myself. Most of the old guard I ran with have put the pedal up."

The phone rang in the back of the office and a woman hailed the manager, said it was a salesman in Rochester wanting to know why the crew hadn't arrived yet.

"Eighteen months," the manager said, stroking his moustache. "Then I'm going fishing for good. Gonna give those walleye hell. You be careful out there, Ubi. From what I'm hearing, this strike could happen sooner rather than later. And you got enough kooks out there, could get ugly."

Ubi and the young man spent the day delivering furniture to a third-floor apartment with a long, uphill walk out front. It was dark when they returned to the office, and the manager had already left. Ubi parked out back, paid the man cash, and filled out his logbook. He headed toward the outhouse, found it locked, and circled the building. A small mound of snow remained under an overhang where the sun seldom shone. Ubi stopped behind the building, unzipped his khakis, and urinated in the ice. The ice melted and caved in, forming a small ice volcano with steam rising from its mouth.

The next afternoon, Ubi loaded a small shipment at a Milwaukee suburban home—an antique dining set stashed in a garage—and fought his way south through Chicago rush hour traffic. Uneven lanes dropped off at any moment. Sometimes the rig listed to one side, the passenger seat higher than the driver's. Orange cones and barricades squeezed four lanes to three and then three became two. Whenever Ubi left adequate stopping space, a couple car lengths, some idiot zipped in front and hit the brakes. Stop and go. Run through a half-dozen gears, get rolling and then another brake check. Sitting with an arm out the window, it was cold, but not that cold.

Finally rolling again, Ubi sat on the edge of his seat. The broken road pitched his truck up and down. The road atlas and logbook he kept on the doghouse kept slipping toward the passenger side floorboard. Several times Ubi grabbed them just before they spilled over the edge. In the bunk, his thermos, shaving kit, and assorted city and state maps all inched forward bump by bump, like they were mischievously crawling out, planning to make their escape. On the city's south side, closing in on the Indiana state line at fifty miles an hour, Ubi hit a deep pocket in the road and the truck felt like it was breaking apart. The logbook and atlas crashed to the floorboard on the passenger side. Ubi's coffee thermos rolled out of the bunk and wedged between the shifter and the doghouse. The shaving kit Ubi forgot to zip that morning at the Eau Claire truck stop exploded. A small plastic shampoo bottle flew onto the doghouse, and an aspirin container blew its top, sending little white pills across the cab like hail stones.

"For crying out loud."

Ubi let off the accelerator and slowed the rig. With the cab in disarray, he found a steady rhythm at about forty-five miles an hour. Hanging on to the big wheel, he timed the bumps, about a tenth of a mile apart, and raised his rear end just before each impact. *Thump thump*, the beat continued, *thump thump*, across northeastern Illinois, interrupted only by long lines at tollbooths. Pull up, wait. A little more. *Look at the jerk in the Grand Am, cutting in line. Finally my turn. Seventy-five cents to ride on this washboard road? You gotta be kidding? Yes, I want a receipt. I'm writing this off at tax time. Crying shame to pay extra to drive on a road like this.*

Across the Indiana state line, the road opened up, no more construction and tolls, and traffic thinned. But the roadside looked bleak. Rusted steel buildings lined both sides of the highway, separated by row after row of grimy apartment buildings. Graffiti everywhere: on rail cars parked at scrap steel yards, on overpasses and bridges and concrete embankments, and on rusted-out automobiles with no wheels or windshields that littered the highway shoulder and side streets. Ubi looked out the passenger window down empty alleys and avenues. Looked like everybody just packed up and left.

Continuing eastbound at dusk, Ubi found a steady clip, about sixty, and on the AM radio a country station out of southern Michigan broadcast a song about Saginaw and a fisherman. Driving in the far right lane of the four-lane interstate, Old Ironsides passed a slow-moving Ford Galaxie 500 that for some strange reason was plodding along in the far left lane like he was taking Mama to the country on Sunday afternoon with a bucket of fried chicken and jug of iced tea. *Come on, buddy, even four-wheelers know the left lane is the passing lane, the hammer lane, the show-off lane. Move over. And, sure enough, here comes a long-nosed Freightliner barreling along in the same lane.*

The coal-black truck was dressed in an oversized chrome bumper that almost dragged the ground. A mechanic once told Ubi those monster bumpers cut off airflow under the truck and could make transmissions and engines run hot. Both sides of this rig were adorned with yellow marker lights by the dozen, end to end, light after light. Safety regulations require all rigs to have a minimum number lights on tractors and trailers, but some drivers go all out. *Hope he's got a hellacious alternator to pump all that current. And you better not leave those lights burning very long without the engine running, they'll drain your batteries lickety-split.* To Ubi, all this glitter was like bragging on the CB or at the truck stop coffee counter: Loaded in Vegas one day, delivered the next night in Buffalo. Ain't nobody gonna' believe that fairy tale. And sure, you want to drive a good-looking rig; there ain't nothing wrong with tacking on a few extra lights, sprucing up the truck with some custom lettering and pin stripes. But do you really want to drive a circus wagon? And of course, this joker's gotta have those chrome silhouettes of skinny naked ladies on his mud flaps. What would Amber say about that? What a disgrace, dressing up that beautiful rig like a ten-dollar whore.

The sun dropped behind the vacant buildings as the gaudy rig inched up on the Ford. To the driver watching in his rearview mirror, the massive bumper looked like it was riding in his back seat. The trucker flashed his brights; once, twice, but the car wouldn't move over. *Sheesh, just go around, driver. You got three more lanes. Take your pick.* But the big rig continued to dog the Ford. Bright lights glared into the Ford driver's rearview mirror. Ubi felt the hair on his neck twitching. His face felt warm, then hot, like he was back in Texas the previous August, stacking furniture inside the stuffy trailer. He fingered the CB mike, ready to bark at the tailgater. Hell, never mind, last time he intervened he got into a running argument across half of Georgia. Still, that's enough to make you want to jerk that driver out of the truck and—*ah forget it, some people are going to be what they're going to be.*

Suddenly the Ford took to the shoulder, driver working the steering wheel back and forth like he was washing windows. The car kicked up a cloud of dust and gravel, peppering the immaculate rig's front bumper, huge chrome grill and windshield. Ubi smiled. *The four-wheeler's got spunk.* But the Freightliner driver then jerked the wheel to the right, hit the accelerator. Black smoke billowing from twin stacks, he pulled in front of the Ford. Returning the favor, he swerved onto the shoulder and stirred up a whirlwind. Ubi watched in disbelief: *That driver's gone too far.* Now the Galaxie was gone, disappeared into that cloud of dust. The driver had no choice and backed her down, out of the cyclone. But he charged again when the air cleared, hit his brights, and aimed them into the rig's side view mirror. Then the shoulder disappeared, so the rig could no longer throw up a smokescreen—no more ammo. *Boy, if this ain't one of the strangest confrontations.* Ubi again fingered the mike. *Aren't we the pros? Aren't we 'sposed to set the example. The highway is our workplace. These four-wheelers, they're just amateurs.*

For another five miles, Ubi followed the confrontation at a safe distance. The tractor-trailer was still in front, but the trucker apparently grew tired of the brights in his rearview mirror. He acted like he was going to exit, turned on the right blinker, crossed two lanes, and headed toward the ramp. But when the Galaxie passed, the driver pushed the Freightliner right up against the car's rear bumper, bright lights burning. At a safe distance, Old Ironsides kept up with the dogfight, Freightliner versus Ford. Then, *wow,* the Ford shot across four lanes and down an exit ramp. Just like that, the battle was over. Continuing eastbound, the Freightliner was almost out of sight when a plain brown wrapper taking pictures forced the driver to slow down. Ubi closed the gap. A little further down the road, the trucker ran up on another slow-moving four-wheeler in the left lane. The trucker hit the brights and moved in for the kill. This car, a new Volkswagen Rabbit, quickly merged right, so the rig continued unimpeded.

The Freightliner and Old Ironsides then hit a major cross-roads. An interstate running out of Indianapolis, another one headed toward Detroit, and a toll road leading to Cleveland all came together. Inside this giant, concrete-and-asphalt spaghetti bowl sat two truck stops. Rows of diesel pumps stretched across parking lots. Huge repair shops resembled airplane hangars. And a dozen restaurants offered a variety of chow: steakhouse, Chinese, Italian, fast-food burger and fried chicken franchises, twenty-four hour pancake house, and Mexican. (After a gut-wrenching experience in Missouri, Ubi never trusted Mexican food north of Fort Worth or east of Houston.)

Ubi followed the black Freightliner into the larger truck stop. The rigs pulled into adjacent fuel bays. Ubi climbed down, reached into the magic box, as Amber called it, and snatched a small billy club, called a tire bumper, that truckers use to bang against their rubber to check for flats. Even experienced drivers could walk past an under inflated tire. The Freightliner driver looked about thirty-five years old. Wearing pointy-toed cowboy boots with high heels, he was almost tall enough to wash the windshield from the ground without climbing on a stepladder like other drivers. Arms like tree trunks, the man inserted one fuel nozzle in the driver side, hundred-gallon-tank and circled the front of the rig to the passenger side tank. He was unscrewing the fuel cap when Ubi approached.

"Where you headed driver?"

"Indy. Gotta drop forty thousand pounds of steel there in the morning."

Ubi looked the driver over from head to toe and felt a combination of sadness and rage. Rage won over. "What the hell are you trying to pull? I watched you tailgating those folks for the last twenty miles. Blinding them with your brights. What's your problem?"

"Damn fools need to stay out of the left lane if they don't want to get run over."

The trucker narrowed his eyes and scowled. *Who was this old guy in an antique rig, coming down on him about* his *driving?* He grabbed the hose from the diesel pump, pulled down on a black lever, and jammed the nozzle into the tank. Ubi stood flat-footed, holding the tire bumper like a police baton.

"That coulda' been my wife, my daughter, somebody's grandmother, or a kid on their way to senior prom in that car. So what if they don't know to get in the right lane. Don't give you no right to scare the bejesus outta' them."

"Hell, this rig pays more in highway and fuel taxes in one year than that rust bucket back on the interstate is worth."

"What's that got to do with you breathing down their neck?"

"Lead, follow, or get the hell out of the way, that's the way I see it," the driver sneered, from under a brown cap decorated with some kind of wings and a trucking company logo on it. "Somebody's gotta teach them a lesson."

"And somebody's gotta teach you a lesson."

The driver looked down at Ubi, blinked once, and asked, "Are you supposed to be somebody I have to answer to?"

He stepped over the black hose stretching from the pump to the fuel tank and brushed past Ubi like he wasn't there. The driver then picked up a squeegee from a plastic bucket, but when he looked up, Ubi was right behind him, sizing up the Freightliner like he was going to attack it.

Ubi hitched up his pants. He wrapped the piece of twine attached to the tire bumper around his wrist like a lanyard. The driver had left his engine running and his headlights were still on bright—you gotta be kidding. Ubi knew most long-nosed Freightliners were engineered with the bright lights on the outside and the single headlights on the inside, close to the grill. He glared at the trucker and raised the tire bumper over his head. A quick downward stroke, *pop!*, and the wooden club splintered a head-light. Two steps to the left and *pop!* Ubi shattered the second one. Glass shards rained down on the chrome bumper and onto the asphalt parking lot.

"You can go to Indy tonight all right, driver, but you ain't blinding nobody else this evening," Ubi said firmly gripping the tire bumper in his left hand. "Unless you can install two new high beams right quick."

"You son of a bitch," the man said, pointing his index finger at Ubi's chest. "I'm gonna kick yer ass."

"No you ain't. You're nothing but a big bully. You use that truck to intimidate people on the road and you're trying to back me down now."

"Throw down that tire bumper and let's see if I don't kick yer ass."

Ubi dropped the tire bumper, kicked it once, and it rolled under the Freightliner. "You're twice my size and half my age but I think I can take you," Ubi said. He clenched his fists and held his hands up in front of his face. Veins popped out on his neck. "Your call, hot shot, right here or behind the tire bay, don't make me no never mind."

"You old fart," the driver said. The fuel nozzle then popped and the pump quit chugging. The driver jerked the handle and pointed it at Ubi like a pistol. "You're lucky I ain't got time to mess with you, old man."

"No, *you're* lucky."

The driver slammed the nozzle into the pump, cursed at Ubi while he screwed the cap on the fuel tank, and continued muttering as he plodded inside the truck stop to pay. Ubi was still fueling his rig when the driver returned, sneered, climbed in his rig, and pulled out. The last trailer axle bounced over Ubi's tire bumper. Ubi picked it up, bumped all eighteen tires, stowed it in the magic box where he found a whisk broom. A minute later, the Freightliner hit the entrance ramp, downhill, racing the engine between shifts. Ubi stooped over and swept up the broken glass.

After Ubi filled both tanks, he took advantage of the truck stop's free shower for drivers who buy diesel. Show your receipt, and you're walking down the hallway with a fluffy towel, fat bar of soap, and a door key shaped like a tractor-trailer, a nice change from the locker room showers at many truck stops. And this place had been remodeled; the showers were like mini-motel rooms with a vanity. Sherry would have liked this; put on makeup, blow-dried her hair and everything, right here. She didn't take many trips, but she hated truck stop showers, especially because it seemed like there was always one driver who just had to leer at her in the lobby.

Back in Old Ironsides, with a full coffee thermos, Ubi figured he had another hundred miles left in him that night. He had mastered pouring Java on the go. Using the doghouse like a counter top, he tipped the thermos slowly until the hand-painted porcelain mug, a Father's Day present, was almost full. Now the hard part, timing the bumps so he wouldn't burn his lip.

A few cups down the road, Ubi knew the waitress must have given him decaf. He rubbed his eyes, held his head out the window, and turned up an oldies radio station. But Chuck Berry and Fats Domino couldn't keep him alert. The next rest area, and it's *Goodnight, Irene. You been pushing it too hard. Logbook's behind too. You're gonna' get a ticket or have to shut down if the ICC catches you.* Twenty miles later, Ubi pulled into a new rest stop jammed with cars and vans and recreational vehicles. This place had just opened and it was already overflowing. The truck and bus areas with long parking spaces were full, too. Ubi pulled in the back of the line, his trailer partially extending into the exit ramp.

TEN

BAM, BAM, BAM. Someone was beating like hell on Old Ironsides' door. Can't a feller get some rest without getting hassled? Ubi peeled back the sleeper curtain and squinted into the bright daylight. The rest area was almost empty, except for a lean man with a Florida tan wearing a Deaton Van Lines cap tilted to the left. Chewing a cigarillo and standing flat-footed in the lot, he held his hands above his head. The silver chain dangling from his neck swayed from side to side.

"You got the whole parking lot to yourself, why you parked in the middle of the driveway?" the man shouted. "Why you parked in the middle of the driveway?"

Ubi kicked off the covers, slipped on his khakis and grabbed a flannel shirt. The knocker was an old friend and driver everyone called Repeat because he said everything twice. Bare-chested, Ubi stuck his head out the window. "Whatever you're selling, I ain't buying."

"What are you doin' with your ass end sticking out in the road?"

Repeat grabbed a handrail and pulled himself up on Old Ironsides' front tire. He reached in the window with his free hand and started rubbing Ubi on the top of his head. "How the hell you been, Ubi Sunt? You old road dog. I thought you woulda' got smart, got off the road by now, got off the road by now."

"Some people never learn." Ubi pushed the man in the chest. "And git your ass off this truck, you know I don't let no highway tramps in Old Ironsides." Ubi shoved both arms in his flannel shirt, slipped on his boots, and climbed down into the parking lot. "Repeat, what the hell are you doing? I thought one of your ex-wives, the IRS, the ICC, the DOT or Donner Pass would've got you by now."

Early in his career, Repeat had gotten to popping pills to stay awake on the long runs. He developed an addiction that almost cost him his job, and left a permanent stutter that he tamed by learning to repeat the last few words of almost every sentence. Of course, with a trait like that he had to develop thick skin. Ubi warned him several times on the road that he was burning the batteries down too low and, unlike a flashlight, you can't just drop in a few new D cells and everything would be okay. Dispatch finally got wise and started making him pee in a cup once a month. He raised hell, threatened to sue, threatened to quit, but the company wouldn't back down. The former owner, Don Deaton, caught him at the Denver dock one day, took him aside and gave him a two-hour ass chewing. Told him if he was going to take road dope, he could unhook that trailer right now and pull out. As long as his name was on that equipment he wasn't going to put up with no pill poppers. That put an end to the road dope.

Nobody remembers who dubbed him Repeat. But that moniker had twice the significance because Repeat went through Peterbilt truck tractors like he did wives. He ran his trucks hard and bought a new one every three or four years, or when the ashtrays filled up, as Ubi liked to joke. This new rig had to be about the fifth Peterbilt he had owned.

Repeat started driving for Deaton a few years after Ubi signed on. He was one of those barges Ubi complained about, sought out coast-to-coast loads and tried to turn them as fast as he could. Repeat's favorite quip: "Never let the sun set on an empty trailer."

He preached *get it on, get it off.* It was all about volume, turning tonnage. "Sheeeut. Ain't nobody can keep up with me, keep up with me," Repeat often bragged.

Several years back, Repeat blew past Ubi in Montana, both drivers westbound toward Puget Sound. Repeat emptied out in Seattle, reloaded in Tacoma, and passed Ubi before he made it to the Washington state line. Repeat loved telling that story to anyone who would listen; dispatchers, waitresses and other drivers when he held court on the CB late at night, leading a pack of rigs down the highway.

Traffic backed up on the ramp behind the two Deaton rigs as Repeat described his new girlfriend to Ubi.

"She's a smooth piece of highway, long and lean with soft curves and gentle slopes, soft curves and gentle slopes."

Then the two men heard horns honking and looked up at a man standing outside a Volkswagen van waving his arms. "Pull on up," Repeat said. "I got some fresh coffee in my truck. Brand new, plug-in coffeemaker works like a champ. Looks like you could use some. Looks like you could use some."

"That ain't no lie," Ubi said. "Had a bad experience with decaf last night. Almost nodded off."

Ubi cranked up the diesel and waited a few seconds for air pressure to build in the brake system. Ubi pulled up, followed by Repeat in his new rig. Ubi climbed in the passenger side. Settling in the front seat, he sank in a high-back velour captain's chair with two armrests. Repeat handed him a Styrofoam cup, filled to the brim with black gold. Steam curled toward the plush, carpeted ceiling. Ubi looked over the cab: electric windows, heated mirrors that would prevent icing and fogging, stereo speakers mounted above, below and behind, ashtrays and cup holders everywhere.

"Reach between your legs. Reach between your legs," Repeat repeated. "Push that valve and the air will raise the seat."

Ubi squeezed the valve, and the seat hissed like a tire with a nail in the sidewall. It shot upward and Ubi's head brushed the ceiling, knocking off his cap.

"Too much," Repeat said, flashing a gold tooth with a quarter-moon in it. "Now you got to lower it. Now you got to lower it."

Fiddling with the knob for a minute, Ubi found the right elevation and relaxed.

"Where's the TV?" Ubi asked. He thought he was being funny.

"In the bunk, got a cable connected to a little antenna I hang out the window at night, hang out the window at night. Can't wait to get one of them satellite dish attachments. Watched that movie about Butch Cassidy and the Sundance Kid last night. Got good reception, good reception."

"Color?"

Repeat rolled his eyes like he'd been insulted.

"What you think? I'm gonna chinch on a TV?"

Suddenly Repeat bit his lip and lowered his eyes. "Sorry about the missus, Ubi. Afore I found out, it was a month too late. I never forget that time I run into the both of you in Miami looking like newlyweds, looking like newlyweds."

After an awkward pause, Repeat changed the subject. "You musta' been the last one in last night, parked way out in the ramp. Good thing nobody rear-ended you. Had to dodge ya' my own self. I mean, here I am coming down the exit ramp, I'm dropping gears like a lot lizard dropping her drawers, and I'm not believing there's the ass end of Old Ironsides coming up real fast, coming up real fast."

Repeat's gold tooth flashed in the bright light. Ubi sipped coffee. This was not decaf, all right, and it was starting to kick in.

"You should get one of these here coffeemakers, Ubi. Got mine at the Barqs Brothers truck stop in Omaha for fifteen bucks, fifteen bucks."

Ubi changed the subject. When you seldom see old friends, you got to get in the news quickly. "You hear about Ben Johnson? Ditch Dragon got him on Cabbage Mountain. They found him inside that old Kaywhopper, bottom of the grade. Rig smashed to hell. Mick Thorton told me when I was in Denver last week."

"What the . . . ? No stuff?"

For once, Repeat was speechless.

"Too bad for his wife. I heard he was fixin' to call it quits. Retire." Ubi caught Repeat staring out the windshield.

"I never thought the Ditch Dragon would get old BJ," Repeat muttered. "But if it can happen to him, it can happen to any of us."

"What about this strike?" Ubi asked. He felt the need to again change the subject. "You going to shut down?"

"Aw, hell yes. Hell yes. I ain't goin' to have nobody shooting at my truck. You shutting down too, ain't ya?"

Ubi stirred the coffee with a finger, licked it clean, took another swallow.

"Aw hell, you would be just the type to make a stand, talk about all that freedom stuff, one man, one truck. I know you. You're going to keep running, Ubi Sunt. You're going to keep running."

"When someone else is making my truck payments, they can tell me what to do."

"Aw hell, Ubi, everybody knows you ain't made no truck payments in twenty years. How long ago you paid off that rig? How long ago you paid off that rig?"

"Come on, Repeat. You know what I'm saying. Damn good Java, by the way. So it's like this. I'm paying for tires, fuel, insurance, taxes and labor. And a bunch of yahoos gonna' tell me to strike 'cause diesel's gone up a couple pennies?"

Repeat smirked and gave Ubi one of those *don't bullshit me* looks.

"Okay, more'n a couple cents. But here's what I'll tell 'em. First thing, quit idling yer engines. You walk through any truck stop, most rigs are left running with nobody inside 'cause they're all bellyaching to each other in the café 'bout high diesel prices. And if they quit blowing down the road like Johnny Law's on their tail they might get a little better fuel mileage. Finally, you could buy enough diesel to run from Miami to Miles City, Montana on the money some guys blow on all that chrome crap they don't need."

"Don't talk bad about my baby moon hub caps, my baby moon hub caps."

"You got them too? I didn't notice."

"Why, hell yes. I bet you still got the first dollar you made, Ubi, the first dollar you made."

"Maybe so. Anyway, I hear on the CB, the independent owner-operators might be trying to block some truck stops and organize a slow-moving convoy to Washington."

"When that happens, I'm gone fishing, gone fishing."

Ubi felt the cab shake slightly. He turned to his left and watched the sleeper curtain zipper come down and a woman's face appear. She had long, black eyelashes, thin nose, fat lips.

"Coffee smells good."

"Sweet Pea, this is Mr. Ubi Sunt, Mr. Ubi Sunt. His truck is like the Statue of Liberty, it may be old but you gotta' respect it. It's a one-of-a-kind. And boy can he load a rig. One year, he moved the whole state of New York. The whole state of New York."

"That's where we're going, New York," the lady in the bunk said. "We're getting married in Buffalo and going to Niagara Falls."

"Now hold on, Sweet Pea," Repeat said, holding out his hand. "Hold on, Sweet Pea."

"You said, after your divorce was final."

"I know what I said."

Ubi took the opportunity to refresh his coffee. "This sonofagun coffeemaker does a better job than some truck stops. Repeat, put it here, my friend. I got to get my logbook straightened out and head to Erie."

"You need an extra comic book? Sweet Pea, open that cabinet behind the TV and get this man a logbook. All you gotta' do is dummy up last two weeks in case you get checked, Ubi, you know that. Then when you get on down the road, and got enough hours of rest, go back to the real one, go back to the real one. Just remember, don't give no state trooper the wrong one, and sure don't mail in the wrong ones to safety and compliance back in Big D, they'll have a heart attack, they'll have a heart attack."

Ubi was familiar with the practice of running two logbooks, but like taking road dope, it wasn't for him. First, road dope makes you too nervous—chain-smoking and tingling hairs on your head and the back of your neck—and later you come down like an anchor dropping. After taking two Black Mollies one time, Ubi climbed Tehachapi Pass in a wind and dust storm, made it okay, but the next day he had to rent a room in Fresno, shut the curtains, and take the phone off the hook. Took six hours to go to sleep and then he overslept until the next afternoon, almost missed a delivery. As for logbooks, keeping up with two was complicated; a good liar has to have a good memory. But more than that, Ubi didn't like lying. The times he'd been caught for not having logs current, he never made excuses. He just paid the ticket, or pulled over for a catnap. Ubi told Repeat "no thanks" for the extra logbook. Like most drivers, he carried several, because one lasts just eight weeks and you might not make it to the home office before running out.

Repeat had to hustle into Cleveland to deliver that day, so the two clasped hands like a tire tool ratcheting down on a lug nut. The lady in the bunk brushed her hair. Ubi climbed down from the Pete and walked around the gleaming chrome bumper, looked down at his reflection.

"You look rough, old guy."

Repeat hung his head out the window. "You be careful, Ubi Sunt. If we go on strike, some of those boys—they don't play," Repeat said. Ubi turned and watched Repeat light a cigarillo. Hazy smoke billowed out the driver's side window and from the truck's twin stacks. "Some of those boys—they don't play."

"You keep the shiny side up, and greasy side down," Ubi hollered, and pointed his left index finger at his old friend.

Repeat let out the clutch and stepped on the accelerator. Unlike some drivers who shook their truck on almost every gearshift, Repeat gently eased through the low range gears. Shift after shift, the mighty rig barely twitched as Repeat pushed it up the entrance ramp.

Twenty minutes later, Ubi had his logbook and mileage report current—just enough hours to make Erie, Pennsylvania. Late that afternoon, Old Ironsides lumbered down an exit ramp, and after several miles and three wrong turns, Ubi found a two-story motel with yellow paint peeling from wood siding. Ubi backed the rig into a nearby gravel lot, up on a slope. From the driver's seat, he saw blue water stretch to the horizon. Water and sky, you can't tell where one stops and the other starts. Nothing but open space, as far as Ubi could see. After several minutes, a seagull flew across his line of vision and broke his trance. Down on the ground, digging his canvas bag out of the magic box, Ubi couldn't stop staring at the blue expanse.

The motel lobby was empty. Behind the counter, a television newscaster's voice drifted through an open door. Dim light flickered in the attached room. Ubi waited a minute, glanced at several framed pictures of a white brick lighthouse that hung from the paneling. He shouted hello, waited, picked up a brochure that celebrated the lighthouse's hundredth anniversary, and yelled hello again, a little louder. Then, from the TV room, a scraping noise—perhaps a chair scooting across the floor—followed by a long, loud honking sound like someone was blowing his nose. A large human shadow appeared in the doorway, and a heavy woman, about seventy, with short white hair and dark bags under her eyes entered.

"I'm sorry, sir. How long have you been standing there?" the woman asked, wiping her nose with a crumpled tissue.

"Not that long."

"We had a fire at the Canadohta lighthouse—one hundred and one years old. Looks like an old chimney sticking out of the ground now," the woman said. She stopped talking long enough to steady herself and wipe her nose. "My grandparents lived there for seven years, back in the '20s. Now they say it's not worth restoring. Our lighthouse has burned out."

The woman shoved a pen and a small card across the counter. "Fill this out," she said, looking over her shoulder into the TV room. "This place is nothing without that lighthouse. Nothing. It was the only thing that kept us going. Business is bad enough. Now, we'll dry up and blow away across the lake. Just like we were never here. Just like nothing ever happened."

That evening, Ubi fell asleep on a sagging mattress, a black-and-white wallet-sized photo of sassy Sherry Sunt on the nightstand.

The next morning, Ubi picked up a helper at the local Deaton franchise, which was a mildewed red brick warehouse, locally owned. His helper wore a ponytail down the back of his neck that stretched almost to his waist. His pockmarked face bore the scars of an adolescent bout with acne. The helper introduced himself— "Mississippi Hippie," he proudly said, holding out a calloused right hand.

Out at the residence, Ubi and The Hippie dropped the shipment from Colorado in no time—*this kid's got more hustle in him than Pete Rose*. Next, they picked up a shipment from a home on the edge of town in a decaying neighborhood with numerous empty houses. Elbows flying, hands zipping up and down, Mississippi Hippie wrapped six armchairs like Christmas presents while Ubi went over the moving contract with the homeowner.

Holding his clipboard, Ubi watched The Hippie drape two furniture pads over a china hutch and tuck and fold the edges in perfectly straight lines. No edges flopped over or dragged on the floor. Hippie had a dozen large black rubber bands cut from old truck tire inner tubes dangling from his neck He stretched two across the hutch like ribbons to keep the pads tight against the polished cherry wood.

It had been years since Ubi had a helper who could wrap sticks like that. Local moving companies typically assign part-time and inexperienced workers to road drivers and keep their best men for themselves. Unless a driver carries with him a full-time helper, he has to cope with whatever help he gets from the local agent: students, inexperienced friends and relatives of the office staff, or someone just looking for a day's pay that he'd spend on booze that night. Ubi often felt like he was training the rookies for the local moving companies. And if he didn't keep a close eye out, he risked drawers sliding out of dressers and splintering on the ground, or upholstery hanging up and ripping on doorjambs. But this hippie guy was smooth. He even lined the entry and hallway with cardboard to keep from tracking up the house. So Ubi let The Hippie load, and marveled at his craftsmanship. Straight and square, the tiers rose from the trailer floor: first, heavy pieces like dressers, followed with night tables and small chests on top, topped off by chairs neatly stacked with one kneeling inside the other. After loading, Ubi drove his rig to a truck scale to determine what the shipment weighed. Back at the agent, Ubi paid The Hippie cash.

"Where you headed?" The Hippie asked, folding the cash and tucking it into his jeans pocket.

"New York and New England. Got about a dozen shipments to drop. Then on to Philly where I got a couple grandkids. Take a week or so off to catch up."

"Catch a ride? I'll help you peddle those loads."

The clerk handed Ubi the freight bill and he clamped it to his clipboard. An experienced hand would be a blessing. Plus, he wouldn't have to call ahead every day setting up labor.

"Suit yourself, if you don't mind sleeping in the trailer."

The Hippie disappeared into the driver's lounge and returned with a battered black guitar case, duct tape strip across the top like a Band-Aid. The latches were broken, so a black rubber band, like the ones used for wrapping furniture, was doubled and stretched around the case to keep it closed.

Ubi and The Hippie rode Old Ironsides across northeastern Pennsylvania into New York State. They eased up to a tollbooth near the state line and a toll worker with a sour face and three days' beard handed Ubi a toll ticket.

"Thirty-six bucks to Albany? Ya'll must be awful proud of this tollway."

"You can take the back roads, if you don't like it."

Ubi muttered, "Don't tempt me."

Throughout the evening, cars zipped past Old Ironsides, bumper stickers with red hearts proclaiming motorists' affinity for the Empire State. Ubi stewed about the expensive toll. Finally, he decided to shake it off and find out a little about his new helper.

"What kinda' guitar you got, Hippie?"

"Aw, heck. I don't own a guitar. That's my suitcase. It helps me get rides, hitchhiking, you know. People see me, they think they've discovered another Kris Kristofferson."

"You think that's right to deceive folks like that?" Ubi asked, his foul mood showing through. "I mean, don't they get upset thinking ya'll are going to roll down the highway like Bobby McGee, just to find out you're a fraud?"

"Ain't no goddamn fraud," The Hippie said. He sat up straight and clenched his teeth. "Lost my handmade rosewood Martin sleeping in a roadside park outside Tulsa. Some drunk-ass Okies thought it would be fun to rob me, beat me up and cut my hair.

It was too hot to sleep in my pup tent, so I stretched out on a concrete picnic table. Woke up with one fat bastard sitting on my chest, two more pinning my arms to my side. Another one, with black teeth and dog breath, was snipping away with a pair of pruning shears." The Hippie's hazel eyes caught fire. "Know what the sheriff said the next morning?"

Caught by surprise, Ubi said nothing.

"Want to know?" The Hippie's voice screeched. "Well, do ya?"

"Sorry about that. I didn't mean to imply nothing."

"He said . . . he said . . . they shoulda' took a little more off the top."

After that uncomfortable exchange, the duo rode in silence for a while. Ubi didn't mind that, normally, but something about The Hippie intrigued him and he felt bad about the haircut story, an episode that The Hippie obviously hadn't been able to put behind him.

"What are you doing way up here in Great Lakes country? Long way from Mississippi."

"Well, let's just say me and the old man didn't see eye to eye. So, I took off, started out playing at county fairs and festivals for whatever folks would drop in my case. Some nightclubs too. Landed in jail a few times, mostly it was bullshit. I was doing good last year, had a little jingle in my pocket, staying out of the pokie. Had a gig lined up at Coffeeville, Kansas—that's where them Doolin-Dalton boys got shot up in that bank robbery about ninety years back—was going to play some songs about that at their annual festival. But them inbreds pulled over to piss at the rest stop where I was sleeping and . . ."

The Hippie turned his head and looked out the window. "I already told you that story," he said, still facing the glass. "Ain't nobody going to hire a folk singer with no guitar and fucked up hair like mine, so I started catching trucks, loading furniture, just kicking around, working enough to get by. That's all. Grew my hair back, but still ain't saved enough to buy a decent guitar."

It was late October and the New York countryside rolled past, decorated with thick woods—sassafras and oaks and dogwood tree leaves turning gold and scarlet.

"How'd you learn to load sticks like that? You're better'n anyone I seen in a long time," Ubi asked.

"My old man owned a moving company. Worked on the trucks since I was fifteen. At twenty, he said I was a coward for protesting the Vietnam War. Said I embarrassed him. Turns out his bidness friends complained. They saw me on TV news. I was up in Oxford, at an anti-war rally. I'd been playing guitar for a couple years. Studied Jimmie Rogers, the singing brakeman, you know he's from Mississippi, too. I know all his stuff. So, when the old hypocrite came down on me, I hauled ass." The Hippie said. He finally turned away from the window. He looked straight ahead, but not toward Ubi.

"Just turned thirty and I ain't been back since. Catching trucks, humping furniture, making enough to get by, get a gig or two on the way and keep moving."

The Hippie looked down at the white stripes disappearing under Old Ironsides. "Moving," he said again. "Long as I'm moving, I'm okay."

"You ever thought about a rig of your own?"

The Hippie curled up his lip and shook his head no.

"Well, I'm proud to have you work with me until I get all these shipments delivered. Then I'm going to stay in Philly like I said, with my daughter, son-in-law and twin grandkids."

The duo rode in silence until Old Ironsides rumbled into Utica, a city of about seventy-five thousand in the heart of the state. Ubi parked in a vacant lot overgrown with weeds, adjacent to what looked like a once-booming factory of some sort.

"Three stories high, two blocks long, and every window broken," Ubi said, frowning and shaking his head.

That night, The Hippie slept on a stack of moving pads in the trailer, nestled between bicycles and a barbecue grill, the last things loaded back in Erie.

In Utica the next morning, they unloaded furniture that belonged to an elderly widow from that town. Only ten months earlier she had moved to "glorious" Colorado to please her son and his family. She did not like it. Sure, the grandkids were adorable, and the mountains picturesque, *but who are you kidding?* Mee-Maw is not getting on a pair of skis at age seventy. And that's all the family did—ski, ski, and ski. Every weekend. But more than anything, Colorado wasn't home. No bridge club with best partner Bernice, no familiar church friends, and none of her favorite Italian and Greek restaurants. And back in Utica, she could visit Daddy at the cemetery whenever she wanted.

After setting up the woman's modest home, Ubi threaded Old Ironsides through residential streets lined with cars on both sides. Twice he stopped to squeeze the rig under low-hanging telephone lines; The Hippie assisted from the ground, using a two-by-four to push the wire above the top front edge of the trailer.

"What do you think about that grandmother moving back home?" The Hippie asked as the truck approached the interstate.

"Rip a tree out of the ground without the roots and it'll die when you replant it. All the water and fertilizer ain't going to help," Ubi said. He checked his mirror for a tailgating motorcycle. The bike zipped into the oncoming lane and passed.

"Does that include you?" The Hippie asked. He turned his head, looked at Ubi.

"I'm a tumbleweed, Hippie, you should know that by now."

"So, um, what would happen to a tumbleweed that was planted in fertile soil, watered staked and pampered?"

"I give it a week."

After another night camping in the truck, Ubi, The Hippie, and Old Ironsides approached the George Washington Bridge at sunup. Hippie looked down on the broad Hudson River. "She's not the Mighty Mississip, but that's a lot of water down there."

Ubi exited the freeway and pulled in line at the tollbooth behind a truck that had tomatoes painted on its rear door. A tall, pale man wearing greasy jeans and a New York Mets cap jumped in front of the rig wielding a spray bottle and squeegee. He reached up, grabbed a windshield wiper, climbed onto the bumper, and sprayed wildly at the glass. Hanging onto the wiper blade with one hand, he stabbed at the windshield with his squeegee, leaving a long smear directly in Ubi's line of vision. Ubi dug into his khakis for loose change. He held his hand out the window, and dropped the coins in the man's clutches. The man staggered backward, almost fell, and pointed to Old Ironsides.

"Mother fucking dinosaur."

Ubi wedged the rig across the edge of Harlem and down Broadway into Manhattan. Skyscrapers blotted out the sky. Sirens echoed down long corridors of tall buildings. Taxicabs zipped in and out of traffic. Whenever Ubi left stopping distance between Old Ironsides and the car in front, a cab squeezed in, almost clipping the rig. People moved in swarms down the jammed sidewalk. Buzzing, jumping, zigzagging, humming, the New Yorkers were in full swing when Ubi found the twenty-eight-story apartment building and double-parked out front. The Hippie remained in the front seat, wide-eyed at the circus going on all around him. Ubi scoped out the situation. He had called the building manager earlier in the week and reserved the freight elevator and a spot at the loading dock out back. No matter. His request was usurped by someone more important.

Arms crossed and blocking the front door, the elevator man said, "Got some hotshot producer, works on Broadway, moving out. Gonna take all day. We bumped 'cha, Tex. Come back tamarra. That's how it is in New Yawk."

Ubi sized up the elevator man. Tall. Trim. Silver mustache. About sixty. Navy blue uniform. "Why are you running the elevator half empty?"

"Whattya tawking about?"

"The elevator," Ubi said. "It's full coming down, but empty going back up. Don't make no sense. In Texas, we'd have that thing loaded both ways."

"We don't care how you do it in Texas. This is New Yawk."

Ubi reached into his wallet and pulled out a twenty. With both hands, he held up the crisp Andrew Jackson at eye level. "Is this how you do it in New York? I need about three, maybe four hours to get this shipment delivered to the twenty-first floor."

"Keep it down."

The elevator man took four quick steps to the heavy wooden door and unlocked it for a woman carrying an oversized shopping bag. The door slammed shut and he approached Ubi, standing near the curb. "Put it here," he said, with his left hand dropped to his side. Ubi slipped the twenty into the elevator man's leathery palm and he made it vanish.

"Now you understand," he said with a nod. "*That's* how we do it in New Yawk."

While Ubi and the elevator man were negotiating their deal, traffic stacked up behind Old Ironsides. In a rush, drivers honked, yelled, and gesticulated out open windows. Sticking their front bumpers into traffic, they pushed into the next lane and around the big truck. One dark-skinned cab driver—rosary dangling from his rearview mirror—stopped, opened the driver's side door, and put one foot on the pavement. Leaning across the hood, he cupped both hands around his mouth like a megaphone and yelled above the din.

"Hey, buddy, when you get done which ya' moving job, take that jalopy down to the Smithsonian in D.C. Ha!"

Ubi ignored the catcalls and chaos until a city bus approached. Squeezing past the eighteen-wheeler, the bus driver failed to allow space for his passenger side mirror. Screeching metal on metal made Ubi's spine twitch. He raced around Old Ironsides' front bumper. The exhaust fumes made his head swim, and for a few seconds he felt like the pavement was moving under his feet. Ubi propped himself against the driver's door with his shoulder, inches from traffic. The bus driver left a deep gash down the side of his rig, right through the Deaton logo.

Ubi had been to Manhattan before, so he knew what to expect—another world. And he had learned the ropes the hard way. On his first trip here, after delivering a young rabbi's furniture to a synagogue, he found himself trapped on the island. His trailer was too tall to exit any of the tunnels. On subsequent visits he learned his way around, which bridges could handle his truck, and picked up some high-paying loads other drivers turned down because they wanted no part of the Big Apple.

Now that Ubi had lost his place at the dock, he had to unload from the street. Double-parking, he blocked about a half-dozen cars. The two men quickly set up shop; they extended the walk board out a trailer side door, and squeezed it between front and rear bumpers onto the sidewalk. Trip by trip, Ubi rolled the furniture dolly down the ramp, up the sidewalk, dodged pedestrians, and dropped the items off with The Hippie stationed near the elevator. Then he hustled back to the rig before someone ran off with a TV or night table.

Returning from the elevator on one trip, pushing an empty dolly, Ubi found a city cop with a double chin, hands on his hips, scowling.

"What's a matta whichya? You can't leave this ramp in da' sidewalk like this. Somebody's gonna trip and break their neck."

"They've been stepping over it okay," Ubi said.

"I bedda not come back and find this ramp here," the policeman said, wagging his finger in Ubi's face. Then a woman loaded down with shopping bags gingerly stepped across the walk board. "Dat's what I'm talking about. You gonna' hurt somebody."

Although he had delivered to Manhattan before, Ubi felt like an alien, like he had somehow landed in a place where normal had been turned upside down. Working without the ramp dragged out the job because he had to climb up and down from the trailer again and again. Four hours later, Ubi signed paperwork upstairs while The Hippie buttoned up the truck.

Sifting his way through traffic, Ubi closed in on the George Washington Bridge. After sitting through several turns at one stoplight, he found the freeway ramp and ran up the rpms, slipping through the low gears.

"There's some kids chasing us," Ubi said, looking into the side mirror. "Looks like one's carrying a set of hedge trimmers. What are you gonna' do with hedge clippers in New York City?" Ubi hit the air-activated splitter, shifted to high range and the rig surged forward. The kids peeled away and slowed to a walk.

About sixty miles up the interstate in Connecticut, Ubi parked in a jammed truck stop called The Patriot that featured an oversized illuminated billboard with what looked like an American Revolutionary War soldier driving an eighteen-wheeler. Suspicious about what happened back at the freeway ramp, Ubi and The Hippie walked behind the rig. The padlock dangled from the door latch, about to fall off. The hasp was almost cut through. Ubi fiddled with the lock and it fell open. He wiggled it free and turned toward The Hippie. "Another turn sitting at the stop light, and those kids might have found some goodies for the pawn shop."

"Yep," The Hippie said. "That's how they do it in New Yawk."

ELEVEN

THE MORNING AFTER the New York delivery, Ubi and The Hippie left before sunlight. Rolling into Massachusetts, before Ubi had a second cup of coffee from his thermos, he saw a man wearing a police uniform and flat-brimmed hat waving him down.

What's this joker want? Oh, brother, a speed trap. Ubi pounded the steering wheel and stepped on the brake pedal. On the shoulder, a baby-faced state trooper pulled himself up the side of Old Ironsides and stuck his nose in the driver's window. He asked for Ubi's driver's license and his eyes lit up when he saw Texas printed across the top of it.

"Okay, Tex. Let me see your bills, your pills and your shooting iron."

Ubi handed over his permit book, logbook and a small satchel stuffed with freight bills. Panting, the young trooper clutched a handrail, still perched on the side of the rig. He wasn't ready to climb back down, and had to hang on until he caught his breath.

"I got you doing sixty-two in a fifty-five," the trooper said. "Surprised this old tub can go that fast. Radar musta' caught you on the downhill."

"You need to get off my truck."

"Beg your pardon."

"You got bad breath. You're not funny. And I'm old enough to be your daddy, God forbid I had a son that talked to his elders like you. So go back to you car and write up the ticket. I'll sign it and be out of this state before you can make it back to the donut shop."

"You can't talk to me like that," the trooper said. His face turned red, and his tired arms quivered from holding himself up on the truck's steps. "I'll take you downtown."

"For what? Going seven miles an hour over the speed limit? I'm sure that will impress your sergeant."

Watching the altercation from the shotgun seat, The Hippie's mouth dropped open and his eyes looked like he'd seen Paul Revere riding down the frontage road yelling, "speed trap ahead, speed trap ahead."

The trooper caught The Hippie staring. "What are you looking at?" he asked. The Hippie looked away and said nothing.

The trooper said he'd be right back and shimmied down the truck. During his descent, his uniform caught the door handle and he popped a shirt button. Ubi watched the boyish trooper straighten his uniform and march toward the patrol car.

"I guess you told him how the cow eats cabbage," The Hippie said.

"What a shame. Young fella' with such poor manners," Ubi said, shaking his head. "I know I'm crotchety, but I'm old."

Ten minutes later, the trooper stood below the rig, reached up, and handed Ubi a speeding ticket. Ubi signed the back and grabbed a gear. Old Ironsides pumped black smoke from both pipes.

"Bet he's glad to see us go," The Hippie said. "That's a side of you I ain't seen before, Ubi. Made me want to crawl up in the bunk, hide under the covers."

Ubi slipped into traffic. Pushing the rig harder than normal, he rushed a shift and the transmission growled, made a large clunk and shook the cab. The rig shuddered and lost momentum. A man driving a van a few car lengths behind the rear bumper braked hard.

"I guess I'm losing my touch, or my patience. I can't remember the last time I missed a gear."

That afternoon and early evening, Ubi and The Hippie dropped one shipment in Massachusetts, one in Maine, and a third in New Hampshire. Ubi never got over how close together these New England states sat, and small too; some West Texas counties were bigger than Rhode Island. He could deliver in three states in one day, no problem.

At dusk, Ubi found a deserted shopping center near the Vermont—Massachusetts state line. He parked in a far corner. The unlikely duo hiked a quarter-mile down the shoulder of a tree-lined boulevard, cars whizzing past, until they found a small grocery next to a state liquor store. They soon returned with dinner and a six-pack of Canadian pilsner beer in snub-nosed bottles. Washing hands and faces, the road grime and dust and dirt from a day of moving, they drained Ubi's two-gallon insulated water jug. Ubi saved the last few ounces of Rocky Mountain river water and poured it down his throat. Colorado and that great Western expanse seemed a world away from the dense Northeast.

With the trailer now more than half-empty, Ubi had room to set up a makeshift dinette. He took two flattened dish cartons, taped them up like he was going to fill them with stemware, and set them side by side to make a kitchen table. Ubi then folded furniture pads into a tight square and used them as seat cushions for milk crates that were filled with straps and rolls of tape. Ubi dug into his stash of plastic knives, forks, spoons, and napkins saved from various take-out diners across the country. He pointed a large flashlight upward in the middle of the table. It cast long shadows on the trailer walls. The Hippie held his hands up, one in a fist, the other flat, and made a low, groaning sound. A shadow that looked like a tractor-trailer rig moved across the trailer wall. "Here comes Ubi Sunt and Old Ironsides, last of a breed. They don't take shit off nobody, especially a greenhorn Smokey from Connecticut."

Ubi positioned himself on the milk crate, leaned against the trailer wall, and sipped the beer. Sometimes the road can get under your skin; he'd seen that the last few days. Now, there in the trailer, he relaxed. He had made his living with this big wagon, and kept the inside swept and clean, furniture pads always stacked and strapped to the wall. Back when Jeanne was elementary school age, and Ubi was home for holidays, or maybe a birthday, he would stretch two-by-four wood beams wall to wall like ceiling joists and throw a plywood sheet across them. Jeanne would climb the stepladder into the tree house where father and daughter pretended they were camping in some remote national park. They played Go Fish by flashlight, snacked on Cheetos, and drank Dr Pepper. Now, The Hippie was making a shadow figure that looked like the Massachusetts patrolman. "Gimme your guns, Tex, this ain't the Alamo." Those days seemed like a dream.

The Hippie peeled back a sardine can lid, speared a tiny fish with a plastic fork, laid it on a saltine cracker, and shoved it in his mouth. Forgoing the napkins, with a quick turn of his head, The Hippie wiped his mouth on his jacket sleeve. For twenty minutes, the men ate in relative silence, both growing weary as the long day and alcohol set in.

Ubi and The Hippie zigzagged across New England and New Jersey for two more days. They grabbed truck stop showers in the evening, meals on the run, eating, driving, reading maps and directions scratched on note pads as they rolled down the road; their only downtime was when Old Ironsides caught a breather near a pay phone where Ubi set up delivery appointments. He had one shipment left to deliver, the preacher's piano from Colorado, but couldn't find the nephew who had inherited it. Parked in a New Jersey truck stop near Trenton, he settled up with The Hippie. The two men had agreed on a deal that paid according to weight, riding time between jobs, and extras for stairs and long walks where Ubi couldn't get the rig close to the house or apartment. He counted out the cash and double-checked the figures he had scratched on an envelope were accurate.

"You going to shut down, like most of the other drivers?" The Hippie asked, sliding the cash back into the envelope Ubi had given him, and cramming it into his front jeans pocket. "You heard that guy on the CB yesterday talking about blocking some tollbooths."

Ubi dangled his arm out the window. "I'm taking a little time off. Visit my daughter and grandkids in Philly. But I don't call that going on strike. These fellas want to make a point, but that ain't how you do it, stirring up trouble. If you're serious about getting something done, write your congressman, or call your senator."

Ubi ran his fingers through his thin hair, scratched the growing bald spot at his crown. "I don't have any answers, but I ain't going to let somebody tell me when I can or can't run. I been independent too long. If I was a kid just getting started maybe that would be different."

"Fella last night at the coffee counter said fuel prices are ridiculous."

A mosquito buzzed near Ubi's ear and he brushed it away. "Yesterday, my dispatcher said we're fixin' to get a fuel surcharge tacked on to the bottom line of every load we haul, if these hotheads don't pull some stunt and piss off the politicians first."

The two sat quietly for several minutes. Although Ubi had only known The Hippie for a few days and wasn't inclined to get close to someone that quickly, saying good-bye was harder than expected. He had made the job easier and was good company without whining about living out of a rig. Recent showers had left puddles in the gravel lot, and trucks sloshed through, dripping gray mud from wheels and mud flaps. More mosquitoes buzzed inside the cab. One landed on Ubi's arm. He slapped it and blood splattered.

"When do these blood suckers go away? It's October, for crying out loud."

"I've been lumping sticks for bed-buggers for a good while," The Hippie said, "and I've never heard so many drivers looking for a fight like they are now. They're mad at everybody, Arabs, that Georgia peanut farmer in the White House, each other. When this strike happens, and I heard some drivers are already blocking truck stops down South, it's going to get nasty."

"Like I say, I'm taking time off for family, not for fuel," Ubi said. He swatted and missed a mosquito hovering above his head. "What about you, Hippie? You're one of the best furniture men I've worked with."

"I've been saving. I might buy another guitar," The Hippie said, patting the envelope in his front pocket. "Might have to start out on the sidewalk, or washing dishes. But I might land a regular gig at a little bar."

"Thought about going home?"

A mosquito landed on The Hippie's forearm. He watched the insect sink its needle deep into his flesh. After the mosquito had swelled with blood, The Hippie suddenly slapped it. He held up five bloody fingers, looked at Ubi. "Hell no."

"Sorry if I touched a nerve."

A vein is more like it, The Hippie thought.

"You did. But that's okay. You're at a crossroads too. You missed that gear yesterday, and forgot to lock the trailer door after we dropped that shipment in Burlington. I didn't say nothing, just locked it up. And I seen you adding oil to Old Ironsides two days in a row."

"I don't think I can live back East," Ubi said. "Much as I want to see them little shits grow up, I'd feel boxed in."

"Why don't you settle down back home? Texas, right?"

"You don't understand," Ubi said, shooing another mosquito off his face. "This is home."

TWELVE

JEANNE SUNT GRADUATED salutatorian at Paisano High School. Six feet tall, with a figure like an ironing board, and studious, she never had many dates. But her stellar grades and senior project about how a district attorney prosecuted illegal migrant workers while employing some at his ranch earned her a four-year scholarship at a private university in Philadelphia. In her sophomore year, a graduate student named Martin Taylor read one of her essays in the student paper and sought her out. The theme, growing up head and shoulders above your peers, both in physical stature and intellect, caught his attention.

Martin had earned his master's degree in political science the same spring that Jeanne graduated with honors earning an anthropology degree. A year later, Ubi walked his only daughter down the aisle at their small Catholic church back home. The newlyweds got a deal on a fifty-year-old bungalow on the city's west side, in a neighborhood with a tavern and a church on almost every corner. Jeanne and Martin remodeled the wood frame home and settled into professional careers. Martin worked long hours editing a monthly muckraking journal that called itself a government watchdog, shining a light on fraud, waste, and corruption. Jeanne worked at a downtown Native American history museum. The couple agreed: no children, until they had a grip on how their careers would work out. But that plan was turned upside down nine months after a long spring weekend at a waterfront hotel on Cape Hatteras, North Carolina.

Molly came first, kicking and screaming on an icy February thirteenth, just before midnight. Jeremy entered the world a few moments later, but he was born February fourteenth, smiling and cooing. Their personalities reflected their birthdays. Molly, born on Friday the thirteenth, was mischievous, rowdy, and skeptical. Much to her muckraking father's delight, she questioned everything. Her skepticism wasn't the typical grade school doubts over Santa Claus and the Easter Bunny, but stuff like: *Why did the alphabet start with A, not Z? Why don't we have a bridge from Philadelphia to London?* And watching the baseball playoffs with Daddy, she asked, *why players always run in the same direction? Why can't they run either way, depending on where they hit the ball?*

On the other hand, Jeremy, born on Valentine's Day, thought life was like Silly Putty, you could mold it into whatever reality you wanted. Mom and dad fighting behind closed doors didn't happen; their TV was turned up loud. Their cat, Pocahontas, wasn't really poisoned when the teenage boy across the street intentionally left out a plastic dish with antifreeze in it; she just got sick and died. And the lady pushing the squeaking rusty grocery cart past their house every day wasn't a homeless alcoholic, she was probably somebody's maid going to work.

Despite their contrasting personalities, Molly and Jeremy both worshipped their mysterious Grandpa Truck. Their young eyes were accustomed to seeing Mom and Dad dressed in slacks and starched shirts and blouses. When Grandpa Truck visited, he always wore khakis and a green work shirt with a patch that read "Ubi" just above the left pocket. Mom rubbed creams and lotions on her face, especially around her eyes, and had pretty skin. The skin around Grandpa Truck's eyes was wrinkled and red and rough. And hugging that stubbly face felt like rubbing a toothbrush across your cheek. In the evening, Mom and Dad poured wine from tall slender bottles into funny glasses that had skinny stems and wide bowls. With just an itty-bit in the bottom, they sniffed and sloshed the wine and took tiny sips. When Grandpa Truck visited, he always brought with him a six-pack of Schmidt's beer and gulped it straight out of the little opening in the top of the steel can. Mom and Dad opened thick hardback books on their laps in the evening. The only thing the twins saw their grandfather read: magazines with pictures of huge rigs on the cover. Rigs that pulled rocket ships. Rigs that carried giant logs. And a rig that carried the world's biggest Christmas tree to the White House. Sometimes, Mom and Dad pushed tiny cassettes into their stereo and listened to strange music with no words, just lots of horns and strings and a pounding piano that sounded like what they heard on Saturday morning cartoons. Riding in Old Ironsides, listening to the scratchy AM radio, the twins heard people singing with poor grammar about things like white line fever, White Freightliners, and white lightning. Instead of violins, they heard fiddles. Instead of a harp that sounded like an angel was playing it, they heard a strange guitar that sounded like a faraway train whistle. Instead of a deep, deep string sound from a giant guitar standing straight up, the twins heard a high-pitched, clankity banjo.

Mom and Dad were the best parents in the world, sure, but Grandpa Truck, well, he was like a character in their history book, or from a movie that was filmed in black and white.

* * *

Sitting in the family's new Saab station wagon at the mall parking lot, Jeanne and the twins heard a low rumbling behind them. Jeanne looked in her rearview mirror. A red diesel rig with a large front grill like a locomotive ambled forward. The hairy, sunburned arm hanging out the driver's window was her first glimpse of Daddy since the funeral. The twins leaped out of the car, left the doors open, and raced toward Old Ironsides. Ubi stopped the truck and set the brakes. Popping air valves sounded like firecrackers to the twins. Ubi turned the key in the dash, and the diesel engine coughed, sputtered, and shook the cab before its last gasp. Ubi then pulled a cable hanging from the ceiling near the driver's window and a blast that sounded like it came from a gigantic tuba echoed across the almost-empty parking lot. The twins stamped their feet, clapped their hands and rushed the truck. Ubi climbed down and held his arms out wide. Squatting down, he wrapped an arm around each grandchild and then stood up, holding them on his hips.

"You guys get down from there," Jeanne said, approaching her father. "You're going to hurt his back."

Ubi loosed his grip and the kids slid down his torso like they were scooting down a tree trunk. Ubi kissed his daughter on the cheek, held her close, and pulled back for a good look. The little girl who ate Cheetos and camped out with him in the trailer was a full-grown woman and mother. About the same height, their eyes met. Jeanne looked away first, over her father's shoulder. The kids were already frolicking in the cab, climbing over the seats, dog-house, in and out of the bunk. Jeanne closed her eyes and a voice inside her said: "Daddy, Daddy, Daddy. You and Old Ironsides. What are we going to do with you?"

Then a mall security guard pulled up in a tiny, foreign pickup and told Ubi he couldn't leave his truck there overnight. "No, problem," Ubi said, "Let's go to Sid's."

With Molly riding shotgun and Jeremy bouncing in the bunk, Ubi took the mall's back entrance and headed down a state highway toward Sid's Truck Stop. Sid was an old friend, and Ubi knew he could leave the rig there for several days. Jeanne followed alone in the Saab for about a mile, but then pulled up beside Ubi at a stop sign.

"You're going the wrong way, Daddy," she shouted out the open passenger side window. "Follow me."

Jeanne was sure she remembered the old dive, Sid's, just the kind of place Dad would like. It was down the Allentown Highway, so she turned left, and Ubi followed. About three miles down that road, doing about fifty miles an hour, Jeanne scooted under a railroad overpass with a yellow sign on it that read: *Low Clearance—13 feet 4 inches.* Following close behind, Ubi braked hard. Jeremy somersaulted out of the bunk and bumped heads with his sister. Jeremy's brow split open. Blood trickled down his face. Both kids started crying. Ubi slowed the rig to a crawl and handed Jeremy his bandana. Molly rubbed her forehead and through sniffles and teary eyes asked Grandpa if her head was bleeding, too. Ubi assured her no, dabbed Jeremy's wound with the bandana and said they both would be fine. Then he poked his head out the window and looked up at the bridge's underside; his CB antenna was bent back, rubbing.

"Sheesh, come one Jeanne, I can't get under this bridge," Ubi blurted out, exasperated. "Why did you insist on going this way?"

Ubi looked ahead. The Saab was nowhere in sight. He edged forward at a snail's pace, watching the bridge's belly grow closer to the top of the trailer. The tractor made it through okay and the rig slithered up a small rise, exiting the underpass like a snake shedding its skin. About five feet before the back of the trailer was clear, the sound of screeching metal on metal pierced Ubi's ears. He set the brakes.

"Are we stuck?"

"Yep."

"What are you gonna' do?"

"Dunno. How's your head?"

"I'm okay."

"Me too."

"Are you scared, Grandpa?"

"Naw. I'm just' gonna' go back and push up the bridge a little bit. We'll be out in a minute."

"How are you going to do that?"

"Get on top of the trailer, lying on my back, and push the bridge up with my arms."

Ubi smiled, rolled up his shirtsleeve, and bent his elbow. His bicep popped up. To the kids it looked round and hard, like the foul ball dad caught for them at a Phillies game.

"Hey, there goes Mom, the other way."

Ubi turned his head. The Saab flew past in the opposite direction and made a U-turn, jumping the curb and concrete median, then pulled onto the shoulder, four-ways flashing. Ubi climbed down, and faced his daughter on the street.

"Why didn't you say something, Daddy?" Jeanne asked, holding her arms out, palms upward." I don't know how tall your truck is."

"Why did you change the route?" Ubi asked. Only one hour into the visit and things were already going wrong.

"Look, you might want to check the kiddos," Ubi said. "They bumped heads when I hit the brakes."

Sherry's eyes shot darts at her father. She jogged toward the rig, and with spider legs, easily climbed into the tall truck. Ubi pulled a tire gauge from his shirt pocket and squatted at the trailer's rear axles. Air hissed from each tire, one by one, until he had eight flats.

Meanwhile, a traffic light down the highway had turned green; cars, buses and trucks, some honking, piled up almost a mile behind the rig. One paunchy motorist wearing a sweaty green Philadelphia Eagles t-shirt that barely covered his belly walked up and waved his hand in disgust. "Come on, mister, get this rust bucket out of the road. They got a scrap yard over on Lancaster Highway. Geez, gimme a break."

Ubi hustled to the cab and climbed in. Jeanne was sitting between her children, in the bunk, pulling them close toward her small breasts. Ubi dropped the transmission in the lowest gear, called the Granny Gear, because in that position your rig creeps along like a grandmother on an afternoon stroll. The truck eased forward, and the last few inches of trailer scraped the overpass. Ubi took a chance, romped the accelerator, felt a tug, and then the rig rolled free. Ubi limped the rig along for a couple hundred feet and pulled onto the shoulder.

"Grandpa, how'd you do it?"

"Pushed up the bridge. Just like I said."

"You can't push up a bridge."

"Sure, you can."

"Then, how will you put the bridge back?" the kids asked, laughing. Ubi smiled.

"Hadn't thought of that."

Aware what Ubi had done, Jeanne refused to play along. "How are you going to air up those tires, Daddy?"

Ubi held up his index finger. "I got something in my magic box," he said. The twins looked at each other: Grandpa has a magic box?

Down on the street, Ubi uncoiled a long rubber air hose and attached it to a metal connector called the glad hand, which carries compressed air from the truck to the trailer, and inflated the eight trailer tires. Meanwhile, Sherry walked back to retrieve her car. She insisted the twins ride with her, strapped in by seat belts. The small convoy arrived at Sid's about dark.

The twins woke early the next morning. Rubbing sleep from their eyes, they charged into the guest room where Grandpa Truck slept. He was in bed, shirtless, reading by lamplight a truckers' tabloid he picked up last night at Sid's. Molly reached up, flipped the light switch near the door. Ubi blinked twice, rubbed his eyes with his fists, put down the journal. His arms rested on his lap. Jeremy pointed at his grandfather like he was a cartoon character.

"Grandpa, your arms are different colors," Jeremy said, cocking his head. "One's brown like Miss Sanchez and the other's white like Miss Churchill. That's funny."

"You look like a zebra with one stripe," Molly said. She approached the bed, poking Ubi's left arm, the brown one.

"No, you look like opposite man. A man who has opposite color arms for doing opposite things," Jeremy said. He climbed on the bed and held up the brown, left arm. "This one's for talking on the CB to truckers who sound funny."

"And this one's for shifting big gears—rumm, rumm," Molly said. "I bet you're the only person on the planet with different color arms."

The kids had now closed in on Ubi and he saw his chance. The left brown arm swooped around Molly's waist and lifted her on the bed. The white right arm went straight to Jeremy's ribs. Suddenly both kids were on their back, giggling.

"Help, it's Grandpa Truck's tickle attack!" Molly squealed. She squirmed on her back, kicking her feet in the air.

"And I can tickle with both arms. See?" Ubi said. He quickly switched his arms back and forth. "Brown tickler. White tickler. Brown. White. White. Brown."

Suddenly, a shadow at the bedroom door. "You guys are going to be late for school," Jeanne said. "And you've got to get dressed in your costumes. Remember, this is Halloween."

"Tell us a ghost story, Grandpa," Molly demanded, now sitting up straight in bed.

"But not too scary," Jeremy said, sitting cross-legged at the foot. "And don't tell us about the Ditch Dragon. We already heard that one. A big, green monster comes up out of the slime and grease—"

"Okay, Jeremy, we all know the story. You don't have to tell us," Molly said, like a big sister, with a touch of irritation.

"Have you heard about Phantom 309? That's a good one," Ubi asked, leaning against the wooden headboard, arms folded.

"Not that old story," Jeanne said. "I heard it on the radio when I was a kid. A truck driver named Big Joe gets killed when he drives his rig off the side of the mountain to miss a school bus full of kids. Then one day, a hitchhiker shows up at a truck stop down the road, says he got a ride from Big Joe. Turns out, Big Joe is now a ghost trucker. He's been giving hitchhikers rides in his rig, called Phantom 309, on that road ever since the crash."

"You didn't tell it right, Jeanne. You gotta build up the suspense, talk about the rain and cold and fog and everything," Ubi said, his voice trailing off.

"Never mind," Jeanne said, clapping her hands twice like a gym teacher. "Get dressed in your costumes if you want to wear them to school. Now."

"I'll tell you the rest of Phantom 309 tonight," Ubi said.

"But not too scary," Jeremy reminded.

"Not too scary."

With the house to himself all day, Ubi read newspapers, watched TV, and caught up on the truckers' strike. Some owner-operators, or independents, were holding rallies in the larger truck stops across the country. Others had blocked a tollbooth in New Jersey. And a small convoy drove the interstate across Ohio at thirty miles an hour to back up traffic and gain attention. Ubi called dispatch back in Denver, said he had one shipment left to deliver, and reminded them he had asked for time off to visit family. *Looks like this is a good place to wait out the strike, see what will happen.*

That evening, Ubi escorted the Statue of Liberty and Albert Einstein up and down the low hills and narrow streets in the West Philadelphia neighborhood. After their mother took away their candy for the evening and made them brush their teeth, the kids knelt down for nighttime prayers.

"I pray Grandpa Truck comes to live with us," Molly said, hands folded.

"Me too. But he needs to shave, like Dad," Jeremy said. "My face hurts."

That evening, lying in bed with her husband, Jeanne rolled over and turned on a reading light. She pulled out a folder from a nightstand, and thumbed through copies of documents from several state and federal agencies and a Baltimore history museum. The light woke Martin. He rolled over and draped an arm around his wife's waist.

"You going to talk to him tomorrow? Like we said?"

"That's the plan. You take the kids shopping for new shoes and we'll be alone."

"I don't think he's going to like it."

"We'll see. You know, he's still telling the same lame ghost stories he told me as a kid. The one he adapted from one of his favorite trucker songs, by Red Sovine, about Phantom 309," Jeanne said. She shuffled the papers again, making sure everything was in order. She closed the folder, set it on her lap.

"You seem conflicted, Jeanne."

"Huh?"

"You want him to settle down and live nearby, but don't like him bonding with the kids. There are a lot more lame stories coming from Grandpa Truck, and to the kids, those tall tales will be fresh and raw and funny and sad, and they'll love him for it. Sure, someday they'll grow out of it, like Puff the Magic Dragon, but until they're a little older, let them have their fun—all three of them," Martin said, looking at the digital alarm. *3 a.m., geez.* "There's something enchanting about Ubi. I see it. The kids see it. It's a shame you don't."

Jeanne slid the folder in the nightstand, turned out the light. "Well, it's just . . . it's just. . . he needs to grow up."

"Why did it bother you this morning, the laughing and giggling coming from Ubi's room? You just had to go in there," Martin said. "I saw your face after you broke up the party. I hate to say it, honey, but it looks like you're jealous."

Jeanne ripped back the covers, stomped into the living room, and flung herself face down on the couch.

THIRTEEN

IT WAS ALMOST DARK when Ubi returned from Sid's truck stop. Riding public transportation was a challenge. Reading bus and train schedules and following color-coded routes was a different cup of coffee to someone who knew by memory every interstate and most U.S. highways, coast to coast. But he made it back to Jeanne and Martin's, a six-pack of cheap beer under one arm, and a remote-controlled, battery-powered toy truck he bought at Sid's under the other.

Ubi used the key Jeanne had given him the day before to unlock the front door. *Hmm, nobody home. Wonder why.* He slid the six-pack onto an empty refrigerator shelf. Then he heard the front door open. Jeanne dropped her umbrella in the brass stand at the door and met Ubi in the kitchen. She set her briefcase on the table and pulled out a beige folder with *DAD* written across the top.

"What's that?"

"Daddy, we need to talk," Jeanne said, taking a deep breath, her stomach full of butterflies. "I've been doing some research, and I think I know where you were born."

Jeanne slipped out of her tan jacket, draped it over the back of the chair. "You ever heard of Orphan Trains?"

Ubi's eyes glazed over. "I know I'm an orphan, I never hid that. But what's this about, Sweetums?"

Sweetums, Jeanne hadn't heard her father call her that since she was in grade school. Jeanne and Ubi huddled at the table, flipping through a couple dozen copies of old railroad schedules and New York, Philadelphia, and Baltimore newspaper stories from the early 1900s. "Remember those stories you told when we camped out in the big truck? You told me about dreams you used to have, said you would hear the clickety-clack and feel like you were rocking along like a baby? You said when you were a little boy, the priests at the boys ranch would play train sounds on an old phonograph to lull you to sleep. You slept in the room with the sloped floor and they took turns rocking the bed until you drifted off. I thought that was just another story, like Phantom 309, and Teddy Bear, that you got from Red Sovine, but it's not."

Ubi propped up his chin with an open hand. "What are you driving at?"

"I've been corresponding with the boys ranch. They wouldn't release their records, but I got an attorney," Jeanne said. She flipped to a copy of the letter her attorney wrote to the boys ranch director. "The ranch kept a log of all the boys, when they arrived, and how. The priest who picked you up at the San Antonio depot wrote in his remarks all the other kids on the train had been picked over, taken to new homes, except you. Said parents thought you were odd because you were always twitching, shaking, even if someone rocked you in their arms, you wouldn't relax. So, the priest took you back to the boys ranch and gave you the name Ubi Sunt."

"I guess you looked that up, too, what Ubi Sunt means?"

"It's Latin. No surprise there. After all, the Jesuits were Roman Catholic. Roughly translated, it means: Where are the snows of yesteryear? I'm sure you checked it yourself," Jeanne said. She looked up at her dad. She reached across the table and pushed back the corn stalks growing out of his scalp. "I love you, Daddy. That's why I'm doing this."

"So I was shipped out on an Orphan Train from the East Coast," Ubi said, sliding back his chair and bouncing his left leg up and down. "I don't know why it matters now. Me and your mother learned to live with not knowing. Maybe some things are better left alone."

Ubi stood up, opened the refrigerator door, and wrestled a can of beer from the plastic ring. He held one up and looked at Jeanne. She nodded. He grabbed two. *Unbelievable, Jeanne drinking a beer.*

"The priest who picked you up in San Antonio recorded the day, and time, and what train you came in on. I backtracked from there. Someone, probably your parents, put you on that train in Baltimore," Jeanne said. She popped open the can, sipped and swallowed, careful not to let her eyes give away her distaste. "The train made lots of stops, and people picked over the kids like shopping for fruit at the farmers market."

"And I was like a peach with a big bruise. Is that what you're saying?"

"Patching together a history from the railroad's records and the priest's log, it looks like you were on that train for almost two months. Just riding and riding," Jeanne said, again sipping the beer straight from the can. "Riding and riding."

Ubi stood up and turned toward the kitchen sink, leaned toward the window. He pushed back the white lace curtains. Light rain had soaked the street outside and mist hung in the air, a wet blanket. A small car, one of those Toyotas, or some foreign brand, drove past, wiper blade swishing, tires spewing water onto the sidewalk.

"Daddy?"

"What is it, Sweetums?" Ubi asked. But he wouldn't turn around and face her. *Why did she have to push this? Why couldn't she leave the past alone? Is this why she went away to college? So she could torment the old man, show off how smart she was, digging up all this stuff, hiring lawyers, writing letters. Sheesh. No, not, sheesh, but Godamnit. Why was she doing this?*

The answer came before he could turn around.

"I want you to quit the road. I found an apartment, real close. You can walk here in about fifteen minutes. Together, we can put the final piece in the puzzle, find out who your parents are, who my grandparents are. Daddy, this is where you are from, here on the East Coast."

"I don't know. I've lived all my life not knowing, why now?" Ubi asked. He felt two hands on his shoulders, rubbing with long fingers the way Sherry did when he came in from the road stiff from sitting long hours in a truck seat.

"You got your mama's hands."

"Please, Daddy. Even if we never find who your parents are, we want to see you more often. Maybe you can drive locally, or just take day trips. Be home at night."

"I don't know, Sweetums. I just don't know."

"Pretty please. The apartment's vacant. It won't hurt to look."

FOURTEEN

UBI WOKE EARLY. It was Sunday. He went straight to the toilet and leaned over it. His stomach churned but nothing came up. Small bumps like ant bites had popped up on his forearms. And looking in the bathroom mirror, he was disturbed by the red rings around his eyes. Ubi showered and dressed in starched khakis and a long-sleeve white dress shirt. He walked alone to nearby St. Francis Catholic Church. At the boys ranch, Ubi attended Catholic Mass daily and often performed altar boy duties. He would slip on a black-and-white gown, ring the small, brass bells, and recite Latin at the appropriate junctures, unless his mind wandered. In that case, a cough and a stern look from Father brought him back to the present time and place.

Outside in the cool mist, Ubi rounded a corner and pulled up his jacket collar. It seemed like every neighborhood had several churches and beer joints—oops, taverns—like Martin called them. The taverns often looked like residences. Without the beer signs hanging out front—Schaefer and Lucky Lager and Rolling Rock—you'd think it was somebody's home. And that was sometimes true because the proprietor often lived in an apartment above the business. With the churches, however, there's no doubt what purpose these buildings serve. Cement and stone spires reached several stories above the concrete and asphalt floor. Straight up they grew, like trees in a forest competing for sunlight. Hurts your neck looking at 'em. Inside St. Francis, the towering statues and high ceiling made Ubi feel insignificant. He slid into a long, wooden pew near the back door and used his toe to pull down the padded kneeler. He dropped to his knees and grimaced when the left knee cracked. The wrinkled lady wearing the black scarf in the next pew heard the loud pop and turned her head. Ubi ran his fingers from his forehead to his waist and then quickly touched both shoulders. He dropped his head. Closed his eyes.

During Father Bartholomew's sermon about how St. Paul was on the road, traveling to Damascus when God struck him deaf and dumb, the woman in the scarf again turned around, looked at Ubi like he was a kid squirming in the pew. Then a man in a navy blue suit with a gold-plated nametag pinned to his chest appeared in the aisle. He leaned into the pew and placed his hand on Ubi's shoulder.

"Sir, you're shaking the whole pew. This is a Catholic church. Maybe you're in the wrong place. The Society of Friends meet on the corner of Franklin and Delaware, seven blocks down."

"Sorry," Ubi whispered, and looked down at his bouncing right leg. During communion, when most worshippers lined up and received the body and blood of Christ, Ubi slipped outside.

Across town in a suburban shopping center, celebrants at a rented space clapped and swayed side to side in rhythm to drums and electric guitars. Jeanne and Martin liked this church for its modern approach to spirituality. Come as you are. No kneeling. No dogma. No guilt trip. And the twins seemed to enjoy the Sunday school class, gluing macaroni crosses to colored poster board and pencil coloring bearded men wearing long robes.

After lunch, back at the house, Jeanne, Ubi, Martin, and the twins hopped a city bus and met a real estate agent at an empty apartment that was carved out of an old, three-story brick home. The building sat only a few feet back from a boulevard eight lanes wide. Even on a drizzly Sunday afternoon, the sidewalk was teeming with pedestrians huddled under umbrellas. And little old cars kept swishing along, honking and weaving, brake lights casting red shadows on the wet road. Inside the apartment, an excited young real estate agent slipped out of a double-breasted black trench coat and draped it over his arm. He bounced from room to room opening closet and cabinet doors, jabbering nonstop about the Picasso art exhibit he had seen yesterday.

Ubi poked his head into the two bedrooms, then the kitchen, which looked like a closet with a stove in it. The kids had found a toad in the small courtyard out back and were nudging it along with a stick. Jeanne was in the living room chattering with Martin about decorating ideas. Ubi joined them, but soon grew irritated with the conversation. Jeanne was acting like this was a done deal. She was already picking out colors for the curtains. Standing by the thick, wooden front door with three deadbolt locks, Ubi stared out the plate glass window. A red city bus pulled up across the street and people squeezed inside like sheep into a livestock trailer. The real estate man commented about the great location on a major thoroughfare—easy access to museums, theaters and parks. His voice echoed off the hardwood floor.

Ubi turned from the window. The real estate man asked Ubi if he had made up his mind. Two couples were scheduled to look later that evening, you know, so if he wanted to lease it, he should act now. Places like these don't stay vacant very long.

"What's the deposit?"

"Eleven hundred. Same as the monthly rent."

Ubi winced. He could refuel Old Ironsides, five, six times for that, drive from Florida to Seattle and back. "How long is the lease?"

"Eighteen months."

"Eighteen months? You can't be serious. Eighteen months?"

"Daddy, that's typical. You won't find anything around here shorter than that."

Ubi turned away, stepped toward the window and looked across the busy boulevard, showing his back to the real estate man. The red bus pulled away. Eighteen months of watching that?

"Daddy, do you know how hard it is finding a location like this? You can walk the kids to school, take the bus, meet me for lunch, go to baseball and basketball games, plays, concerts, the library. It'll be great."

Ubi continued staring out the window. More drizzle. More people. After a long, cold silence, he faced the real estate man. "We'll think about it and get back to you."

Jeanne looked at Martin for help, someone to plead her case. Martin looked at the floor. Frustrated, she stomped to the back door and yelled at the kids: "Time to go, you guys."

Those two words, "you guys," caught Ubi's attention. When did she quite saying y'all? The gang climbed down the half-dozen concrete steps out front, into the soft rain.

"Remember, I've got two more people looking today," the real estate man called after them, pulling on his coat. "You've got my card."

That evening, the twins rubbed Grandpa Truck's whiskers for good luck and went to bed. After Jeanne said bedtime prayers with them, she went straight to her room. Deflated from her father's cool reaction to the apartment she had spent weeks researching, she wanted to be alone. Martin refused to get involved. And to Jeanne, that meant her husband was on Daddy's side. Tacit disapproval of her plan.

Out in the living room, the men sat stone-faced in front of the TV, neither one laughing at a comedy with people living on top of each other, cramped in tall buildings in a big northern city. After the late local news, Martin got up and headed toward the kitchen.

"How about a beer, Ubi? Never mind, only one left," he said, peering into the fridge. "Why don't we grab a cold one at Domenico's? I got a day off tomorrow and I'm sleeping in."

Ubi looked at his left arm, the tan one, draped over the side of the orange, flowered upholstered chair like it was hanging out the truck window. He then noticed his fingers were steadily drumming, out of control, dangling in the air. Ubi looked up and caught his son-in-law staring at the quivering hand. "Good idea. Been sitting here so long, my hands are shaking and my feet are numb."

Outside, the rain had stopped, but the air was cold and damp. The men walked briskly and Martin explained the story of the local hangout. Domenico was born in Naples, but left there when Mussolini took over Italy, said he probably would've been arrested and hung for treason if he hadn't snuck out through Switzerland and into France. Altogether, he spent three months on the road, hiding, running, living in the mountains. After the war, he immigrated through Ellis Island and joined his uncle's family there in Philadelphia.

Inside Domenico's, the bartender tilted two large steins under the Lucky Lager tap and set them on the long wooden bar. Ubi looked around at the dim room. Framed black-and-white Frank Sinatra and Sophia Loren photographs hung from dark paneling, drooping to one side or the other. Above one wooden booth, a faded and blurry picture of a man hanging from his heels caught Ubi's attention.

"Mussolini, the son of a bitch," the bartender said. "Got what was coming."

Martin grabbed his foamy beer and pointed to an adjacent room. "Pool?" The duo walked across the empty tavern, uneven, wooden planks creaking under their feet, and stepped down three steps into the pool room. Martin dropped a quarter in the horizontal slot, pushed, and fifteen balls crashed down the chute. Ubi loaded the balls into the triangular rack and picked up a cue stick that was leaning in the corner, bent slightly at the tip. He then heard the front door bang shut and voices ordering beer at the bar. Martin slammed the cue ball into the formation and it exploded; two balls flew past Ubi, hit the wall and rolled around on the bare concrete floor. "Sheesh. Whattya' got in that stick, Martin, dynamite?"

Martin picked up the green number fifteen that had lodged under the pinball machine. Ubi dropped to one knee, groaned, and reached under the pool table. Extending his left arm, he rolled the stray ball forward with his fingers until he had it in his palm— the shiny, black number eight. *Didn't need to see that.*

Ubi slipped a quarter in the slot and commenced to re-rack.

"I've never seen anyone break like that," Ubi said. "Take it easy, next time. Somebody could get hurt, balls flying through the air like that."

The two men who had just arrived now stood at the door, looking down the steps into the pool room. Both wore plaid flannel jackets. The husky one sported a black beard and red bandana tied around his head. The other was rail thin with several days brown stubble sprouting from his face and neck. "You fellas wanna play doubles? Couple bucks a game?"

"Just a friendly game," Martin said. "You can have the table after this."

The bearded man took a slug from his beer and wiped foam from his moustache. A white splotch hung above his lip. His flannel jacket sleeves stopped halfway between elbow and wrist; the front remained unbuttoned, hanging loose.

"Aw come on now, don't tell me you and Gramps can't handle a couple of games for a few dollars. We always throw a little money around at this pool table; sort of like house rules. If you can't handle a little competition you ought to sit in the corner there."

"Just a friendly game, like I said."

Martin set the cue ball on the table and aligned it for his shot.

Ubi nervously worked a cube of green chalk across the tip of his cue stick, back and forth. The bearded man nudged his elbow into his friend's ribs, nodded toward Ubi and winked. The block of chalk squirted out of Ubi's hand, hit the floor and bounced up against the bottom step. The bearded man quickly stepped down into the pool room, picked up the chalk and held it out for Ubi.

"Looks like you better get something stronger than beer, Gramps. Hey, Domenico, get this guy a shot of vodka, put it on my tab," the man yelled over his shoulder. "He's got the shakes like that bum who lives under the Central Street Bridge."

The second man came down the steps, grabbed a wooden chair and spun it around. He sat in it backwards, arms folded across the curved top, beer mug dangling from his right hand. "We ain't seen you boys around here before. Where you from?"

Martin lined up the cue ball, placed his left hand on the bank to guide the stick, leaned over the table, and reached back like he was pulling a bow string. Irked at not getting an answer, the man let out a loud belch and then said: "I asked you a question. It ain't polite to not answer."

"And it's not polite to interrupt when a man's shooting," Martin barked over his shoulder. "Can't you see I'm breaking?"

Martin had visited this tavern several times before, shooting pool in the early evening with a friend from work. He'd never seen these guys. They looked like hustlers, not the usual crowd. But Martin had never stayed past happy hour, so maybe this friendly neighborhood watering hole took on a different personality late at night.

"Better hurry up and break. Your pal's about to have a nervous breakdown over here," the bearded man said. "Domenico, where's that shot of vodka?" he yelled up the steps. "Got a fella' here about to go into the DTs."

The bearded man turned up his beer mug and emptied it. He picked up a cue stick that was leaning against the wall. Black nose hairs cascaded from his nostrils into his mustache. A brown crumb, probably from lunch, was embedded in the unruly whiskers above his lip. The whites of his eyes had faded to a jaundice color. Ubi had run across blowhards like this, mostly at truck stops. spewing smoke until someone called them out. But, on occasion the fists started flying, like in Omaha at the Gray Wolf fuel stop when two drivers took a CB argument over a parking spot into a lot behind the tire bay. If things got out of hand here, these guys looked like the type to start swinging cue sticks. And by the way, what happened to Domenico? This was his place.

"We ain't playing doubles. Period," Ubi said, looking into the bearded man's yellow and glassy eyes. "Go on and break, Martin."

Martin leaned over the opposite end of the table from Ubi and the bearded man. He slid the long stick back to line up his shot and slammed it into the cue ball. The white cue shot forward and crashed into the yellow number one ball. On impact, the cue left the table and zoomed toward the bearded man's face. The man froze. Martin froze. The man sitting backwards in the chair froze. To Ubi, the ball moved in slow motion. His left hand sprang from his side and snatched the cue ball inches from the bearded man's nose. Ubi held the ball directly in front of the man's face, hand still like a statue.

"You need to be on your toes, partner," Ubi said. "That cue ball could a' done a number on your front grill. I don't know what dental work goes for up here, but back in Texas it ain't cheap."

The man exhaled. His beer breath permeated Ubi's nose.

"At least you had a little pain reliever so it wouldn't have been that bad," Ubi said, nodding at the empty beer mug hanging from the man's hand. Ubi then walked around the table, clinching the cue ball.

"Like the man said, you boys want to play pool, you're gonna' have to wait."

Ubi dropped the cue ball on the table with a flick of the wrist and the backspin caused it to ricochet off the bank.

The bearded man's eyes opened wide and darted toward his buddy, then to Martin, then to old Gramps. How did this codger with the shaky hands move so quickly?

"Let's go somewheres else," he said. "These sonsabitches think they're too good to play pool with us."

The two men scampered up the steps and out the door before Ubi could take his turn. Then Domenico, white apron around his waist, appeared at the pool room door holding a tray with a shot glass on it.

"Hey, who ordered the vodka?"

FIFTEEN

SOMEWHERE, A BELL WAS RINGING. Ubi rolled over, head pounding like a rig rolling along with a flat tire, and fell off the couch. He groaned and stood up, rubbed his eyes, and looked around a strange room. This uneasy feeling, waking up not knowing where he was, had happened before, usually after Ubi had been running hard and finally had time to cool his tires. Look, on that coffee table, there's a picture of the twins. *Oh, that's right; still in Philly.* Ubi then heard someone talking in the kitchen. He steadied himself and walked in that direction. The voice was coming from a little box by the telephone. *Aw heck, it's the answering machine, the nephew in Baltimore, looking for his piano.* He had been out of state on vacation and just now got the message Ubi had left at his workplace last week. Ubi leaned over the kitchen sink and splashed water on his face. He wiped his forehead with a towel, and pressed the flashing red button on the machine. The voice repeated the information. Ubi called back, and later that afternoon he was driving down the interstate to Baltimore.

Pushing Old Ironsides harder than normal, Ubi weaved through southbound traffic. The pavement dropped several inches when Old Ironsides crossed the Maryland state line and the airborne truck hit with a jolt. Ubi thought he heard something crash inside the trailer. Sheesh, an almost empty rig rides rough, no weight to hold her down.

An hour later, at twilight, Ubi found the white brick town home, sitting shoulder to shoulder in a row of them, all alike except for numbers painted above front doors. The nephew and two friends waited in the front porch light.

Ubi unlocked and opened the side trailer door. It was dark inside, but Ubi clearly could make out the piano's shadow. It was lying flat on the trailer floor. Two straps that had held it in place dangled from the wall.

Ubi and the men lowered the walk board from the trailer to the sidewalk, lifted the piano, strapped it onto the piano board, and rolled it through the front door into the living room. Following Ubi's orders, the men raised the piano and attached all three legs. The underside was roughed up from the fall. While attaching the foot pedals and two wooden dowels, a splinter embedded in Ubi's left thumb. The attachments no longer fit snug in the holes and hung limp. The nephew tinkered with the keys for a few minutes, frowned and closed the keyboard cover. He leaned over the piano, his head hung low.

"What happened?" he asked, without looking up.

"I unstrapped it when I delivered another shipment in Jersey, and I guess I didn't get the straps snapped back into the wall like I should. I'm sorry. I promised your uncle nothing would happen to this piano and I let him down. I let us all down."

"You got insurance?" one of the nephew's friends asked. "Surely you wouldn't ship a piano like this across the country without insurance."

Ubi handed the nephew his clipboard and pointed out the thirty thousand dollar policy his uncle had purchased. The nephew relaxed a bit, but Ubi felt like crawling inside the piano bench and closing the lid on top of himself. He spied a phonebook and flipped through the Yellow Pages to pianos. When the nephew saw what Ubi was looking for, he patted him on the back.

"It's okay, sir. I know someone who can fix it. How do I file a claim?"

Ubi explained the claims process, pointed out the toll-free number on the freight bill, and apologized again. He shook hands with the young men, all polite and careful not to levy charges of incompetence, and wandered through Baltimore streets until he found the interstate. Back at Sid's truck stop, Ubi found a pay phone in the rear of the building, near a coin-operated washer and dryer. The tumbler was spinning and something inside was banging like hell, probably a pair of tennis shoes. Ubi found the reverend's number located on the freight bill's top left corner and dialed long distance, shoving quarter after quarter into the slot.

"Hello."

"This is Ubi Sunt, the truck driver who picked up the piano last month. I delivered it in Baltimore today, but I damaged it and wanted to apologize to the reverend," Ubi said, his heart pumping. "I wanted to be the one to tell him because I guaranteed safe transportation, and I . . . well . . . I failed."

"Who's this?"

"Ubi Sunt, the trucker that moved the reverend's piano. Can I speak with him please?"

"No you can't, honey chile."

Ubi now recognized that voice—the housekeeper who gave him the eight-track.

"I'm sorry, but he passed away early this morning. Another stroke. We still notifying fambly. I guess it's okay to tell you, since you thought enough of him to call."

Ubi staggered back to Old Ironsides and climbed in the rig. He rummaged through a shoebox stuffed with eight-track tapes, spilling them onto the mattress. *Where is it?* Then he rifled through the sleeper. *Where? Where the hell is it?* Sheets and pillows and a dirty work shirt, shaving kit, state maps and logbooks flew up in a tornado. *Where, where, where. Damnit, where?* Freight bills and a coffee thermos, pliers and a Phillips screwdriver, caps from the Peterbilt dealer in Denver, all whirled inside the cab, caught in a vortex of arms and hands and elbows thrashing about. *Where is it?* The mattress upended, flipped and landed half in and half out of the bunk.

Then the storm subsided and the old trucker, with fire in his eyes, emerged from behind the mattress holding up the eight-track tape. He inserted it into the tape deck's open jaw and a jazz piano sprang to life. He slithered into the bunk, headfirst and listless, and burrowed himself face down in a heap of clothes and bedding and papers. How did those straps come loose from the wall? Maybe The Hippie did it, a parting shot at a cantankerous old fool. *Now you're being paranoid. And that's not fair to The Hippie and his work ethic. You did it. You fucked up. You old coot. Admit it. You're getting old. Listen to your daughter. What do you have to prove? What the hell is wrong with you? You stayed too long at the party and now you're sloppy drunk. An embarrassment to yourself.* Ubi covered his head with a pillow, bent it almost in half, and wrapped it around both ears. Yet the muffled piano found its way into his eardrums, into his head, into his heart. The image of the reverend kissing the piano good-bye came alive, like he was there inside the sleeper with him.

The sobs came low at first, and he pushed them back through will power. But they grew stronger, louder, and soon he had no control over this relentless force that had taken hold. It wasn't pain like screaming kidneys from drinking too much coffee or a sore back from years of humping furniture. He could block that out. This ache surged up from nowhere and surrounded him. It shook him, attacked from all sides, and pierced deep inside. It ran up and down his body, from his toes through his legs and spine; it made his neck tingle and his scalp throb. He wrapped his arms around his head, squeezed, curled into a fetal position and sobbed until he was out of breath, throat dry and tight, panting and claustrophobic from being buried in a mountain of clothes and sheets and pillows.

The eight-track continued emitting the jazz throughout the night. The trucker continued writhing in the bunk, catching fitful rest, still buried in the big mess. Just before sunup, the thin, brown tape tangled and choked and died.

SIXTEEN

IT WAS LATE MORNING at Sid's truck stop. Old Ironsides was parked out back, but Ubi hadn't come in for morning coffee. *Maybe he's sick, or back at his daughter's house. Better go check.* Sid Quatro banged on the truck door.

"Hey, Ubi, you all right? You in there?"

Sid pulled the door handle. The steel hinges opened quietly because Ubi kept them well-oiled. Sid grabbed the guardrail and pulled himself up on the first step. *What the hell happened? This place is turned upside down. Somebody killed my old friend? Oh, my God, there's the body in the bunk, half under the mattress. How did that happen? Wouldya' look at this disaster? Shit everywhere. Ubi put up a hell of a fight, one old tough sonofabitch. And no blood, thank the Lord, no blood.*

Sid slipped back to the ground and hustled inside to call the cops. Shortly after he hung up the phone, Ubi trudged in, plopped himself down on a stool and propped his elbows on the breakfast counter.

"Coffee. Black."

"Jesus! What happened to you? To your truck?" Sid asked, grabbing a white porcelain mug, and with shaking hands, filled it with hot java. "I thought you were dead. I called the cops."

"Couldn't sleep. Tossed and turned all night."

"Musta' been a helluva' itch. Who scratched it? Is that lot lizard coming back around here again?"

"You know me better'n that, Sid."

The coffee was too hot to touch, so Ubi scooped two ice cubes from a water glass and dunked them in the cup. Steam rose toward the ceiling tiles, which were stained brown from years of cigarette smoke.

"I gotta find me a load, and pretty quick." Ubi sipped carefully at first, but the coffee had cooled and he took a big swallow. "You still make damn good coffee, Sid."

Ubi carried the cup and a yellow pad and pen to the same pay phone he had used the previous night. Denver dispatch now had lots of loads; many drivers had shut down.

"Where you wanna go, driver?"

They had a government load of office furniture sitting on a dock in Wilmington, Delaware, enough to fill his trailer. One stop in Cincinnati, one in Birmingham, and one in El Paso. A stretched out load, but the linehaul revenue was decent. Ubi returned to the front of the empty truck stop. Sid topped off his cup, came around the counter and sat in the stool next to Ubi.

"Cops just left. I told 'em you were like Lazarus. They didn't appreciate that until I loaded 'em up with Styrofoam cups full of Folgers. Then they cut out."

Sid tore open two sugar packets, turned them upside down and shook the granules into his coffee. His spoon clanged against the sides of the mug and echoed across the empty dining room.

Ubi worked on his second cup. Warm coffee in his belly, and the notion of a full wagon going down the road overrode concern about the strike. Plus, he couldn't wait to get that bad taste out of his mouth from the damaged piano. The best thing now was to get back in the saddle.

But what about Sid? He had this truck stop when Ubi made his first trip to the East Coast thirty years ago.

"This strike putting the hurts on you, ain't it Sid?"

Sid shrugged and looked around the room. One man seated at a back table was reading the paper. That was it. "Been like this almost two weeks. Nobody's buying fuel. Nobody's eating. Laid off both my waitresses three days ago."

"An empty truck stop is about as sad as an empty trailer," Ubi said, staring across the counter at a wooden shelf lined with upside down coffee cups.

A few minutes later, Sid broke the silence.

"I hope you didn't get no load. You won't make it past the Walt Whitman Bridge. Driver fueled here last week. While he was in the restroom, someone pulled the pin on his fifth wheel. He made it two blocks, lost a forty-foot flatbed loaded with steel pipe—trailer dropped to the ground rounding the corner right there," Sid said, pointing out the plate glass window. "Almost took out a light pole."

"If a fella wants to shut down to protest, that's fine with me," Ubi said, looking into his cup. "But there's other ways to make a point. Write a letter to the board of directors at the company you lease to. Meanwhile, you can just watch your pennies."

The coffee was going down good now and Ubi had almost finished his second cup. "Sid, I'm tired of hearing this strike talk. I ain't shutting down. Period."

"Your head is harder than a tire bumper, Ubi. Other independents are striking. Got a couple rigs out back, drivers parked 'em last week. They're sitting at home now."

Sid pulled a black comb out of his rear pocket and ran it through his slick gray hair. How he hadn't lost his scalp with all the worries of running a truck stop, Ubi couldn't understand.

"Difference between me and them is," Ubi said, "they're probably intimidated and brainwashed. Intimidated by some renegades on the CB raising hell, making threats. Brainwashed by that DJ on the all-night truckers' radio channel who's talking trash, and by some old boy publishing a rag he calls a magazine who's raising hell, claiming high diesel prices are killing us. What's killing us . . . we're spoiled. You want to sleep in a high-dollar motel ever night, and when you deliver freight, you just open the doors, bump the docks and let a forklift do all the work."

Ubi turned up his mug. The caffeine had done the trick. Now it was time to leave yesterday's nightmare behind. "We'll work through this thing. Heard on TV news there's talk in Washington of a fuel surcharge, going to pass on the rates to the customer. Anyway, most of the folks instigating this strike couldn't drive an eighteen-wheeler around the block."

"You're a stubborn man, Ubi Sunt. Stubborn to a point you could get your ass hurt."

The two men sat in silence for several minutes. There was nothing left to say and there was no need to make small talk just to keep the conversation going; Ubi and Sid had passed that point in their friendship long ago. They were comfortable with quiet.

Ubi spent the rest of the day working on Old Ironsides. He borrowed Sid's power washer and gave the rig a bath. He rolled under the trailer on a creeper, and with a flashlight, found an oil line that rubbed against the frame and was dripping. He disconnected it and hiked eight blocks to a parts house where a chattering and chain-smoking thin woman cut a new hose. After installing the new line, Ubi checked air pressure in all his tires, aired up the low ones, and adjusted all the brakes. He used a full bottle of Windex on the glass, and a bucket of soapy water and three rags to clean the cab. He put the sleeper back together. Swept the trailer from end to end. By late afternoon, his stomach had settled down and he plowed through one of Sid's Philadelphia cheese steak hoagies. Ubi then showered and washed a load of uniforms. It was late in the evening when he caught the train and bus back to Jeanne and Martin's.

The twins were sleeping when Ubi turned the key that Jeanne had given him in the front door. Martin and Jeanne lay in bed reading, and heard footsteps on the wooden floor.

"Daddy? Is that you?"

Jeanne threw back the covers and slipped on a long cotton nightgown. She found Ubi on the couch pulling off his boots and sat beside him. "I got your note. How did the delivery go yesterday? And why didn't you call? We expected you last night."

"I took a load for El Paso, Jeanne," Ubi blurted, point-blank, and looked into his daughter's sagging eyes. "I know you're disappointed, but if I stay here much longer, I'll go off my nut. It's too crowded. It's too loud. And everything happens too fast."

"But you just got here. And we only looked at one place," Jeanne said, tilting her head to one side. "Maybe we can find you something out in the country. I know a place where there's horse stables and woods and green grass and. . ."

Jeanne's voice trailed off when she realized Ubi was shaking his head, side to side, like he did when his mind was made up, set in concrete. Jeanne wiped away a tear, *damned emotions*, and rested her hand on her father's knee. "What about some help? I talked to a friend. A psychotherapist. She can see you tomorrow. Or next week."

After a piercing look from her dad, Jeanne held up her hands in a defensive motion. *Don't push it*, she told herself.

"You mean a shrink."

"Daddy, there's got to be an answer why you're always twitching and itching. Martin told me about what happened at Domenico's. But I've seen it in you all my life. When I was a girl, and you came home, you were there, but you weren't *there*."

Again, Jeanne placed her palm on her daddy's knee. But this time, Ubi placed his gnarled fingers, with a little grease under the nails, on top, and squeezed his daughter's hand.

"They have prescriptions too, Daddy. Maybe that can help."

"You want to put me on drugs, Sweetums?"

"No, oh no," Jeanne said. She leaned back, held her palms up. "But . . . I mean everybody needs a little help sometime. Half the people I know take some kind of antidepressants."

Ubi wrapped his arm around his daughter and she leaned against his shoulder. "Before I leave, I want to bring Old Ironsides to the twins' school. For show-and-tell like I promised. I need to call their teacher and make sure it's okay."

Jeanne sighed, stood up slowly, and walked into the kitchen. Ubi heard her blow her nose, and a drawer slam shut. She returned with a small piece of paper, a phone number written on it in red ink.

"Daddy, you're turning your back on the only family you got," Jeanne said. "I don't understand."

"Sweetums, *you* don't understand. You're asking me to be someone I'm not."

"Someone like a real father? A real grandfather? "

No sooner had Jeanne said "like a real father," she wanted to take it back, gather up the harsh words like the papers that spilled from her arms at work today, and paper clip them back into a neat bundle. She stared out the window, long thin arms folded across her chest.

"Jeanne, you like everything partitioned and organized into neat categories," Ubi said, "like at the museum." He stood up and ran a hand through his hair. "But Daddy won't cooperate. Daddy won't settle down like a normal person. Daddy won't stay in the exhibit where he belongs." Ubi felt this anger welling up inside and he couldn't control it. *And here it comes again.*

"Over here, ladies and gentlemen, we have the grandfather exhibit. He hasn't missed one soccer game or school play or birthday and he is right on time for dinner every Sunday afternoon."

Jeanne placed her hands on her hips. She'd pushed him too far and he was pushing back, hammer down. Still, he had missed much of her growing up, and he was doing it again with the grandchildren. And who knows what could happen with him out on the road during this strike?

"For God's sake, Daddy. At least wait a couple weeks till this strike blows over. Are we that bad to live with?"

"I'm sorry, but I have to get back out there. Don't you know that I still . . ."

Ubi's tongue grew heavy and thick and he couldn't complete his thought. Instead, he stared straight ahead. Silent.

Jeanne handed him the notepaper with the phone number and said good night.

SEVENTEEN

THE NEXT MORNING, the twins swooped into Ubi's bedroom and yanked on his arms and legs and begged him to "Walk us to school, puhleeze."

Ubi explained he was going on a long trip. But before he left, he would bring Old Ironsides to school, if the teacher said okay. That worked the kids into a frenzy. But Jeanne, watching from the doorway, wondered if the twins had even heard what their grandfather had said about going back on the road. Did they understand he wasn't going to live nearby after all? Did they understand things would return to how they had always been? Postcards and phone calls and an occasional visit, maybe once in summer and at Christmas? Did they understand no grandfather at school plays or soccer games like many kids had? Just a Santa Claus—like character that didn't come around very often, and didn't stay long when he did? Did they understand what they were missing? Did they understand their hero was really a sad, lonely man who couldn't relate to people? Did they understand he needed professional help?

Jeanne watched the kids pull at their Grandpa Truck's arms and hold them side by side and laugh how one was golden brown like toast and the other white like milk. She leaned against the doorjamb, slipped her hands into her sweatpants pockets. The kids had launched another tickle attack, but Grandpa Truck held them at bay. The pale arm had Jeremy squirming and flailing and the tan one had Molly giggling.

No, they didn't understand.

That afternoon, Ubi amazed the Westview Elementary second-graders and their teacher with road stories about snowstorms and tornadoes and hurricanes and heat so hot that tires melted on the highway. He rattled off names of state capitals, mountain ranges from east to west, rivers flowing north to south into other rivers, and then bays or gulfs, and finally oceans. He described forests choked with trees where sunlight never reached the ground, and deserts where the heat baked the ground so almost nothing would grow, except thorny cacti. With Ubi rattling on about American geography, the young teacher, brown hair piled on her head like a cinnamon bun, and fresh out of college, pointed with a ruler to a wall map, nodding and smiling.

The ensuing truck tour brought the event to a climax. Kids scrambled up the driver's side, honked the air horn, rolled around in the bunk, and crawled out through the passenger door. Ubi set out the walkboard so the youngsters could climb up into the trailer. When the three o'clock bell rang, the teacher thanked the old trucker, but the kids wouldn't leave. Some parents waiting out front had to drag their youngsters away by the hand, but others inspected Old Ironsides for themselves. One dad called the diesel rig "a piece of American transportation history."

After the parking lot cleared, Jeanne pulled up in her green Saab, and for the second time in one day, Ubi said goodbye to his family. Still buckled in the front seat, Jeanne blew her father a kiss and mouthed "I love you," with one hand on the steering wheel. She had only a few minutes to drop off the kids at the after-school center and get back to the museum. Ubi held one twin in each arm, kissed them on the cheek and loaded them into the car with a promise of more postcards from the road. Walking back to Old Ironsides, he heard his grandson screaming.

"Grandpa, hey, Grandpa."

Jeremy had escaped the Saab and was racing toward the truck. In a moment, he was standing at the front bumper, looking up and grinning at his Grandpa Truck. "Grandpa, don't let the Ditch Dragon get ya, ha, ha. Don't let the Ditch Dragon get ya."

The Saab pulled up and Jeremy scrambled in, expecting to get an earful from his mom. But after the kids turned and waved at Grandpa Truck out the back window like they were riding in a float on Thanksgiving Day, Jeanne drove through city traffic for a half mile without a word.

"Mama, when is Grandpa Truck coming back?"

"I don't know."

"Mama, when can we go see him?"

"You can't go see him, because we never know where he is."

"Mama, why are you crying?"

EIGHTEEN

AFTER LEAVING THE ELEMENTARY SCHOOL, Ubi drove down the
interstate to Wilmington, parked across the street from a warehouse, and crawled into the bunk. When the warehouseman rolled
up the overhead steel door the next morning, Ubi backed up to
the loading dock. Office furniture was always a good load. Steel
filing cabinets and wooden desks were big and heavy and loaded
fast, especially from a warehouse—no stairs or elevators or long
corridors to slow down movers. At three o'clock that afternoon,
a short, dark-skinned warehouseman with a cigar stub inserted in
his cheek signed fifteen pages of inventory, and handed it to Ubi.

"It's your baby now," the warehouseman said. "Can't believe
the guberment's paying to ship this junk halfway across the country. If it was up to me, I'd have a helluva bonfire. You could buy
new stuff cheaper'n what it costs to ship twenty-five thousand
pounds of this crap out west."

Ubi rolled up the inventory sheets like a newspaper and shoved
them into his back pocket. He leaned and pushed against the hand
lever that closes the rear trailer doors, but the latches on the top
and bottom wouldn't catch. Furniture pads wrapped around a row
of filing cabinets hung out the back door like a woman's slip showing below her skirt. So Ubi opened the door again, tucked the
pads up inside the trailer door and then asked the warehouseman
to back his forklift up against the trailer doors so he could squeeze

them shut. Ubi then strapped his six-foot wooden stepladder and several dollies to the tailgate.

"Now that's a full wagon," the warehouseman said. "Ida bet fitty bucks you woulda' left an overflow. Don't get me to lyin'. I just knowed you was gonna spill this load, leave some of this junk on my dock for the next driver to clean up."

Later that evening, Old Ironsides sailed across the Maryland line into West Virginia. Ubi steered her into a truck stop and backed into a parking spot in the rear. For the first time in months, Ubi crawled in a bunk with clean sheets.

* * *

That same night, back in Philadelphia, Martin handed Jeanne the *Philadelphia Weekender*, a glossy magazine that arrived every week packed with a big bundle of ads, editorials, comics, news, and travel tips that made up the Sunday newspaper. It took a few days for the couple to digest it all, and their weeknight bedtime reading usually included combing through the Sunday sections.

"Does that look like anybody you know?" Martin asked, in his typical deadpan manner (one of several little things he did that annoyed Jeanne).

On the cover, in dim, reddish light, a once-tall man, now slightly stooped, wearing khakis and a cap with a high crown, faced the front of a diesel truck. The rig had a flat front with a huge bumper, two headlights, sort of spooky, like big eyeballs, and a massive grill that, at the top, was above shoulder level with the man. Above the grill, the truck's bubble nose recessed and two windshields looked down on the man. Although the man's face was unclear, he appeared to have a whimsical look, staring at his rig like he was saying goodbye. Between the truck and the trucker, a two-lane highway weaved its way into a backdrop of hills, growing small and distant. The red and pink and purple hues made the photograph somewhat ambiguous; you couldn't tell if it was sunup, or sundown. Across the bottom of the page, in white, block letters, Jeanne read aloud:

"The Myth of the American Trucker."

Jeanne slapped at the pages in a panic until she found the story. *Oh, my word. How could Martin read this right beside her in bed and be so calm?* The introduction explained that two college kids from Florida had spent late summer and early fall on the road interviewing and taking pictures for their master's thesis: "Does the rugged American individual still exist?" Out of their experience, came this essay that was picked up by a few weekly magazines across the country.

Poetry and Jazz Rides on Eighteen Wheels

Before this trip, we believed truckers were road hogs roaring down the interstate tailgating anyone who had the misfortune of being in the wrong lane at the wrong time; big bullies hell-bent on getting from A to B ASAP.

All that changed when Ubi Sunt and his eighteen-wheeler, called Old Ironsides because it's indestructible, pulled our red convertible out of a Rocky Mountain stream. Our car had been reduced to scrap, so we rode with this Texas trucker for a few days.

We were broke and hungry, yet, he insisted we earn our way by helping load and unload furniture. *Keep the drawers facing up*, we were told, and *never roll a dolly down a ramp backwards, unless you want an intimate relationship with that filing cabinet. Heavy boxes on the bottom, for crying out loud, you just put books on top of a lampshade. Fold the moving pads neatly.*

We learned a new word, a clean word, to express frustration. Whenever this widower and grandfather of two grew exasperated, he exclaimed "Sheesh!" in a high-pitched voice that sounded odd coming from a man who could parallel park a big rig better than most of us can back up a Ford Pinto.

We weaved through the South Dakota Black Hills inside a thirty-four ton tractor-trailer with an eight-track emitting Duke Ellington standards. We rode up and down with the tempo, pulling, pulling the grade; then at the top, working the stick shift in unison with the jazz piano (how he knows one gear from the other we still have no idea), he grabs the right gear, one out of thirteen, without using the clutch, and you feel and hear the engine purr as the rpms drop, and you lope along until another hill and another downshift and a puff of black smoke that you see in the mirror. And then a low, growling sound rises up from below, from the engine under your feet, because in this rig, called a cabover, you are literally riding on top of a 350-horsepower diesel. And that's when you understand why some men live for the freedom of the open road. Anything else would be incarceration.

One night, the gallant trucker slept in the half-empty trailer and surrendered to us his bunk. That's how we discovered his nighttime reading—poetry. He keeps an anthology of Whitman, Dickinson, and Frost, wrapped in brown paper, tucked into the corner of his sleeper.

We often slept in turnouts and rest areas, kidneys howling late at night, because it was too much trouble to climb down from the rig. We woke in the morning, snug in a cocoon of moving pads, the vapor from our breath forming funnel clouds. We slugged down coffee black, always black, because, "You put all that sugar and cream in there you might as well drink a Dr Pepper." In the warm afternoon, we rode and rode, wind blowing in our faces and swirling in the bunk, maps and old newspapers and logbooks flapping nonstop inside because Old Ironsides has no air conditioning and Ubi Sunt likes to hang his left arm out the window.

Before this trip, we believed truckers drove in long convoys, town-to-town with their buddies, leering down from their cabs at women with low tops and high skirts. We thought they all had chrome silhouettes of naked ladies on their mud flaps.

Before this trip, when we thought of truckers, we thought of potholes and potbellies.

Instead, we found a Renaissance man, someone who can shepherd a tractor-trailer rig across the continent, but also enjoys poetry and jazz. Now that's the spirit of the rugged American individual.

Jeanne closed the magazine and placed it on her lap. She looked down at the cover. Old Ironsides. Daddy. Ubi Sunt. Southpaw. Renaissance Man. *Sheesh.*

NINETEEN

WEST VIRGINIA MOUNTAIN ROADS twist and turn and dip and dive so you can hardly get enough momentum coming down one grade before you have to climb another. Weaving through a fall forest of sugar maples, dogwood and sassafras trees, Ubi felt like he was driving inside a kaleidoscope. The baby blue sky above was a constant backdrop, but all around him, the bright and stunning shades of red and yellow and orange and brown popped out just for him, like he'd been watching life in black and white, and for the first time his eyes could interpret color. It was early November, and with the temperature in the low 40s, Ubi kept the driver's side window rolled up and both hands on the wheel, except when shifting. No arm hanging out the window now. Just plodding along about forty miles an hour, trying to keep from getting distracted by those bright tree leaves fluttering in the cool breeze. *But oh, you just gotta look.* And what difference—all this brilliance—from the dank and dim city, those days in Philadelphia and New York, boxed in by office and apartment buildings, twenty, thirty, forty stories high. And sure, up in New England, they have beautiful fall foliage too, but clouds scudding in from the Atlantic had hung low, blocking the sun, when Ubi and the Mississippi Hippie were up there delivering furniture.

With a deft flick of an elbow and wrist, Ubi maneuvered the stick shift and found a gear that would pull most grades yet hold back the rig on the downhill. Frequent shifting was working against the terrain, fighting the mountains, a waste of time. And Old Ironsides sounded so sweet, purring, pulling a heavy wagon like this with no trouble. For the first time in weeks, Ubi felt like his old self. No jitters. No bloodshot eyes. No churning stomach.

And another thing: driving these back roads across West Virginia was a good way to bypass the busy interstates up and down the East Coast where the striking truckers were likely to cause problems. *That ain't my fight,* Ubi said to himself. *Just let me be.*

Ubi soon moved up into the high country. So it's not as close to God as the Rocky Mountains at ten-thousand feet and above—it's still sitting-on-the edge-of-your-seat truck driving. The two-lane road had no shoulder, just a drop-off down the cliff on the outside lane, and on the inside, a wall carved from stone going straight up where they dynamited into the mountain's limestone guts. They built some guardrails, but look at 'em, all busted up. And look at those skid marks and the gash in that hickory tree—hate to see what happened to that rig and that driver. *Uh-oh, here comes a rig in the other direction. Hug the shoulder, but not too close. Okay, he's past, pick up the CB mike and warn him about that rock-slide a few miles back.*

Finally, you catch a break, the road widens into four lanes—a patch of new highway—but you run about twelve miles and it's back on the goat trail. Yeah, this Blue Ridge Country has rolling, tree-covered hills broken up with some nice farms and big old barns with chewing tobacco ads painted on the sides, and it's a nice change from those Northeastern toll roads, but you gotta be patient, and you gotta be on your toes all the time. Driving the back country through West Virginia in a full rig, now that's a challenge even on a dry day. Throw in some rain, ice, or snow and you got a white-knuckle ride; better know how to handle a rig, or keep to the big road and pray for sunshine.

Nearing the Ohio state line that afternoon, Ubi saw the weigh station sign ordering commercial vehicles to stop one half mile ahead. The previous night, when he had entered the state, the port of entry for commercial vehicles was closed and he had breezed past. But now, no such luck. Below the weigh station exit marker, an *OPEN* sign dangled from a rope. Ubi downshifted several gears, idled toward a small platform scale and a tin shed with a stovepipe sticking out of the roof. A white-haired man with a skinny nose like the beak of a chicken, a cheek crammed full of Levi Garrett, and wearing a brown state highway patrol uniform, stepped out of the hut. He walked around the front of Old Ironsides.

"The scales is broke," he yelled above the diesel engine's clattering pistons. Ubi then reached for his logbook, expecting the man to ask for it, because next to Missouri, West Virginia was the most notorious state for writing logbook violations. Instead, the man pointed to a long white stripe with a thick red line at the end painted on the cracked concrete.

"Pull over thar."

The man then tried to take off running, like he was racing Old Ironsides; but, gasping for air, he soon slowed to a clumsy gait, until he caught and passed the rig. Standing in front of Old Ironsides, he wagged his finger until Ubi eased the front bumper even with the number zero. Then the trooper raced his forefinger across his neck, like slashing a throat. Ubi pulled two levers on the console. The brake chambers popped and hissed, and the truck came to a compete stop.

"Looks like you might be stretched out a little bit," the man said, grinning and looking up at Ubi through the driver-side window. "You know West Virginia is a fitty-five-foot state?"

The man walked toward the back of the rig. Ubi climbed down and followed. Walking with his head down, Ubi realized someone had painted a giant tape measure on the concrete. It started where he was instructed to align his bumper and stretched well beyond the back of his rig.

"You're wasting your time, officer," Ubi yelled after the man, who was now walking past the trailer wheels. "My truck's fifty-five

feet long. Drove it across forty-eight states and half of Canada.
I should know."

The man took several more steps, turned and faced the back
of the rig. Ubi was suddenly at his side and the two looked up at
the equipment strapped to the trailer's rear doors.

"You sure about that? With these here dollies and stepladder
hangin' off'n the back, you're at lease fitty-six, maybe even fitty-
seven-foot long."

The man bent to one knee and peered down at the markings
on the concrete. "See that, right thar? Anywhere past that, you're
too long and gonna get fined."

"That equipment's not part of the vehicle," Ubi argued. "I tied
it on because the trailer is stuffed full."

"Don't make no difference. Anything strapped on is part of
the rig," the officer said, writing the trailer license number in his
ticket book. "You could have bull horns on the front of your rig
for all I care. Still gonna git a tickit."

"How about I tie 'em underneath?"

The man shook his head and kept writing.

"What about strapping 'em between the tractor and trailer, on
the frame?"

The man acted like he didn't hear.

"I drove all the way across the state like this, now I'm ten miles
from the Ohio line and you're gonna fine me?"

"You need to come into my office," the officer said. He turned
and walked toward the steel shack. Ubi set on the man's heels.
Inside, the officer sat in a swivel armchair before a wooden desk,
furniture that looked like what Ubi was hauling.

"Forty-five bucks," he said, pushing the ticket book across the
desktop for Ubi to sign. "Cash."

Ubi yanked at his wallet, jammed with notes and receipts and
thick as a telephone book, but it was wedged in his back pocket.
He yanked again and it finally broke free and hit the floor. He

typically kept about fifty dollars on hand, for tolls or small repairs or a motel room if he just wanted to get out of the truck. Ubi pulled out three crisp twenty-dollar bills, straight from Sid's truck stop, change from when he had fueled. The officer leaned over and spit at a quart coffee can that had tobacco juice oozing down the side from a couple of near misses. The wad landed directly inside, and the man, pleased with himself, took the money Ubi had laid on the desk and opened a cigar box. Ubi saw thick stacks of fives, tens and twenties inside it. The officer lifted a small tray, stuck the twenties in the bottom, and closed the lid.

"Nice doing bidness with you," he said, holding out three crumpled, dirty, and damp five-dollar bills. "Come back agin."

Ubi took the cash and his receipt and slowly tucked them in his wallet. He looked around the shack, at the wood-burning stove, cigar box and coffee can, the pungent smell rising up from it like out of a latrine. Sometimes a man's gotta speak out, but sometimes a man's gotta choke on it. Ubi shoved his wallet in his khakis and stepped outside.

Back on the road, after running through several gears, a cabover International passed in the opposite direction. Both drivers nodded. Ubi picked up the CB mike.

"Eastbound, that chicken coop ahead is open and the old hen's got her hand out."

Old Ironsides and Ubi Sunt continued down a two-lane crooked highway with no shoulder. The rig rolled past trailer homes and rusted cars on cinder blocks and wooden, one-room churches with tall steeples that grew out of high bluffs overlooking a wide and swift river. Approaching a small city, Ubi looked out at road signs clustered on corners, sending mixed messages to travelers unfamiliar with the area. Black and white, square, oval, and rectangular, the wooden and steel markers were stacked one above the other and bolted onto tall posts. At times, the U.S. and state highways, local and county roads, all morphed into one.

Then they'd split. Arrows pointed left, pointed right, and pointed straight ahead, marking various routes to different communities.

Ubi leaned forward, the truck seat creaking under his weight, and squinted out the windshield, careful to follow route 40. *Looks like a right turn, right now.* With an eye out for oncoming traffic, Ubi swung the truck wide into the left lane and turned the wheel hard, back to the right to negotiate a tight corner. A four-wheel drive pickup that had been tailgating for several miles saw an opening, and it tried to squeeze around the corner on the rig's right side, before the hole closed. Ubi's trailer tracked around the same corner and squeezed the pickup toward the curb. The driver leaned on his horn, put two wheels up on the sidewalk, and stomped the accelerator. White smoke gushed from the tailpipe and the four-wheel drive shot past the trailer, careening down the street. Ubi continued, unshaken; cars and trucks trying to sneak past big rigs on the right was a never-ending battle. (At one time, the safety department at Deaton asked drivers for suggestions on how to cut down the number of accidents related to this problem. Most of the owner-operators urged the company to print warning decals they could stick on their trailers. Ubi wrote in, suggesting all rigs should be modified with a long, wooden arm like at a railroad crossing that would drop down on the right when a driver used the corresponding turn signal. He got no response.)

So what else can you do other than use your turn signal and keep a close eye on that blind spot on the right side? If you don't swing out wide on narrow turns, you could take out a street sign, a light pole, or fire hydrant on the right.

Ubi next made a left turn down an avenue thick with coin-operated laundries, small grocery stores, and taverns. Probably the working-class side of town. Wood-frame houses leaned and sagged, and although the occasional brick home stood at attention, long wet winters and humid summers had left them stained with an olive-colored mold. Rusty bicycles and grocery carts littered front yards. Faceless pedestrians in hooded sweatshirts, hands stuffed in pockets, skirted down cracked sidewalks and ducked down alleys. A gray four-door sedan, long and low and covered in rust, ran a stop sign across Ubi's path and hit a pothole. The rear end jerked up and down. Brown rust flakes fell to the pavement.

Keeping a keen eye on the highway signs, Ubi weaved through city streets in a low gear. He found the sign most important to him: *BRIDGE WEIGHT LIMIT AHEAD - 76,000 POUNDS.* No problem. Ubi flipped the air switch, goosed the accelerator, and maneuvered the stick shift to another position, thus spurring Old Ironsides up an incline and onto a thin, steel bridge that spanned the chocolate-colored Ohio River. The steel girders ran in all directions: to the right, to the left, and above the rig, forming triangles, rectangles and some odd geometric shapes Ubi did not recognize. The rig growled along at a steady pace. Ubi could feel the cantilevers swaying under the big truck's weight.

As a young trucker exploring the Midwest, Ubi marveled at great bodies of water like the Missouri, Mississippi, and Ohio Rivers. He would slow down on the long bridges and drink in the view like the first time he saw the Gulf of Mexico. Back in Texas, most of the rivers' headwaters begin within the state. Draining parched West Texas, the rivers flow sporadically until they pass the ninety-eighth meridian, an imaginary line that works like a giant shower curtain, dividing rainy East Texas from arid West Texas. During summertime, sections of Texas rivers such as the Leon and Colorado sometimes go dry for many miles and many weeks. Crossing them, even on major highways, takes only a moment. A quick glance from the driver's window as you cross the bridge reveals a tree line, a dry gully, and then you're back on hard asphalt. But not these mighty rivers. Wide and wild, muddy and meandering, they made waterways back home look like creeks.

Halfway across the Ohio, a ten-wheel garbage truck approached from the opposite direction. Ubi kept the windows rolled up, his left hand steady on the wheel. He eased the rig to the right, and the outside mirror squeezed within a few inches of the steel girders. Down the center stripe, both trucks' mirror brackets passed within a hair of each other. *No waving or head nodding toward the oncoming driver here. Keep a true hand on the wheel and focus straight ahead.*

After the garbage truck squeezed past, Ubi turned the wheel slightly to the left. He tilted his head upstream. What a panorama. For miles and miles, barges hanging on docks. Docks and high trees hanging on riverbanks. Riverbanks, sometimes eroded and precipitous, others sloping and gentle, faded into a distant haze. And look at this muddy, swift current, forty feet below. Whirlpools too. If Old Ironsides broke through the railing, the mighty river would suck her down with barely a ripple.

At the bottom of the bridge, Ubi passed a road sign announcing he was in the Buckeye State. And *thank God* the weigh station was closed. West Virginia's rugged terrain eventually gave way to open, rolling hills dotted with large farms. The gray sky turned black early in the evening and Old Ironsides' headlights showed the way across southern Ohio. Ubi parked the rig at a small truck stop just north of Cincinnati.

The next morning, Ubi and Old Ironsides again crossed the Ohio River, this time on a wide and modern bridge. Ubi delivered three thousand pounds of office furniture to a downtown Cincinnati warehouse. Then it was back on the interstate, the big road, and southbound, across hilly Kentucky. It was wet and overcast all the way into Bowling Green where the left windshield wiper squealed and ripped apart. Strips of black rubber, flapping back and forth, couldn't keep up with the steady rain. Then up ahead, a giant sombrero decorated with flashing green and red lights welcomed weary amigos to Little Tijuana Travel Plaza. Ubi exited and entered a long driveway lined on both sides with light poles shaped like palm trees. To the left, a small carnival beckoned vacationers with rides and games and a water park complete with slides and fountains. On this dreary day, however, the park gate was chained shut. But, to the right, a massive complex of buildings that were painted bright yellow and blue and red and turquoise made up the new travel plaza.

Inside, Ubi wiped his old boots on a large mat. Rainwater dripped from the bill of his red Peterbilt cap. He trudged down a wide corridor, past three Mexican restaurants and several gift shops, including one that sold bullhorns, bull whips, and bullshit repellent spray that came in an aerosol can,. Thirsty for a Dr Pepper, Ubi slogged into a small convenience store. No luck. Had to settle for a root beer. Gulping the foamy soda from an aluminum can, he marched past the Pancho Villa Motel, a barbershop, a mini movie theater, and an arcade. *This place looks like Six Flags back in Dallas, not a truck stop.*

After wandering for fifteen minutes, Ubi asked the tall, blonde shoeshine girl in tight leather pants and low-cut tank top for directions to the parts counter. He had to leave the building and hike past the fuel bays about three blocks away. Over at the parts house, the part-time college student behind the counter couldn't find wiper blades to fit a '56 Peterbilt so Ubi bought a modern set. Working in a steady drizzle, he leaned against the truck frame and cut the wiper blades to fit his truck. Ubi then grabbed the stepladder from the trailer and wiggled the homemade wiper blades into the metal holders.

Back on the road, Ubi saw the sky for the first time that day. North of Nashville, a patch of pale blue poked through the gray blanket for several miles and then disappeared. A tease. An hour later, Ubi reached Guitar Town. He followed highway signs that ordered interstate truck traffic onto a detour around the city. He weaved Old Ironsides between orange barrels and jostled with rush-hour four-wheelers and delivery vans in stop-and-go traffic, finally leaving the city in his rearview mirror about the time the afternoon radio talk shows wound down. Late that evening, about forty miles north of Birmingham, Ubi pulled into a truck stop that featured a giant coffee pot on stilts like a water tower near the entrance. Shelby Brothers Truck City was one of Ubi's favorites, owned and operated by the same family since he'd been on the road. A long-nosed white Pete sat perpendicular to the row of fuel pumps, blocking all but one. A forty-foot banner draped on the trailer read: *SHUT UP OR SHUT DOWN.*

Ubi pulled into the open fuel bay, climbed down from his tractor and pressed the intercom button beside the diesel pump. An attendant asked if he was sure he wanted to buy diesel. Ubi said yes, hell yes, and please send someone out here with a receipt book to take his money because he wasn't leaving his rig unattended for one minute. With two fuel pumps churning out diesel into the Pete's saddle tanks, Ubi slid into the front seat and grabbed the CB microphone.

"If anybody's watching and got some funny ideas, let me tell you, I ain't shutting up and I ain't shutting down. You got a problem with that, I'm right here at pump number one, fueling Old Ironsides. They call me the Southpaw, and I got my tire bumper here in my left hand. Ten-four."

The CB remained quiet while Ubi finished pumping, paying, and remained silent when he drove back up the ramp onto the interstate. Another twenty miles down the road, he pulled into a rest area and crawled into the bunk. Lying flat on his back, he pulled off his khakis, folded them, and stuffed them under his pillow. It had been a long day—splashing through heavy showers, performing a rain-soaked repair, following detours in thick traffic and messing with this damn strike—but it beat sitting around in a suffocating city, locked in an urban, concrete cage. He closed his eyes. His hands lay flat and still at his side on the mattress. Breathing steadily, he thought about what Jeanne said, settling down in Philadelphia, and his hands started tingling and twitching. Ubi rolled over on his side, tugged on the thick moving pad he used for a blanket. Why couldn't she understand?

TWENTY

THE CHEVY NOMAD STATION WAGON prowled the truck stop parking lot looking for prey. The Nomad had a green, hand-painted reptilian figure crawling across the vehicle's hood, mouth breathing fire like a dragon. The wagon was decked out with leopard-skin seat covers, white shag carpet on the dashboard and a pair of pink women's underwear hanging from the rearview mirror, a souvenir from a dancer named the Pink Panther who worked at the Eureka Club, or at least that's what the driver, who called himself the Chameleon, told everyone. A voice on the AM radio speaker blasted the news that the Los Angeles Dodgers had just swept the Milwaukee Braves behind a spectacular lefty named Sandy Koufax. Weaving between rows and rows of trucks, bottle of Budweiser between his legs, the Chameleon chatted on the CB.

"Polishing, painting and pills. Anybody want to talk to the Chameleon? Come on, now. We got the polish for that dull chrome, we got the paint to personalize your rig, and we got the pills to keep you at the craps table all night. Come on now, bring it back to the Chameleon."

In the rear of his wagon, the Chameleon kept his acrylics and paintbrushes in several metal kits that looked like fishing tackle boxes. An electric polisher sat piled high on coiled-up extension cords with black tape wrapped around spots where the insulation had worn through. A plastic bucket overflowed with rags saturated with various amounts of paint, grease and grime, used for wiping down and hand-rubbing chrome and steel.

It was mid-afternoon in late summer and the punishing Las Vegas sun had stymied most outdoor activity. The truckers were either hovered over the one-armed bandits, Black Jack and craps tables inside the air-conditioned casino, or dozing in their bunks, truck doors open wide to catch a breeze. The Chameleon trolled the rows of trucks, sipping Bud.

"Breaker, breaker, this truck stop looks like its ready for the undertaker. Come on now, anybody awake? Anybody want to talk to the Chameleon? Life's too short to drive a dull truck. Let the Chameleon hand-letter your CB handle on your rig and shine up that bumper. Talk to me, trucker, talk to me. How about that white Kaywhopper on the front row? Fix you up with some orange and yellow flames down the side? Ten-four?"

"Shaddup," an anonymous voice bounced back. "Ain't nobody interested."

"Come on now," the Chameleon continued, unfazed. "Whatever your handle, I can make it come alive with my artistic aptitude. I painted some of the finest rigs to come through Vegas. Who wants the honor of having their rig decorated by the Chameleon? Come on. Talk to me."

Still nothing. So the Chameleon turned around at the fuel pumps and headed toward a back aisle. On the corner, he saw a furniture wagon with doors open on both sides. The driver was hanging wet furniture pads on ropes stretched from wall to wall like a clothesline.

The Chameleon worked his eight-ball shifter into neutral, killed the engine, and crawled out of the front seat. "Hell's bells, driver, how'd you get those pads wet out here in the desert? Musta' left the doors open when you went through the truck wash."

The trucker slapped another wet pad up on the rope like a housewife hanging out sheets. He jumped from the trailer, landed flat-footed on the asphalt parking lot.

"Monsoon hit San Francisco yesterday. Rain came down sideways, soaked a stack of pads near the door in about sixty seconds flat."

"They'll be dry in no time. Sun out here can turn a grape into a raisin quicker'n a Black Jack dealer can deal himself twenty-one. Big old beast like this, you need a little personality on this rig. What's she called?"

"Old Ironsides. Built to last."

"What's your handle?"

"Don't have one. Just got a CB last year for Christmas," the trucker said. He crossed his arms, sized up this character. "Wife says I ought to be Lefty because I hang my left arm out the window."

"Well, you gotta get a handle and you gotta get it painted on your rig. But Lefty, well, that ain't no good. Too common. Listen here, that Koufax pitcher for the Dodgers, they call him a southpaw. So why not Southpaw? Can't go wrong with that. Koufax just got through mowing down the Braves like it was the St. Valentine's Day Massacre. Whattya' say, trucker? Let me show you my professional portfolio."

The Chameleon reached into the front seat and snatched a binder stuffed with plastic pages that held truck photographs. Standing in the only shade available—a shadow cast by the semi-trailer—the Chameleon leafed through the pages.

The Chameleon had painted smiling caricatures on each side of a long-nosed, blue Freightliner rig. *Big Baby* was painted on the passenger-side door, next to a short, heavy woman with a wide face. On the driver's side, her husband, *Big Daddy*, had eyebrows that looked like caterpillars and a nose like a braunschweiger. The Chameleon turned the page and pointed to a picture of a cabover

KW, a black man in a tuxedo standing with arms crossed and his handle, *Chocolate Chip, Kenner, Louisiana*, painted on the side of the sleeper.

Loose Screw beamed from the driver's window of a yellow, long-nosed Mack, pointing down at a large bolt painted on the side of the cab. Another trucker that was leaning against his rig's front grill was so tall he could almost see inside the windshield of his red Peterbilt. Long, bold, black letters that spelled his handle, *Tall Boy*, traveled straight up from the bumper to the windshield. And a driver about five feet tall, wearing baggy pants that hung low on his hips, stood beside his GMC with a befuddled look; his CB handle was painted in purple letters on the sleeper compartment—*Low Pockets*.

The Chameleon kept jabbering and flipping pages, pointing out that his art had national exposure riding the highways on the fronts and sides of eighteen-wheelers. "Museum? Screw a museum. Who's going to pay all that money to look at some stuff that looks like a retard drew it? My stuff's free, and on permanent, outdoor, traveling exhibits across the U.S. of A. Looky here."

The Chameleon flipped another page. "Here's the Big Banana from Gulfport, Mississippi, the Village Idiot from Gila Bend, Arizona, and Black Streak from Detroit. This is Americana. Who needs a museum and all those art snobs with their noses stuck in the air like their drawers don't stink when you got the Chameleon right here. This is folk art, you hear me? I said folk art."

The sun had moved straight overhead and the two men lost their shade. The Chameleon suddenly remembered his beer and circled around to the station wagon.

"All that advertising works up a thirst," he said, turning up the glass bottle until only foam was left in the bottom. "Here's what I'll do. Since I like you, I'll make you a deal. For twenty bucks, I'll paint Old Ironsides with flames on both sides of the truck."

"But I'm not a fireman or devil-worshipper."

"I didn't say nothing about no pitchforks or Dalmatians. Okay then, how about a desert scene with Saguaro cactus and a coyote chasing a roadrunner? Eighteen dollars. And that's with *beep beep* painted in blue block letters."

The trucker shook his head no, and watched sweat roll down the Chameleon's face.

"I can paint a rocket ship with the moon in the background. President Kennedy says we'll be there this decade."

"Reckon not."

"How about a John Wayne? It's one of my most popular, the Duke sitting on Trigger."

"Trigger was Roy Rogers' horse."

"Same difference. Whattya say? Fifteen bucks? And you get free touch-up for a lifetime. When you're in Vegas, you just break on the CB for the old Chameleon."

The desert sun glared off the assorted rigs' windshields and chrome bumpers. The Chameleon wiped his forehead with the back of his hand, pulled a pair of sunglasses from the v-neck of his t-shirt, and put them on. "Okay, here's what I'll do. Look here."

He then grabbed Ubi by his left arm and pulled him around to the front of his rig. "Put your left palm up against the truck and don't move."

He grabbed a pencil from his back pocket and in a flash traced an outline of Ubi's left hand on the front of the truck.

"I'm a genius," he said. "Another Norman Rockwell. I just think up this stuff like nobody else can. See, now, we'll paint that in whatever color you want and write "SOUTHPAW" in bold letters above it with your hometown below. Like I said, I'm an artistic genius."

"How much?"

"Twenty."

"You already offered John Wayne for fifteen. How's my hand-print gonna cost more'n that? Tell you what. I'll give you ten," the trucker said. "And you got to paint my wife's name on the passenger door."

What's her name?"

"Sherry. But I want to you paint Sassy Sherry because that's what I call her."

"That's eleven letters," the Chameleon said, counting on his fingers until he ran out of digits. "Eleven bucks and you got a deal."

TWENTY-ONE

THE GREEN SAAB SCREECHED into the front fuel bay reserved for four-wheelers at Sid's Truck Stop. A tall, thin woman wearing blue jeans, sneakers, a windbreaker, and an old cap from a Texas truck stop climbed out of the driver's seat and thrust the gas pump nozzle into the tank. Her upper lip quivered and she frowned like her shoes fit too tight. Her eyes looked red from crying. With dollars and cents scrolling past on the pump dial, she stepped over the hose, past a pothole filled with standing water and yanked open the glass door. A small, silver bell jingled to life and Sid Quatro's face appeared in a long, narrow window behind the coffee counter.

"You sell CBs?" the woman asked, barely inside the door.

"Got a few," Sid barked through the opening, as he scooped two flat sausage patties from the grill and placed them on a plastic plate with scrambled eggs and white toast. "I'll be right out."

He pushed through the chrome-plated swinging doors into the dining room and slid the order before a man wearing a matching sweat suit and sitting at the coffee counter, newspaper folded back to the sports page.

Sid escorted the lanky woman past a metal floor rack stuffed with assorted brochures that touted trucking job benefits: *Home every weekend. New equipment! No-touch freight. Fuel and insurance discount. Take control of your destiny. Be your own boss. Run with the best!*

In the back corner, next to gallons of blue and yellow plastic oil jugs and tire bumpers, Sid wiped the dust off a locked glass cabinet that held several radar detectors and four CB radios. "Got this Cobra and three Midlands."

"Which one's more powerful? Gets out farther?"

"They're about the same. The key is your antennas. You need two of these."

Sid reached behind a row of black bungee straps and held up two Wisconsin Whoppers, antennas taller than the strange woman standing before him.

"Do you install?"

"I got somebody on call."

"I'll take the Cobra and two Whoppers, if you can fix me up this morning," the woman said, reaching into her wallet and digging out a credit card. "How much?"

By noon, the greasy-haired twenty-seven-year-old radio installer was sitting in the Saab front seat, chatting on channel nineteen. "This here's Monkey Wrench. Somebody gimme a radio check, come on. Yeah I copy that."

Monkey Wrench approached the woman sitting on the hood, her long, crossed legs touching the ground.

"Darn thing gets out good, lady. I can talk all the way to the stadium, about six miles. By the way, where are you going that you need a CB? I thought that fad with the rich folks playing truck driver had passed? Say what? Your daddy's a long-haul driver? No way. And you're going to find him? Well, you're both crazy, 'cause there's a truckers' strike going on. And some of those bastards out there, well, they play rough. Seen on the news last night a sniper in Richmond shot out the windshield on a Coca-Cola truck. Of course, the dumbass with the rifle don't know the difference 'tween a local delivery and long-haul rig. So, anyways, who's your old man? Ubi Sunt? That's the Southpaw on the CB ain't it? Hell yeah I know him. Everybody knows him. Says sheesh all the time and drives with his left arm hanging out the window."

Monkey Wrench waved at Sid through the glass front door and the proprietor stepped outside. "Hey, Sid, come over here. This gal is Ubi Sunt's daughter. She's going to track down her old man. Ain't that some shit? Won't listen to no common sense and wait for the strike to end. Two of a kind. Hard-headed like a two-by-four. Well good luck, lady, but keep your eyes open and your head down. That'll be thirty bucks. Cash, please."

Shortly after midnight, Jeanne steered the Saab, now with a pair of six-foot antennas bolted to the bumper, into the No Tell Motel north of Chattanooga. She had planned on driving all night, but had second thoughts after nodding off near Knoxville. This place was a dump, but it would do for a few hours rest. Jeanne got the last vacancy, a dingy, second-floor room with a single black-and-white TV bolted to the wall, a sunken mattress, and a night-stand with numerous cigarette burns on the top. She opened her small, green suitcase and unpacked: jeans, a sweater, underwear, and the tire bumper that Sid gave her at the truck stop. (Sid was so upset about Jeanne chasing her dad that he insisted she have something to protect herself with.) Sitting on the edge of the bed, Jeanne dialed home. The twins had been asleep for hours and Martin was dozing on the couch, a copy of *The New Yorker* open on his lap.

"Everybody's fine," Martin said, yawning. "My sister picked them up from school and cooked dinner for us. Tomorrow, same thing. Where are you?"

"Somewhere outside the Choo Choo."

"Huh?'"

"Oh, sorry. Chattanooga. Been on the CB all day. Anyway, I got the last room in a dilapidated motel on the interstate. I should be able to catch Daddy tomorrow in Birmingham. I called his dispatcher from Sid's Truck Stop, said it was a family emergency, and got the delivery address."

"Any signs of truckers on strike?"

"Oh, yes. It's all over the CB. Mostly just complaining. Truckers are overworked, underpaid and unappreciated. If you wear it, eat it, look at it, or sit on it, a truck brought it. That sort of thing. Anyway, I'll call you tomorrow, Honey, I'm tired and want to go to bed. And," Jeanne said, looking down at the nightstand, "this bed has Magic Fingers."

"Magic what?"

"Fingers. I haven't seen the Magic Fingers since a trip I took with Daddy—I must've been about nine—and we stayed at a motel that had a vibrating bed. You drop a quarter in this slot, like a pop machine, and the bed starts jiggling. Daddy must've returned to the front desk three times that night for change."

Jeanne opened her pink coin purse and turned it upside down over the nightstand. "Oh, good, I've got a bunch of change."

"How long do you get for a quarter?"

"I don't know, about two minutes. Hold on," Jeanne said, slipping a quarter in the slot. "It works. It works. Just like I remember."

Jeanne ran her hand across the vibrating mattress. "I can't wait to lie down."

"Call me tomorrow," Martin said. "Let me know if you find Grandpa Truck. The twins keep asking."

Jeanne didn't answer, didn't seem to hear her husband.

"Honey, are you there?"

"Oh, sorry. I can't believe they still have Magic Fingers."

"I said, call tomorrow. Okay?"

"Mmmhmm. I will."

"By the way, there's more quarters in the Saab. In the ashtray. Sounds like you'll need them."

Sometime early that morning, hours after the pulsating bed had grown still, a loud thud outside in the parking lot woke

Jeanne. Then another. She peeked out the curtains and it looked like somebody was changing a flat tire. No, wait. They were changing four flats. Those sonsabitches, they've got someone's car up on wood blocks and now they're headed toward my Saab with a jack and a tire iron. Jeanne slipped on the jeans and sweater, grabbed Sid's tire bumper and raced downstairs, heart thumping.

"Get away from that car," Jeanne screamed, raising the tire bumper above her head. "Thieves! Bastards! Get the hell away from my car."

Stretching her long legs and holding the iron guardrail, Jeanne skipped the last two steps and hit the ground in full stride. Her forehead burned and throbbed, felt like it was going to explode. She waved the tire bumper over her head and chased the two men, wearing solid black, toward a tall pickup that was loaded with assorted wheels and tires from a busy night preying on out-of-state vehicles parked at local motels. One man leaped into the truck bed and the other scrambled into the driver's seat. He hit the gas and the rear wheels kicked up gravel in Jeanne's face.

"You sonsabitches," Jeanne screamed. "I better not catch you or I'll bust your head open like a cantaloupe."

Like stars in early evening, lights in several rooms and the manager's office flickered on. Guests peeled back thin curtains and their silhouettes appeared in windows. A middle-aged Hispanic couple then trotted toward the red Buick that sat on wood blocks. A short, heavy woman wearing a pink, cotton nightgown buried her head in her hands and sobbed.

"Por Dios. Como pagamos para cuatro ruedas?"

Her husband stared in disbelief, comatose. His white t-shirt sagged almost to his knees.

A tall man with a rooster tail of white hair and a matching, goatee shuffled out of the office, slippers dragging across the pavement. Standing before the couple's crippled car, he said the police were on the way, he was sorry, but look at the sign by the office door: *Not responsible for accidents, vehicle damage or items stolen from the parking lot.* The Hispanic woman tore loose from her husband's chest and flung herself on the man. She pounded her fists on his chest, shouting incoherently in Spanish.

Backpedaling across the parking lot, the man pleaded with her husband, "Get her off of me."

It took the woman's husband and Jeanne a minute to pin back the woman's arms. By then, all four people were standing under the overhang at the motel office door. No sooner had the woman calmed down when a policeman pulled up and the Hispanic woman cut loose into another tirade, again in Spanish, but this time she targeted the policeman.

"Ladrones," she wailed. "Ladrones, robaron todos nuestra ruedas. Por Dios!"

The young policeman squeezed the woman's thick forearm and led her to the squad car's front seat. He called a bilingual dispatcher on the radio who took her statement and information. After a summer working in Maine on a small farm, the couple was returning to their Mobile, Alabama home. Every week, they sent money back to her parents, who were keeping their five children. Before leaving New England, they bought a set of good used tires and had just enough money for gas, food and one night in a motel. Now they were stuck.

The police radio then jumped to life, something about a break-in at a liquor store.

"Gotta go, sorry, gotta go."

The cop turned on his bubble gum machine and sped off, leaving the couple standing with their mouths wide open in the parking lot.

Jeanne picked up the tire bumper she had dropped by the pathetic-looking Buick and went upstairs to shower and pack. *Might as well hit the road, get an early start.* Checking out at the front desk, she overheard the Hispanic woman on the lobby phone, still upset. Jeanne borrowed a phone book and opened it to the tire section.

An hour later, Johnny's Tire Service pulled up with four Firestones and a set of rims. After the tire man had the Buick back on the ground, Jeanne wrote a check for the entire amount. She then grilled the tire man about the warranty. Gabe and Alma, as Jeanne now called them, were waiting to say *gracias* and *vaya con Dios.*

What now? The Buick won't crank? Jeanne popped the hood and was appalled at what she saw. Green, flaky corrosion covered the positive and negative terminals on the battery. Gabe leaned over the radiator, past the tall white woman and peered under the hood.

"You got a jump?"

In no time, Jeanne had her trunk open. She grabbed a pair of jumper cables that Ubi had given her when she first moved to the East Coast. Jeanne then opened the steel toolbox that came with her father's going away advice: Always *check the water, oil, and air, or WOA.* Jeanne's friends who graduated at that time got gifts like sheets, towels, stereos, or kitchen appliances. She got tools.

Tall and wiry, Jeanne had little trouble reaching under the hood. Using a steel brush, she scrubbed the battery posts to a shine. She attached the jumper cables to her car battery. The old Buick roared to life, blowing gray smoke from the tailpipe.

Alma then approached Jeanne and put her hands together like she was praying.

"Angel de la guarda," Alma said, and buried her head in Jeanne's flat breast. Jeanne wrapped her arms around Alma, jumper cables dragging the ground.

The red Buick and the green Saab, piloted by the guardian angel, traveled together southbound across the northwest corner of Georgia and into Alabama. The couple exited north of Birmingham, but Jeanne continued, honking and waving goodbye out the window as she closed in on the city. But Birmingham threw her a few curves and she spent more than an hour lost. One ramp shot her onto the highway to Atlanta; next, she found herself headed to Monkey Town, then back to the Choo Choo. *How does Daddy learn his way around all these cities?*

When Jeanne arrived at the warehouse, she found an empty loading dock. No Old Ironsides. Only a stooped black man wearing brown coveralls and holding a clipboard. Daddy had never been a lead foot, so it was unlikely he was already finished unloading and had moved on. Maybe he never made it. *No, don't even think like that.*

"You missed him," the warehouseman said. "Left about two hours ago. Don't have no idea which way he headed. Pay phone upstairs, but you got to move that car fust. Cain't be blocking my dock, girl. You say your old man's a trucker? Then you outta' know better than to park there. What the hell's wrong wicha?"

Jeanne took the stairs two at a time and found a driver's lounge furnished with scratched and gouged wooden chairs and mismatched lunch tables. She grabbed the pay phone receiver attached to the wall and dialed the toll-free number to dispatch she had memorized years ago. Daddy was headed to El Paso.

The daughter of a long-haul trucker, Jeanne knew to get prepared before taking off on another leg of a long trip. The restroom was godawful, but she held her nose and entered anyway. She hadn't eaten all day, but the vending machine peanut butter sandwich crackers and a can of Coke would have to do. Oil, check. Tires, check. Fuel, almost half a tank. *That should be enough to catch Daddy.* If not, stop down the road, gas and eat at the same time. Now grab the paper towels and Windex and wipe the bug guts from the windshield. Open the road atlas to the Alabama state map. *Daddy must've taken the interstate to Tuscaloosa and then Jackson, Mississippi. A two-hour head start wasn't much, slow as Daddy drives.*

After a few more wrong turns and more frustration, Jeanne found the westbound interstate and squinted into the Alabama sun. Her visor, flapped down, and her wide-rimmed, plastic sunglasses dimmed the glare. She twisted the radio dial from one end to the other, looking for a National Public Radio station, but no luck. She settled on a Miles Davis cassette, and with the CB squelch turned low to block out interference from faraway traffic, she crossed the Mississippi state line. Thin trunks of endless pine trees grew so thick you could barely walk between them, or see between them. And they cast long shadows across the road, gloomy silhouettes that the Saab cut through in the twilight. Just across the Mississippi line, the sky grew dim and the road twisted slightly. Over her left shoulder, Jeanne saw a half-moon rise above the pine forest. Although she was driving about seventy miles an hour, an eighteen-wheeler decorated with red and amber lights from bumper to bumper roared past her in the left lane. The Saab rocked side to side. Jeanne picked up the CB mike.

"You can bring that large car back over," she said, "you missed me."

The driver jiggled a toggle switch on the dash and the truck marker lights flickered on and off, a silent yet brilliant thank you. Jeanne suspected the trucker didn't respond on the radio because he refused to shut down and wanted to keep a low profile.

As the evening wore on, Jeanne felt the rhythm of the road take hold. Eight cylinders purred under the hood. Four wheels rolled freely in overdrive. Rubber on asphalt, whirring, whining along. The steady hum was almost hypnotic. And then an outline of a big rig up ahead in the right lane. *Looks like the back of a furniture van; you can tell by the low taillights. Looks like it says Deaton Van Lines on the back. Oh my God, that's Daddy's trailer number all right, 83, stenciled on the back door.*

"How about it, Southpaw? You got a copy on this four-wheeler at your back door?"

Silence. *Come on, Daddy, turn up the radio.* Jeanne was now about a dozen truck lengths behind the rig. It was definitely Old Ironsides.

"Break for that westbound Deaton driver. You got a copy? This here is Sweetums on your back door."

Sheesh, Daddy. Guess I'll have to follow you into the next truck stop, or rest area, or wherever you decide to stop. Jeanne fingered the CB mike again, debating whether it was best to pass and wave him down, or just hang back and wait for him to exit. The latter choice could be a while; Daddy was known for driving hours without stopping. Mom used to say his bladder was larger than Lake Superior. *Now, what's this? He's pulling away? What's up with the lead foot?* Oh, no. He's not speeding up, the Saab is slowing down. *Oh my gosh, the Saab is out . . . of . . . gas.*

Back in Birmingham, Sherry double-checked everything. Even the gas gauge. But after that she got caught up in the chase, lost in the drive, like reading a good book and you look up and your late for an appointment, and forgot about refueling. And she hadn't bought gas since the other side of Knoxville, yesterday.

"Break for the Southpaw. Come on. You got a copy on this Sweetums? Come on, Daddy."

Jeanne slammed the microphone against the dash. Old Ironsides disappeared into the twilight. The Saab coasted to a stop on the shoulder.

TWENTY-TWO

"HERE COMES ONE. Eastbound. Inside lane. Big-ass eighteen-wheel dry box, like the broad side of a barn. Come on. Pull the trigger. What are you waiting for, fuckhead? An invitation? There she goes. Out of sight. Why didn't you shoot? Scairt?"

"Ain't scairt. The sonofabitch was going too fast. I want a slow-moving rig, one I can lock in on, like dove hunting, you know, let the barrel follow the bird, and BAM!"

"There ain't going to be that many choices, you dipshit. It's a truckers' strike. Most of the rigs are parked. And I ain't going to sit up here on this hill all morning freezing my ass, waiting on you."

"Gotta' be the right one. I'll know it when I see it."

"I think you're scairt. Like the time you wussed out when me an Bobby broke into the pawnshop. Then you lied, said you was sick."

"Easy for you to say. If we get caught, I'm the one with the rifle. I'm the one left holding my dick in my hand."

"Don't forget, it was your idea. Said you could do better'n that no-shooting ass in Atlanta that hit that eighteen-wheeler. Said you could pick off one of them truckers on the freeway from a quarter mile away, across both lanes of traffic, no problem. We got the perfect spot like you said, up on this hill, in the woods, take the back way out through these pine trees and be back at Floozy's drinking beer before anyone knew what happened. I still think you're scairt."

"I ain't scairt. Gimme those 'noculars, fuckwad."

" Here. Take 'em. See anything?"

"Shut the hell up. I'm looking. Fuck a duck. Get down. A god-damn sheriff."

"Crap. Get the barrel out of the window, dipshit. Never mind. I got it. Sheriff could see that, you know. Dumbass, you coulda' get us busted."

"Okay, he's gone. Probably headed into Shreveport. Gimme the rifle back."

"Here comes one. Westbound, gonna' be a long shot, but he's rolling nice and slow. No traffic either direction too. And would you look at that thing? Like a goddamn submarine on eighteen wheels. Don't choke."

"Shut the fuck up. I got this mother in my sight. Old fart got his arm hanging out the window on a cold day. Fool gonna learn to keep his window rolled up after this. Come to papa, you slow moving whale, come to papa."

"Holy shit! You hit the fucking door. Look, he's pulling over. You nailed his ass. Goddamnit. Let's get the fuck out of here. The law's gonna be here any minute. Come on, hurry up."

"I'm looking for the fucking shell. Got to throw it in the river on the way back."

"You can shove that shell up your ass. Crank this truck."

"Who's scairt now?"

TWENTY-THREE

A TRUCKER WITH FUEL TANKS and coffee thermos topped off, and an early start, can knock out several southern states in one day—Georgia, Alabama, Mississippi, Louisiana. And the terrain and vegetation looks about the same. State after state, loblolly and longleaf pine trees swarm and march across the low-rolling hills and drop a bed of needles on the forest floor. Red, rusty dirt, sometimes with an ochre tint, breaks through the forest floor only where the land has been cut open at construction sites or near freeway exits. Otherwise, it's several hundreds miles of pine forest, trees growing up to seventy feet high, occasionally interrupted by slow-moving black creeks and rivers. One major exception: the Mississippi River sweeps through at Vicksburg, a ribbon of water more than a mile wide that, despite the man-made levees and locks and bridges, can still rise up and wreak havoc on the cornfields and communities brave and stubborn enough to live in its floodplain.

Driving westbound through Louisiana, past Shreveport, you cross the Texas state line and the big green sign *El Paso 800 miles* meets you with intimidation. It takes a driver with an iron backside and steel kidneys to cross Texas, from the Louisiana line to El Paso, in one day. The first one hundred fifty miles of Texas look like what you left behind in Louisiana. Even in fall, the air remains thick and heavy and clings to your skin like a film, and if you spend the night here in your bunk with the window open, the merciless mosquitoes will find you and attack, no matter how deep in the sleeper you burrow. A little farther west, Dallas and Fort Worth can take forever to get around. With its network of consti-pated freeways, everybody races the clock, fighting for a place on the entrance ramp, or exit ramp, or jockeying for position, squeez-ing in one lane or the other. Better not stop to check the tires in Big D, might be an hour before you can get back on the road. Sure it hurts your bladder like someone's sticking a needle in you, but it's best to plow straight ahead. No serious accidents choking traffic and you might make it across the city in an hour. If you're lucky. Then you can stop in Fort Worth—now there's a town where a driver can catch his breath. You got a little wiggle room in old Cow Town.

West of Fort Worth, the land peels back and the sky comes out like opening the curtains on a sunny day. No craning your neck here looking for sunshine. Azure-blue sky, window to window. An hour later, headed toward Abilene, white, puffy clouds drift past and morph into elephants, angels, Abraham Lincoln, a giraffe, a swan, Moses, God. And unlike yesterday's drive where you were bottled up by hundreds of miles of conifers that guard the horizon like wooden soldiers, this endless expanse distracts you from the CB, distracts you from the white lines and mile markers, the tele-phone poles and fence posts, the road kill and gators. Songwriters proclaim the road goes on forever, but that asphalt ribbon would not be possible without terra firma. And that terrain rolls and pitches outside your windshield, which is still smeared with green insect guts from the Deep South. But now, with the gnarled live oaks and mesquites and clumps of junipers widely scattered, you can read the topography like a geologist. See that wrinkle on the hillside where the water runs? Now follow the creek downstream where it has eroded a limestone ledge. Check out how the dif-ferent layers of sediment were deposited over millennia. Now look how the creek widens and disappears behind another hill in the distance, eventually flowing into the Brazos River. And here comes the Brazos now, unimpressive compared to the mighty rivers up north and back east. But she must have inspired the Spanish explorers, because, drawing up the first maps, they labeled the river Arms of God.

Unlike the Deep South, this land is heavy with cattle and dotted with hay fields and those iron grasshoppers that, long after the oil boom went bust, continue to pump petroleum from a few old wells that haven't played out. Up and down like seesaws, they continue around the clock. And then further west, the low rolling hills can catch you off guard. You gotta romp the accelerator, get a good running start or you'll end up bogged down, grabbing gears in the climbing lane stuck behind somebody in a little pickup with an oversized camper hanging over the truck bed, dozens of stickers from assorted states plastered on the back window glass.

Continuing west toward Abilene, the horizon continues to unfold. The sun traverses the sky, now high enough above that you're not looking directly into it. And it's then you feel lonesome, wishing for a passenger to share the sky with; there's just too much space out there for one pair of eyes. And there's still a lot of land, a lot of road ahead. Then, you find yourself talking out loud, to an anonymous rider, like someone was in the seat next to you.

Hey, here comes a roadside park. Let's pull in, take in the sky. No, don't open both doors at once. Can't you feel the wind shaking the rig, rocking it like a cradle? Open both doors simultaneously and you'll create a wind tunnel. All the maps and logbooks, S & H Green Stamp books you've been collecting, they'll end up in New Mexico or Oklahoma. You know, a driver caught up on the East Coast making deliveries for a few weeks, why, he could sit here for a half hour just catching up on sky. What's that? There's nothing out here? That's the appeal. No civilization. No big cities breaking up the horizon. What the hell's wrong with that? Out here, you can get lost in the sky.

TWENTY-FOUR

ABOUT THREE HUNDRED MILES WEST of Abilene, the interstate abruptly ends and a two-lane road detours through a small town with one grocery store made from cinder blocks, a post office housed in an old feed store, and a smattering of adobe houses and trailer homes. Just outside of town, a retired gemologist and his wife opened a campground. They had spent their careers digging for jewels across much of the Western Hemisphere, but caught jungle yellow fever in Brazil and almost died in a long hospital stay there. So the middle-aged couple decided to plant roots in the desert sand here; the dry climate suited their lungs. They bull-dozed a wide entrance to accommodate travel trailers and the occasional big rig. They built stone fire pits and ran electric wires and water pipes through a network of trenches to each camping spot. A cedar and sandstone building near the entrance housed showers, a gift shop stocked with lots of minerals and jewelry, of course, and a small grocery, dusty shelves stacked with food that had long shelf lives. Anything canned was a good choice for a little store that had to order weeks in advance to get a truck in from El Paso. The couple sold sardines in flat, silver cans, Spam in half-round cans, fingerling Vienna sausages in little cans, peanuts in big cans, canned V-8 and orange juice, and coffee in bright red cans. About the only items not in cans were strategically displayed at the front counter. What parent could deny their children candy bars after dragging them out here to no-man's land?

It was late evening when Jeanne's green Saab rolled down the gravel road, past a fifteen-foot steel roadrunner welded together out of rusty truck and tractor parts, and stopped at the entrance. A half-moon peeking over a jagged mountain peak, probably across the Rio Grande in Mexico, illuminated a wooden sign hanging from a rope that stretched between two thick cedar posts.

Welcome to Casita Buena. Congratulations if you are looking for the middle of nowhere because this is it!

Inside the lobby, Jeanne rang the night bell and explained to the clerk that she would sleep in the back of her wagon, but would like a shower in the morning. The sleepy gemologist, still wearing yellow opal earrings, took Jeanne's money and pointed her toward the corner of the twenty-acre tract, near the back of that big rig, parked nose-in toward a dark corner. After parking the wagon, Jeanne opened the back of the Saab and unrolled her sleeping bag. Then a whiff of smoke. A campfire. The sweet smell of burning pinion drifting across the lot—like camping trips in New Mexico with the Girl Scouts. Gotta take a look. Flames dancing and casting shadows in the moonlight. A big campfire. And laughter. A couple pouring wine into paper cups. Kids piercing wieners with long sticks and holding them over the orange and yellow flames. A man drinking from a paper sack. Got to get closer. *Oh my God. That's Daddy's face, flickering in the campfire light. He's sitting on a stump telling stories.*

"It was so cold that my nose hairs froze."

Some kids eating roasted marshmallows giggled.

"I was standing at a pay phone outside and the ink in my pen froze up too. Then I spilled some coffee on the ground, and it turned to ice just like that." The old trucker tried to snap his fingers, but couldn't.

"Where was this?" asked a woman, about forty, bandana tied around her neck. "And when was this?"

"Winter of '63. Great Falls, Montana. Local folks told me it was forty-two degrees below zero. I asked Fahrenheit or Celsius and they said when it gets that cold, it don't matter; they're about the same. One fella, his truck engine died and he did too—froze to death up in the bunk. They found him next spring, frozen stiff, and when they took his body back home to Florida for burial he didn't thaw out until they got him to Tallahassee."

The man holding the paper sack handed it to Ubi. He gulped, swallowed and wiped his mouth on his jacket sleeve.

"When it gets that cold, brakes freeze up. First brake shoes and then air in brake lines."

"How can you freeze air?" asked a pudgy cardiologist from San Antonio, wearing a windbreaker with the collar turned up. "That's a scientific impossibility."

"Well, okay. The air don't freeze, but the moisture, the condensation that builds up in your air compressor and air lines, turns to water. Kind of like a sludge. And it freezes and blocks the air lines so your brakes won't work."

"You mean like clogged arteries."

"Ten-four," Ubi said. "And if that happens, you got to start taking off hoses, looking for chunks of ice. And another problem. That trip was so cold, two nights in a row, my brake shoes froze solid to the drums. Like if you lick a Popsicle and your tongue gets stuck."

"How do you break loose the brakes?"

"Two ways," interrupted Jeanne, stepping into the campfire light. "Dip an old newspaper in the fuel tank and make a torch. Diesel's not combustible like gasoline, it burns low and even. So with the torch, you crawl under the truck and melt the ice from the brake shoes, but careful it's not too hot, or you could melt an air hose or damage the brake shoes."

"What's the other method?"

"Good old-fashioned hammer. Knock 'em loose. Either way, you have to lie on your back, in the ice and snow. Right, old man?"

Jeanne smiled across the fire ring at Ubi.

"How do you know all this?" the San Antonio man asked. He stood up, peered at the lanky shadow. "Are you a lady trucker?"

"Not exactly. And if you're unlucky, you could break through the ice while working on the brakes and soak through your khakis first thing in the morning. Wet clothes, below zero, not fun stuff."

The group watched the newcomer reach for the paper bag, take a swig, and wipe her lips with the back of her hand.

Jeanne circled the campfire. When she was standing next to the truck driver, who was still seated on the stump, she dropped a hand on his shoulder. "This is my father. Taught me everything I know. About trucking, anyway."

Ubi rose from the stump and Jeanne draped her arms over her father's shoulders, looking into his brown eyes, clear and happy, they were unlike the red-rimmed peepholes he was always rubbing back in Philly. Daddy wrapped his right arm around Jeanne and squeezed her until he felt her spine.

"What are you doing here, Sweetums?" he whispered in her ear. "Is everything all right?"

"Yes. I just had to see you. I hated the way things turned out."

"Are you sure everything's okay? The twins? Martin?"

"They're fine," Jeanne said. "Look, I've thought about this for two thousand miles. I know you can't help being who you are any more than I can help being who I am. And . . . oh my God."

Jeanne now noticed Ubi's left arm hanging at his side, wrapped in white bandages from wrist to elbow. "What happened to your arm? You've got it wrapped up like a mummy. What? Tell me, Daddy."

"Just a scratch."

"He got shot driving across Loosiana," said a small boy stuffing his face with a marshmallow, now standing beside the couple. "Some outlaws wiff rifles tried to kill him 'cause he don't want to shut down. He's an independent. Don't nobody tell an independent what to do. You can look it up in the dictionary."

"You are a well-schooled young man."

"Home-schooled," chirped a woman sitting nearby. "We're on a geology field trip."

* * *

Jeanne looked down at the boy and thought about Molly and Jeremy back home. She took Ubi by his right arm and pulled him over to a bench carved from a cottonwood tree trunk. She sat him down like she would the twins when they came in from the playground, pants legs ripped open, knees and elbows bloody.

"A couple yahoos outside Shreveport didn't have nothing better to do, so they figgered it was open season on old Peterbilts," Ubi said. "The law caught 'em that afternoon. Fools got to ratchet jawing at a beer joint and the barmaid called the sheriff. Didn't have nothing to do with the strike. They just took advantage of a situation. Stirring the pot. That's all. Anyway, they nicked me with a deer rifle, thirty-ought six, halfway between the wrist and the elbow." Ubi held up his left forearm and with his right index finger pointed at the spot where the bullet entered. "Just missed a tendon, went plumb through and lodged in the door."

"How serious is it?"

"Not too bad. Got a little round hole just below the handle. Makes a kind of whistling sound at sixty miles an hour. But since the window was rolled down, the bullet broke the glass and tore up the little assembly and I can't roll it up. Might have to get a whole new door. So, I called the Peterbilt dealer in El Paso and they're looking for one. Gonna be hard to find. Glad it hasn't rained."

Jeanne leaned forward and took the wounded arm in her hands. "I don't care about the truck, Daddy. What did the doctor say about your forearm?"

With Jeanne examining her father's bandaged wing, the group that was huddled around the campfire said their goodnights and goodbyes and started to drift away. For the past hour, they had sat transfixed by the old trucker's storytelling and creased face glowing in the firelight. What a journey. Criss-crossing the country like that for thirty years.

"You hear that old trucker? You don't get that in the eight-to-five world, or flying airport to airport in business travel."

A husband clutched his wife's hand as they returned to their pop-up camper, walking shoulder to shoulder. "We got to get out more often. Out of the rut, off the treadmill. I'm talking about freedom. I'm telling you, when the kids are grown, we just gotta explore, ramble and roam. Life's too short. Wanderlust? If that's what you want to call it, so be it. We all got a little wanderlust."

The families retreated to their tents and campers. Ubi and Jeanne watched the campfire burn down. A log softly crumbled, split open. Scarlet coals throbbed and pulsated and hypnotized father and daughter. And the half-moon now stood at full attention, directly overhead.

"If I hadn't run out of gas, this wouldn't have happened. I was right behind you in Mississippi when the car quit. I called you on the CB."

"You got a CB in your four-wheeler, Sweetums?"

"Ten-four, stopped at your old pal's truck stop, Sid's, on the way out of town," Jeanne said. She took Ubi's bandaged arm and laid it across her lap. "Anyway, after I bummed a gas can and bought a gallon the car still wouldn't start—clogged filter. I got it towed and they messed up the front bumper. I spent half a day haggling with the garage and the insurance company. Should have just installed a new fuel filter myself; they're only a couple bucks."

Ubi and Jeanne stared at the bandaged forearm still resting in Jeanne's lap. The campground had grown quiet and they sat alone together on the large timber, their bodies fused almost into one. "Ain't goin' to be no permanent damage, Sweetums. Just a little scar. I got to get it checked for infection, maybe next week."

"Where are you going to find a doctor?"

Ubi shrugged. "Wherever I happen to be."

Jeanne's mind shifted into overdrive. A co-worker's wife back in Philly was a cracker-jack surgeon. Why not let her look at it? Get a second opinion. No telling if whoever patched him up knew what he was doing. Daddy could suffer permanent nerve damage, or disfigurement, or both. *Maybe he can come back with me in the Saab. Maybe I better call first thing in the morning and make an appointment. Maybe . . . maybe . . . maybe not.* Jeanne let the thought pass and downshifted to a lower gear. The couple gazed into the ebbing, crimson coals, silent.

"I'm sure you'll find someone who will take good care of that, um, injury, wherever you are," Jeanne said, handing her father's bandaged arm back to him. "But until then, you better learn to write with your other hand. You know the twins go to the mailbox almost every day, looking for postcards."

"I'm getting better," Ubi smiled. "You can actually read my logbook now. First day, it was a mess; couldn't tell the difference between Mesquite and Monahans. But don't worry, Sweetums, if the post office gets cracking, the twins will have new postcards pinned up on their wall before you get home. Sent a pair from Big Spring this morning."

The campfire continued to burn down. Low blue flames waved in the soft breeze.

"Kinda' funny," Ubi said.

"What's that?"

"The left hand don't hurt near as bad as the right."

Ubi held up his right thumb, plump and purple and infected from the splinter he picked up from the reverend's piano. With his left arm bandaged, he couldn't dig it out, and just today it seemed to explode underneath his skin.

"Sheesh, Daddy," Jeanne said. Her eyelids peeled back. "That looks like Little Jack Horner's thumb."

"Think you can perform a little roadside surgery?" Ubi asked, pulling his pocketknife out of his front pants pocket. "Better sterilize the blade first."

Jeanne held the narrow blade just above the coals until the steel tip turned blue. Sitting next to her father, she propped a flashlight on the log, pointing directly at the sore thumb. She pierced the skin, felt him twitch. "Hold still."

"I'm trying. It ain't that easy."

"No kidding," Jeanne mumbled. She prodded and dug deeper. Yellow liquid oozed out of the tiny wound. More twitching. "Hold on."

In less than a minute, she held up the knife, the tiny wood shaving lying on the blade. "There's the culprit."

Ubi and Jeanne walked to the rig and the old trucker dug into his first-aid kit, looking for the little bottle of rubbing alcohol he carried.

"Where are you sleeping, Sweetums? In the back of that four-wheeler?"

Jeanne nodded.

"Good way to get a backache. I got a half-empty trailer. Lots of thick furniture pads."

Suddenly, the campfire burning down into a bed of red coals caught his eye. "They'll still be hot in the morning," Ubi said. "Just throw a few twigs on, fan it with an old cap and it'll come back to life. If you build a campfire right, with hardwood, it'll always come back in the morning. It may not look like it, but there's heat and warmth buried deep in there."

Late the next morning, Ubi woke to the sound of car wheels crunching gravel outside the trailer. He rolled over on the pallet of pads and saw an empty space where his daughter had slept. He yanked on his old boots, staggered to the trailer door and pushed it open. A green station wagon with Pennsylvania plates disappeared behind a curtain of road dust. Remembering that Jeanne now had a CB, Ubi scampered toward the tractor. He felt in his pocket for the keys. *Gotta go back. Musta fell out of my khakis last night. Sheesh, what am I thinking? Driver's window is broken.*

Ubi climbed in Old Ironsides and flipped the switch on his radio. *What's the chances she would have her ears on? Let's try channel nineteen.*

"Break for Sweetums."

"You got Sweetums. Go ahead."

"Take her down to channel twelve," Ubi said, not wanting his personal conversation aired on the truckers' main channel. "You there, Sweetums?"

"Ten-four."

"Thanks for driving out here to check on me. But what's the hurry?"

"I started to wake you, but you looked so peaceful. Sorry I left in a rush, but I miss my family. I've been gone four days and I've got at least a two-day drive back home. I left you a note in the cab. It's inside your logbook with a magazine article," she said. With one hand on the wheel and the other holding the CB mike, Jeanne pushed the Saab up a steep climb. "A couple hitchhikers you picked up wrote a story about you, Daddy. Took some pictures, too. About sixty thousand readers got to know you and Old Ironsides."

"That must be those crazy kids I met in Colorado."

Ubi flipped open his logbook and found an envelope with *Daddy-O* written on it. "Sweetums. Last night I wanted to tell you something, but I never could."

247

Jeanne rounded a sweeping corner and the Saab dropped into a valley. The voice on the CB faded and static from another channel bled through. Jeanne hit the gas, pushed the vehicle to seventy, and the Saab climbed an open hillside. "I never told you this, Sweetums, and I should have a long time ago . . . " The voice trailed off. "But it just never seemed like the right time. You still there?"

Jeanne pulled over on a patch of sand and gravel. The Saab pitched to the passenger side and an empty Coke can rolled from under the seat.

"Go ahead, you got Sweetums here."

"I said that I . . . "

A pair of motorcycles roared past and drowned out the trembling and distant voice coming through the CB speaker.

TWENTY-FIVE

TWO WORDS, FUEL SURCHARGE, whirled across the country on the airwaves—CB, TV, AM and FM. Fuel Surcharge, like an armistice; the words declared the end of a struggle. Fuel surcharge, published in newspapers that were scattered across truck stop coffee counters from the Gulf of Mexico to the Sierra Nevada to the Adirondacks. Fuel Surcharge, the Interstate Commerce Commission's answer to escalating fuel prices. Two percent of the line haul goes directly to the party that owns the rig pulling that freight. That's us. That's the independents. Fuel surcharge. That'll offset this high-priced imported oil. Fuel surcharge. Finally those bureaucrats in Washington woke up, smelled the coffee.

Fuel Surcharge goes up when fuel goes up, tracks the price of diesel. Dispatch says it'll be a line item on the freight bill. 'Bout goddamn time. Too bad some boys got hurt. That wasn't supposed to happen, those hoodlums throwing rocks from overpasses in Tulsa and taking pot shots on the interstate near Shreveport. But those drivers shouldn't a been out there in the first place. Shoulda' parked it like the rest of us. No matter anymore. Back to work, y'all. Hot loads sitting on docks and in warehouses and in farmers' fields. Gotta make up for lost time. Truck payment due next week. Insurance too. Gonna need tires soon.

Fuel surcharge. Dispatchers got enough tonnage to keep us running steady for several weeks. We showed 'em how the cow eats the cabbage. Bet they got tired of those rigs blocking toll-booths and freeway ramps, and empty shelves at the A & P. Fuel surcharge. Fuel Surcharge. Big ten-four.

TWENTY-SIX

UBI EASED OFF THE ACCELERATOR, downshifted, and Old Ironsides coasted down the flat exit ramp. The engine and transmission hummed. The exhaust purred. A bearded backpacker hiking down the shoulder halted and turned his head. The rig rolled past him just as Ubi dropped another gear, engine throttling down. The low growl echoed off the nearby foothills and the truck cast a wild shadow across an open field. The backpacker continued to stare at the tractor-trailer rig. What a sound. What a truck. Endangered species.

Squinting into the orange horizon, Ubi yanked the sun visor. Still, he had to shade his eyes with his bandaged left hand to make out the yellow, triangular yield sign ahead. He eased around the corner; the glare subsided and he caught a clear view of the Spotto Fuel Stop, known for cheap diesel and greasy hamburgers. A retired trucking company executive had opened a network of Spottos west of the Mississippi. Drag in a double-wide mobile home and stretch some power lines to it. Dig a big hole in the ground and drop a couple fuel tanks in the pit. Lease a few faded billboards, one exit down in each direction, and slap on fresh paint: EXIT NOW SPOTTO CHEEEP DIESEL. Print a little map for the drivers—a black dot for each of the two dozen truck stops. Pick strategic traffic lanes—Joplin, Junction City, Ogallala, and El Paso. There ain't nuttin' near El Paso but rocks and sand and cactus and big trucks thirsty for diesel.

Ubi had grown accustomed to turning down the CB volume when he pulled into a truck stop. The usual banter about parking spots, driver's etiquette and lot lizards had long ago grown old. But today, the small, red needle on the radio that measures signal strength was wildly jumping up and down. Like cattle pushing and shoving at a feed trough, forty-ton beasts squeezed each other for a place in line at the diesel pumps.

"Hey, green cabover Freightliner, wait your turn, good buddy. Like the rest of us."

"I got your good buddy hanging. Shoulda pulled up when you could, instead of jacking off in the back of the line."

After delivering the last of the office furniture that morning at an Army post, Ubi had driven west toward the Spotto, just inside the New Mexico line. He elbowed his way past the crowded fuel desk where several truckers were leaning over the counter, waiting on a single employee to take their money and scratch out a handwritten receipt. Ubi then nudged through more drivers lined up at a grill covered with sizzling hamburger patties and he pulled up a stool facing a half-dozen pay phones bolted to a long wall. *Boy, it's hot in the back of this truck stop.* Ubi dialed the toll-free number to Denver and waited on hold, listening to elevator music. A fly buzzed his nose. It landed on the wall before him, on an advertisement that claimed your engine would last a million miles if you switched to Super Flow heavy-duty oil. Ubi shooed the fly with the back of his hand.

At last, a live voice on the phone and a rookie dispatcher rattling off the weight, origin, and destination of a half-dozen shipments, enough tonnage to fill his trailer. Ubi immediately knew he would have to run more than a thousand miles for this load. From Odessa to Austin and the Rio Grande Valley; six, maybe seven days of hustling. And that wouldn't be so bad except his first delivery was in Lawton, Oklahoma. He would drive more miles picking up loads than hauling them to their destination. Using his right hand, Ubi slowly scribbled the towns and customer names in a spiral notebook. This short-haul stuff is for the regional drivers. Still, he felt obligated to accept the load because he had pulled rank last month to get those shipments out of the Denver area. He had no hole card, no trump, with these new dispatchers. And to be fair, this kid was handing out marching orders that came from area planners. The planners were the ones responsible for getting the tonnage covered on time; just get it off the dispatch board and let the contractor figure out how to make a buck. That's their problem. Hey, look, five o'clock. Happy hour, anyone?

Ubi flipped to another page and wrote down the last shipment he was expected to load—Beaumont.

"You're kidding. Beaumont? That's near the Louisiana line, seven hundred miles from El Paso. One week running all over Texas to pick up a bunch of hot shipments that are going nowhere? Come on."

"You want to talk to my boss?"

"Ten-four. I want to talk to your boss."

Waiting on hold and listening to more elevator music, Ubi clenched his teeth. Guess they forgot about the old-timer who stuck to his guns during the strike, got shot up, but still made his delivery on time. Now, look who gets the leftovers? Suddenly the music stopped.

"Hey, driver, when you want to go to work just give me a call. I don't have time for prima donnas."

The hairs on Ubi's neck stood on end. "What are you talking about? You got me hopscotching across Texas like it was Rhode Island. Or Delaware. I'll run more'n a thousand miles to get loaded. You coulda divvied up those short-haul shipments between the agents."

"Look, just like everybody else, you got to take the good with the bad. I know you'll go over my head like you did before, but you need to learn to be a team player."

"You need to learn to read a map."

"We got maps. And we look at what's best for the whole."

The planner's cold, hard voice was a far cry from the friendly conversations Ubi had with dispatchers in years past, keeping up with their families and joking about bad food and bad roads.

"We have more than three hundred drivers in our fleet. You're no different than anybody else. You're acting way too independent."

"I am independent," Ubi barked into the sweaty pay phone receiver. "And this load is piss-poor planning. You take it for granted I'll accept it, no questions asked."

The fly returned to the engine oil ad. Ubi swatted with his spiral—missed.

"Look, I know you've been driving for us a long time, sir, but I don't need you telling me how to do my job."

"I'm not cleaning up your docks, covering the loads that backed up during the strike. Now that they're running late, you want to put it on my back."

"Okay, that's enough. Like I said, you call me when you want to go back to work, but you better give up that independent attitude, driver. That don't play up here anymore at Deaton."

Holding his pencil with his fist like a dagger, Ubi drew a large X across the page of notes he had written. The paper ripped in two.

"And another thing before you go, Safety and Compliance wants to talk with you. Hold on."

More elevator music. Ubi waited, tore the page from his spiral, rolled it into a ball. Then he heard a soft voice on the phone.

"Mr. Sunt, this is Margaret McCorley. I'm the new safety and compliance manager," a young woman, speaking in monotone, said. "We're upgrading our fleet. We feel that uniformity, with all trucks approximately the same make and model, painted the same color, is best for our public image. We've made arrangements with a local truck dealer who offers competitive pricing and financing on modern equipment."

"I'm not giving up Old Ironsides," Ubi said. "Do you know how long I've had that rig?"

"As a matter of fact, I do," said Ms. McCorley. "It was first registered with our company in nineteen fifty-six. That makes it a quarter century old."

"What's wrong with that?"

"Well, our new policy, which goes into effect next month, prohibits our contractors from operating equipment more than fifteen years old. As I said, we have procured an exclusive agreement with a local dealer that carries some of the finest trucks available."

"What if I don't want to give up my rig?"

"I'm sorry, sir, but we'll have to terminate your contract."

"You're kidding."

Ubi's face turned purple-red. Sweat beaded on his forehead. "How long have you been with Deaton?"

"Six weeks. But that's not important. Do you want the number for the truck dealer here in Denver, sir? Or even better, I can connect you right now. Save you a long distance call."

"Can you patch me through to Mick Thorton?" he asked. This was unbelievable, putting Old Ironsides out to pasture. "His extension is—"

"Mr. Thorton retired last week, sir. Management warned me you would probably want to go over my head and said if you did, there was no grandfathering any equipment. The board of directors agreed on this policy unanimously, Mr. Sunt. I'm sorry; I know that truck is special to you. I've seen pictures of it here in our hallway, but we have secured an exclusive agreement with

Rocky Mountain Truck Sales that would be better than anything you could find on your own. Can I connect you with them?"

Ubi sat motionless on the stool, staring blankly ahead. Talking with this woman was impossible.

"Mr. Sunt, are you there?"

"I don't want a new truck."

"Used is okay, but not too old. May I remind you of the attractive financing and good pricing we've arranged?"

"My payments now are zero. How are you going to top that?"

"Well, you're going to have to do something soon to replace your vehicle, or face termination. Company policy."

"We'll see, Ms. McCorley, we'll see."

Ubi banged down the receiver. He heard something buzz past his ear. The fly. It circled above and landed on the counter before him. Ubi raised the spiral over his head and slammed it down. Fly guts squirted. The countertop shook. The driver sitting on the next stool held his palm over the receiver and shot the trembling man a look.

"Geez, mister. It's only a fly."

TWENTY-SIX

BECAUSE UBI COULDN'T STAND THE IDEA of sleeping in his truck behind the cheap portable buildings at the Spotto—and he wanted a lengthy, hot shower—he deadheaded into New Mexico to a favorite haunt. Arturo's served homemade cheese enchiladas, and their private shower stalls were maintained by Arturo's wife and three daughters. A row of booths nestled against one wall featured what Ubi considered the ultimate luxury—pay phones. You could sip coffee, order huevos rancheros, call dispatch or home, all from the comfort of those old and sagging upholstered benches.

Ubi gathered a couple of the free truckers' tabloids from the lobby and paid three bucks for a magazine loaded with glossy truck photos and how-to articles. He slid into a corner booth and flipped through each one to the want ads in the back.

> *Hey driver, tired of those low-paying loads? Be your own boss! Get your hauling authority—48 states! Haul what you want, when you want. Contact Brown & Brown, Dover, Delaware.*

> *Owner-operators, how much of the linehaul does your company keep? Well, that's too much!*
> *Why let the big trucking companies keep up to 50 percent? All they do is supply the trailer and set up the loads. You can do that and keep it all. We can show you how to be independent.*

Don't delay! Call today! Minzenmeyer and Associates, Shrewsbury, Massachusetts.

Why let the middleman make all the money? Keep more of what you earn with your own authority. Call toll-free today: Jones & Sons, Attorney at law.

Ubi had seen these ads before. A few years back, in the name of competition, Congress made it easier to obtain hauling authority. It also changed the rules so a company could set its rates as low as it wanted instead of following a rigid structure called a tariff in which everybody played by the same rules. The selling tool before was not price, because that was virtually the same, but service. But now numerous large corporations that sold stock on Wall Street had lowered rates and squeezed out lots of little guys—the outfits with only a handful of trucks. Going solo meant going up against the big boys.

It was already after 5 p.m. on the East Coast where the attorneys were located. And it was Friday, so Ubi had all weekend to ruminate making the move toward true independence. He could afford a new rig and keep Old Ironsides, too. Park it somewhere in a garage and take her out for a drive when he had some downtime. And chew on this: His contract with Deaton was the longest-standing relationship in his life. Longer than his marriage to Sherry, longer than his relationship with his daughter. How do you walk away from that?

As for the other option—secure individual hauling authority—maybe a man should consider gearing down at almost seventy years old, not branching out on a new adventure. Still, those stinging words from that planner made it clear he would have to follow their orders, regardless how he felt. New trucks. Warehouses scattered to the suburbs. Pagers beeping at you with unnecessary messages. Talk of placing little satellite tracking systems on rigs. What happened to the freedom of the road?

So, hustling loads through brokers seemed like the best move. Brokers are everywhere, ads at truck stops, in magazines and brochures. Some are crooks, sure, got to be able to sniff them out. But once you make some contacts, provide stellar service, you get repeat business. Now what about the custom furniture van? Probably need a different trailer, a flat floor so forklifts could run in and out, stacking pallets full of consumer goods or raw materials. This would be a new road for an old hand.

Reading in his bunk on Sunday night, Ubi's mind wandered. What would he be doing today if Sherry had licked the cancer? And he couldn't put that argument with dispatch out of his head. *"You better give up that independent attitude, driver."* And what about that safety and compliance lady wanting to put old Ironsides out to pasture? Heck, they probably cut a deal with that truck dealer, getting some sort of a referral fee for all the business they send. And who knows? Maybe the Deaton owners had an interest in that outfit as well. Maybe they owned Rocky Mountain Truck Sales, too. Deaton had backed him in a corner. He didn't ask for this. But just like when he lost Sherry, he didn't ask for that either.

Ubi crawled out of the bunk at 6 a.m. It was already 8 a.m. back east. Time to make a move. Time to cut the cord.

Inside the restaurant, sitting in the corner booth with refill after refill of hot java, Ubi lit up the toll-free numbers at several law firms on the East Coast. They all sounded the same, so Ubi selected the one to represent him because the paralegal he talked with grew up near San Antonio. He then borrowed Arturo's copier. An hour later he had copies of his truck title and registration, insurance and driver's license, all neatly stuffed in an envelope with a three hundred dollar check and was headed to a post office in Las Cruces. Ubi told the woman behind the counter, "Overnight mail, express mail, whatever you got to do, just get it there, pronto." He then opened a post office box. If things went as

Jones & Sons claimed, Ubi would be truly independent in about six weeks.

Back at Arturo's, Ubi decided to call Deaton again, but this time he dialed the switchboard and got the operator to connect him to the warehouse, to Leroy.

"Hey, Leroy, I heard Mick Thorton retired."

"That's bullshit. They fard his ass. I'm probably next," Leroy said from a small office near the break room. "They be cuttin' out all the old-timers. Hiring kids at half the salary. I heard one of them young-blood dispatchers deadheaded a driver in Atlanta to Jacksonville, Florida. But the load was in Jacksonville, North Carolina. I bet that poor driver showed up in the wrong state looking like he'd come out of the rest room with his zipper down. Looky here, Ubi, I got a shipment of packing material to unload so I gotta go, but you take care, and don't let 'em do you like they did Mick."

Ubi made another call, to Denver dispatch, but when the same voice answered that had given him all those shipments spread across Texas, he hung up. Ubi wanted to hand over his sword, but hell, there wasn't anyone worthy to take it. Cornwallis had Washington. Lee had Grant. He had some kid who couldn't read a mileage chart.

Meanwhile, Ubi figured he could trip lease, haul shipments through a truck broker. Don't pay much, but that would be okay for now. Just keep some money rolling in because he would need a new trailer soon. Ubi needed a flat floor wagon, one that could handle pallet loads of groceries one trip, a trade show exhibit the next, and plumbing fixtures after that. Versatility, rather than specialty hauling, was the new modus operandi.

Ubi called a nearby broker who found a load of New Mexico alfalfa hay going to a dude ranch in Alberta, Canada. The owners were stocking up for winter feed and their horses needed high-protein hay-like alfalfa, a crop that thrived in the dry Southwest but not in Alberta with its short growing season.

The next morning, Ubi hired a wiry young man who hung out at Arturo's looking for day labor. They moved stacks and stacks of furniture pads to the trailer's nose and sealed them off with plywood sheets. Old Ironsides then climbed up the brown mountains into the high desert. At the alfalfa farm, the helper laughed when he realized what Ubi had planned.

"You can't stack these hay bales in that furniture trailer, mister. They use flatbeds for that. Then tarp 'em down."

"Don't worry about the mule," Ubi shot back, "just load the wagon."

Working inside the trailer, the men breathed in hay fibers and dust and often sneezed uncontrollably. But Ubi kept a rear-side door open and an occasional gust of cool, dry air cleared out the debris. The two men soon found a rhythm and built tier after tier of sweet-smelling, greenish-yellow alfalfa hay bales. Three on the floor horizontal, and one on the end, vertical. Perfect fit. Flush against the wall. No wasted space. To the ceiling they stacked until there was barely an inch to spare. After they jammed shut the rear trailer doors, the ranch foreman commented it was the most square bales a tractor-trailer had hauled off Enchanted Acres in twenty years.

Ubi dropped off his helper back at Arturo's and pulled on the truck scales to ensure he wasn't overweight. *Sheesh, almost eighty thousand pounds, heckuva lot heavier than a load of sticks.* Ubi then started a new logbook that he bought at the truck stop. The old logbooks had Deaton printed on the top of each page and were of no use. Ubi had one-time hauling authority through the broker, and the facsimile he had picked up at Arturo's proved it. When Old Ironsides lumbered up the interstate ramp, Ubi behind the steering wheel, it was the first time either one had hauled a load that was not under Deaton authority.

Later that evening, near Santa Fe, the truck caught a tailwind and a downslope. The sun was a fireball outside the driver's window, sinking fast on the horizon. The road took a twist in an easterly direction and dropped into a valley. Ubi spurred Old Ironsides into a gallop and the rig roared down the mountain building momentum. With his foot almost to the floor, the truck loped along at the bottom of the grade and tore into the climb. Ubi dropped only one gear climbing, and at the crest he was greeted with a full moon. Bright and yellow and round. Close enough to kiss through the open window. Unbelievable. Ubi eased Old Ironsides back into high gear, sometimes called the going home hole, and the heavy load pushed the rig along. And brother you can feel the difference in how a full wagon rides, floating over the bumps like a clipper ship cutting waves at just the right speed. Instead of jarring and bouncing, the truck lopes along, solid and swift. And doncha' know an engine loves breathing this cool, night air. She runs smooth and quiet, no clattering pistons, because combustion is more efficient with the intake gulping down chilly, evening air. What a feel. What a ride. Ubi sat up straight in his seat. Wind rushed through the open window and threw his thin hair straight back. His face tingled, twitched, felt like someone had rubbed a feather across his nose. This old engine was singing, strumming a sweet song. Ubi looked over his shoulder. The sun had completely disappeared. Tomorrow, adios, Deaton.

TWENTY-SEVEN

UBI MADE DENVER THE NEXT AFTERNOON. He left Old Ironsides on the street, engine idling in front of the Deaton office and warehouse. He found Ms. McCorley in a cubicle on the second floor and handed her the resignation letter he wrote on his yellow legal pad that morning leaning over the doghouse. Their eyes met for an instant. It was obvious this was just a job. Ubi felt sad for her, locked up in this prison. She must have had dreams, goals, yearned for something. And it was a safe bet that she would never understand the euphoria he had experienced last night driving through New Mexico when man and machine and the cosmos were in unison. The phone rang and she said good luck and picked up the receiver.

Walking down the hallway past the dispatch room, Ubi looked through the plate glass windows. Which one was the hard-ass he had talked to a few days ago? And who was that poor kid who had to dish out the ill-conceived loads? Used to know 'em all by name and voice and face. Knew some families, too. Now they're strangers.

Out in the street, Ubi approached Old Ironsides, reached for the door handle. A black sedan with SECURITY painted on the front door pulled up and a man wearing a uniform with a silver badge pinned to his shirt stuck his head out the window.

"Who told you it was okay to park here, driver?"

Ubi opened the door and climbed in his truck, ignoring the man.

"Hey, I'm talking to you. I'll write you up. Who said you could park here?"

Ubi released the air brakes and slipped the transmission in gear. He leaned out the window for another look at this character. He was sure he'd never seen his face before. "You can write me up, but it won't do no good."

"Why's that?" the man snarled.

"I don't drive for Deaton anymore."

"Since when?"

"Since about two minutes ago."

Ubi let off the clutch and Old Ironsides lurched forward. One block down the street and rounding a corner, he looked back. The man was scrawling something down on a note pad.

Denver's truck repair shops, parts houses, and junkyards were all clustered on the city's north side. Zoning ordinances had pushed these eyesores away from downtown, the university district, and desirable neighborhoods. Ubi piloted Old Ironsides down a major boulevard to a junkyard he'd patronized in past years. Last night was cold enough sleeping in the bunk. Now headed to Alberta, he had to replace the broken window. Snooping down rows of wrecked rigs, Ubi felt like he was in a graveyard and those beat-up trucks were tombstones. And because he was looking for used parts, this made him a grave robber. No wait, he was more like a transplant surgeon, extracting an organ from a terminal patient to save another life. Then his eyes came across Ben Johnson's old KW, roof crumpled like an accordion, driver's side smashed flat. But look at this, the other window unbroken, the whole mechanism intact, crank and all. *This should fit Old Ironsides. If not, it can be made to work. Get it quick before you change your mind.*

Grave robber. No, surgeon. *Just do it. But what would old Ben say? Okay, here goes. Take it. But first, down on your knees, Father, Son and Holy Ghost. For Ben.*

Back on the interstate that evening, Ubi learned from his AM radio that an Arctic front was ripping down the eastern slope of the Rockies. It was only mid-November; sheesh, winter was coming earlier than Ubi remembered. The weatherman called it the Manitoba Mauler. It was packing zero degree temperatures, gusts to forty miles an hour, and leaving behind snowdrifts high enough to bury a car. He would have to hustle to make Alberta before the storm hit and buried the highway. That warm New Mexico tailwind was now just a memory. Ubi drove into Sheridan, Wyoming, where the freeway funnels into the old, two-lane road, and found a little truck stop on the edge of town. He topped off both fuel tanks with blended diesel. If it gets as cold as expected, regular fuel, called number two diesel, could turn into a gel in the fuel lines. That would shut down the engine, and could leave the driver on the side of the road with no heat as well. Ubi also poured a bottle of rubbing alcohol down his air lines, at the glad hands. That would prevent the moisture in air tanks and hoses from freezing. A little chunk of ice in the airline or a fitting, and you got no brakes. They seize up and you're stuck. Ubi rummaged around in the magic box until he found the steel milk crate where he stored his snow chains—keep them up front for easy access. Better pick up a couple of extra bungee cords. Those things are great for preventing a broken link from beating against a fender or mud flap.

With his weatherization plan complete, Ubi drove late into the night and got up early the next morning. He fueled again, keeping his tanks full of blended diesel, your life blood if caught in a blizzard. Ubi pushed Old Ironsides into a headwind, across Central Montana. The hours passed quickly, but the miles passed slowly. It was late afternoon, but no storm. Clear blue skies still stretched above distant mountains and the sage-covered prairie. *Uh-oh. Hold on. Would you look at this?* Southbound eighteen's got snow piled on the trailer roof and fuel tanks. See that chunk shake loose and splatter down the highway?

Then a voice on the CB.

"Northbound large car, you better find a place to shut down before too long. That storm is ripping out of the Canadian Rockies with an attitude. Seen one rig jackknife right in front of me. I barely squeezed by on the shoulder."

"Ten-four," Ubi said. "Guess we're gonna' call it a night up here in Great Falls."

"If you make it that far, you'll be lucky."

"'Preciate that, southbound. Where you headed?"

"Florida."

It turned out that the Florida-bound driver underestimated the speed in which the Mauler was invading Montana. Just fifty miles later, the sun disappeared and Ubi drove into light snow. A little farther and the prairie was covered with a white sheet. Ubi eased off the accelerator and flipped a lever on the console. Until now the truck had four wheels pulling, highway mode. But this switch activated another axle and eight tires were now churning through fresh snow. Old Ironsides continued into the teeth of the storm, through an inch of snow on the highway. *Boy, all that weight makes a difference in your traction.* So far, Old Ironsides was making a good snowplow. Visibility was down to just a short piece, but the modified Kentucky wipers were doing their job and there was no ice forming on the windshield. *Not yet, anyway.* Ubi leaned over the doghouse where the road atlas was open to Montana. *Should be a town up ahead, not too far. Looks like it's big enough to have a truck stop.* Suddenly, Old Ironsides went into a skid; the trailer was growing closer in the driver side mirror. Ubi dropped the transmission into neutral and let the rig straighten out. *Oh, brother, looks like time for snow chains.*

On the next straightway, Ubi gunned the engine so he could make it up a slight hill. At the top, he hit the brakes and slid to a stop. Snow was now coming down almost sideways. *Let's get those snow chains on, quick.* Ubi grabbed his winter jacket and a knit ski hat out of the bunk. *Caps are for sun and shade, not warmth. This old rag is kinda worn, but it'll keep the ears from freezing.* Ubi then pulled on his work gloves and, grabbing the icy handrail, rappelled down the side of Old Ironsides. *Grab those chains and lay 'em out in a straight line behind the dual wheels.* Ubi climbed back in the toasty cab, released the brakes, and eased the truck tires onto the chains. Back outside, he yanked the chains up over the top of the tires and snugged them tight with several bungee cords.

With the engine idling, Ubi knew he would have a warm seat waiting when he climbed back in so he decided to take on another chore. He dug deep into the magic box and found the old front grill cover he hadn't seen since last April. He circled the front of the truck and yanked and stretched the vinyl from snap to snap until he had the radiator covered. *Shoulda' done that when I fueled. Oh, well, we're all set now. And would ya' look at this beautiful storm blowing across the land?* Ubi planted his feet wide and stood up straight, facing the storm headfirst. The unbroken wind howled. Fat, fluffy snowflakes swirled about the rig and piled on Ubi's head and shoulders. He turned his frozen face from side to side, absorbing the landscape. Everything, sage and fence posts and highway, all buried in fresh snow. The wind rocked the rig, but that was okay. This was liberty. Face these challenges alone, head-on.

"You hear that Ms. McCorley?" Ubi shouted into the expanse. "I don't need anybody breathing down my neck, telling me to drive a cookie-cutter truck, one like all the others."

The wind shook the truck again. Ubi stomped his feet to shake off the accumulating snow. "This is what it's all about. Working in a cubicle, hell, that's a prison cell. And that lousy job, handing out orders from the front office, that's a sentence, not an occupation.

Out here, you make it on your own or die trying. Like old Ben. Bet he woulda' wanted it that way, going down in that old rig off the side of Cabbage Mountain. Better'n wasting away somewhere in a room."

Ubi felt the wind cut through his jacket. *Shoulda' zipped that liner inside. Sheesh, it must be almost zero and here I am yelling into the wind like an old fool. Let's get on down the road, find a spot to call it a night.*

Old Ironsides plodded down the interstate, snow chains chinking out a rhythm. Ubi could see only a few truck lengths ahead. Even on a low setting, his headlight beams reflected off the blowing snow and back into the windshield. It felt like the rig was standing still, but the speedometer maintained twenty miles an hour. Clanking along, the truck left parallel sets of wide ruts behind. Still, driving into a blowing snowstorm with nothing but headlights to show the way can make you feel like you're on a treadmill, moving, but not gaining ground. Vertigo. *Come on. That little town can't be much farther.*

But the road is disappearing. Everything looks the same. Can't see a thing. Gonna' have to pull over. But where? Right here's gonna have to do. Ride out the storm right here. Going any farther's just asking to get stuck. Might as well hit the bunk. Set the rpms at 900 with the little throttle hookup from that shop in Madison. Old Ironsides' got one heckuva heater. It'll be all right.

Ubi was about to shed his jacket when he heard an odd sound from underneath. Something tapping. Then the familiar smell of diesel exhaust trickled into the cab. He took a deep breath. Exhaust leak, no doubt. Smells like it's getting stronger. Can't sleep in here tonight. Might wake up dead. Better take a look.

Outside in the storm, Ubi pumped the handle to the hydraulic jack that raises the cab. Stroke after stroke, he pushed down on the pipe that he used for a jack handle, and the cab tipped forward over the front bumper. The metal hull lifted higher into the storm and quivered when a gust of wind and snow kicked up. Ubi then took the piece of lumber he used to block the truck wheels and shoved it against the truck frame. Now the cab couldn't come crashing down on top of him if the hydraulics failed. He'd heard that story several times, skulls crushed because someone forgot to prop up the cab.

Even though he was working by flashlight, the leak wasn't hard to find. The clamp connecting the steel, flex exhaust hose to the muffler had broken and fallen off. Ubi pushed the kill switch attached to the side of the motor and went to work. Grab this old expired Nevada license plate off the bumper, bend it, fold it, break it in half. Hammer it and shape it and wrap it around the connection. *Gotta' take a break and warm up next to the engine. She's still hot. Come on fingers. Don't go numb. Now, grab that wire hanging from the fuel tank that you used to hold down the chock blocks; it'll do for a clamp. All set. That wasn't too bad, took maybe a half hour. And warming up down here under the cab made a big difference. It blocks the wind okay and the engine is still warm enough so you can work without gloves. Bet it's down to zero out there, though. Maybe colder.*

Still huddled under the cab, Ubi pushed the switch on the back of the starter and the diesel roared to life. And no leaks. That's right, no leaks. *Gonna be snug in the bunk tonight. Maybe do some reading. Some poetry. So, let it snow. Cain't wait to tell this story to Jeremy and Molly.*

Ubi yanked the wooden block free that he had wedged against the frame to keep the cab from falling and turned a valve. He waited, but nothing happened. A gust rocked the steel hull, still pitched forward and leaning over the bumper, but the cab didn't come down like it should. Come on gravity, do your job. Still nothing. Ubi walked to the front of the truck and shoved, but it was like pushing an elephant. He felt his cheeks tighten in the frigid air, and when he took a breath it felt like he was inhaling needles. Nose hairs frozen stiff, too. The cab rocked again and a clump of snow landed on Ubi's back collar. *Zero, betcha'.*

Ubi brushed the snow from his neck, but a few flakes had already melted and a frigid stream dribbled down his back. He shivered and twitched. *Why won't the cab go down? Got plenty of hydraulic fluid. Checked it the other day and it was full. Wait a minute, hydraulic fluid can freeze up like diesel fuel. Sure it can. It gets slushy in frigid temperatures. Heard that at a shop in Fargo, way back when.*

Ubi looked up at the cab, high overhead. It would be impossible to climb inside with it tilted at a forty-five degree angle like that. Heck, you open the door and it's liable to break off at the hinges. So how to make it through the night? Why not pull some of that hay out of the trailer and sleep back there? Ubi walked in snow above his ankles and fiddled with the frozen lock. *It's going to take some doing to thaw this thing out. There's no way you can light a torch in this wind, and you might freeze before you bust open that lock. Face has already gone completely numb. Trailer might not be that warm anyway, even if you burrowed down into the hay bales. Only one thing to do. Snuggle up next to that warm engine for the night.*

Ubi followed his footsteps back to the tractor, crawled on the frozen ground, under the transmission, and wiggled between the engine and the frame. In less than a minute, he was standing up straight, exhaust hose running behind his back. He could now reach the throttle spring and manipulate the rpms. *Where's that screwdriver? Okay, wedge it against that bracket. Just like that. Now this baby'll purr all night long at nine hundred rpms. Keep everything toasty but my toes. These old boots, kinda leaky. Too bad that gal back in Colorodo stole my new ones. Reckon she needed 'em more'n me. Besides, it's warmer down here than that motel up in Grand Rapids, winter of '62. Might be a long night with this storm blowing, but the Ditch Dragon is going to have to wait to get old Ubi Sunt.*

"You hear that, Ditch Dragon?" Ubi yelled into the night air. "Not tonight you don't. Maybe down the road someday. Maybe slumped over the steering wheel in a Kansas rest area, arteries clogged like a jelled fuel line. Maybe face down in the bunk at a Tennessee truck stop: *kapow!* lights out from a brain aneurism. Maybe at the bottom of a mountain pass, wrecked and entombed in Old Ironsides, like Ben Johnson. But not tonight."

Ubi removed his gloves and leaned over the hot, cast-iron block. He ran his bare hands across the top, warmed his fingers, and rubbed them against his frozen face. Steel pistons churned up and down inside their cylinders. Scalding hot oil circulated like blood, emanating heat and sustaining life. Ubi stood on his toes. His body inches from the pulsating pistons, he could feel the heartbeat.

Not tonight, Ditch Dragon. Not tonight.